BLACK THORNS

RINA KENT

To a deep, raw love that follows no rules.

AUTHOR NOTE

Hello reader friend,

If you haven't read my books before, you might not know this, but I write darker stories that can be upsetting and disturbing. My books and main characters aren't for the faint of heart.

This book contains themes of consensual non-consensual. I trust you know your triggers before you proceed.

Black Thorns is the second book of a duet and is not standalone.

Thorns Duet:
#0 Yellow Thorns (Free Prequel)
#1 Red Thorns
#2 Black Thorns

Sign up to Rina Kent's Newsletter for news about future releases and an exclusive gift.

A lie turned into a nightmare.

She broke my heart.

Broke me.

Broke us.

Only one thing could mend the gaping wound she left behind.

Her.

Naomi.

All mine for the taking.

All mine for owning.

All mine.

PLAYLIST

You Broke Me First—Conor Maynard

The Man Who Can't Be Moved—The Script

Still Loving You—Scorpions

Stuck—Villain of the Story

Decay—Villain of the Story

Someone You Loved—Our Last Night

Falling Apart—Michael Schulte

Into The Fire—Asking Alexandria

Bones—Galantis & OneRepublic

Let Me Be Sad—I Prevail

The Dark of You—Breaking Benjamin

Scary Love—The Neighbourhood

Up in the Air—Thirty Seconds to Mars

Bright Lights—Thirty Seconds to Mars

Why Did You Run?—Judah & the Lion

Fake Smile—Thousan Below

You can find the complete playlist on Spotify.

BLACK THORNS

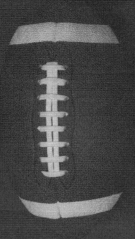

PROLOGUE

Sebastian

Age six

T*HE WEAK ARE MEAT. T*HE STRONG EAT.

Mom bought a painting with that proverb inked in bold Kanji characters.

I don't think she really understands what those words mean. She probably thought it was pretty and fit our house's decor and decided to buy it.

Mommy is that way. She likes things super-fast, then hates them just as fast. And she's not very good at Japanese, but Daddy doesn't like me to say that in front of her.

He's a superhero, my daddy, and superheroes don't like to make other people feel bad.

But like all superheroes, he's busy all the time. Mommy and Daddy work hard so I can eat and study with my friends.

Although I don't really have friends. They call me 'Blondie' in a weird English accent because I have light hair and green eyes like a 'freak.'

I asked Daddy why I don't have Asian eyes and black hair like everyone else, and he told me it's because I'm American, not Japanese. But I was born in Tokyo and that still doesn't make me Asian?

That's stupid. I should look like them so no one will make fun of me.

Or ignore me.

Mommy says that when they have money, they'll transfer me to an international school where there are foreigners like me. But I just want to have fun with everyone in my class.

They look at me funny when Mommy arrives to pick me up in the middle of the day.

I usually go home last. Today, I'm leaving early.

My pretty teacher, Satomi *Sensei*, takes my small hand in hers. She has short hair and a soft smile like the angels from my bedtime stories.

Sensei guides me to the door and everyone murmurs about the 'Blondie' who's ditching.

I'm not ditching.

"Everyone stay quiet, now." *Sensei* stares over her shoulder at them and speaks in Japanese. "Sebastian-kun is meeting his mother. Okay?"

"Okay!" they echo.

"Don't worry about them." She smiles at me.

"Okay," I murmur in Japanese and stare at my feet.

Because I speak both English and Japanese, sometimes it takes longer to figure out what I should be saying, so I just stay silent.

Sensei guides me through the door of the classroom, where my mom is pacing the hallway.

"Is everything all right, Mrs. Weaver?" *Sensei* asks her.

Mommy stops pacing and smiles. "Everything is great. We just miss Sebastian so much and want to have lunch together."

Her golden blonde hair falls down her back and always gets everyone's attention whenever we're in public. That and her name, Julia.

She pulls me from *Sensei*'s side and wraps her clammy hand around mine.

I don't get to wave as we hurry down the corridor. Her heels make so much noise in the empty hallway of the school. She bows in greeting at the principal and one of the teachers and I do so as well.

As soon as we're out of view, her smile drops and her lower lip trembles. She looks like the characters in anime before they cry. Like Gon from *Hunter X Hunter* when he couldn't find his father.

"I still have class, Mommy," I say in English.

She doesn't like me to talk in Japanese at home, even though Daddy is fine with it.

"Not today, sweetie." She ruffles my hair, but it's stiff and hurts.

"But *Sensei* doesn't like us to be absent."

"She'll forgive you this time." She ushers me to the back seat of our car.

My eyes light up when I see who's in the driver's seat. "Daddy!"

"Hey, champ." He turns around and grins at me.

My daddy, Nicholas Weaver, is my best friend. When I told him that I don't have friends at school, he said he'd be my temporary best buddy until I find others. But he'll always hold the number one spot.

He reaches a fist in my direction and I throw my yellow bag to the side so I can bump it, giggling as Mom fusses with my seatbelt.

It's then I notice that there's something beside me.

A painting.

The painting with the bold Kanji letters on it that should be in our living room.

I tilt my head to the side and read it again, out loud, in Japanese, "The...weak...a-are...meat. The s-strong...eat."

"Good boy!" Daddy exclaims from the front seat. "Your Kanji is getting better, Bastian."

"I'm second in my class!"

"That's my boy." He grins, but it's strained, just like how Mommy patted my head earlier.

After making sure I'm strapped securely in my seat, she gets in the front and Daddy drives away from my school.

"Why is the painting here?" I frown.

"It's a family legacy, Bastian." Mom watches the side-view mirror, seeming distracted. "It needed to come with us."

"But it shouldn't be in the car."

"It'll be where we want it. Okay, sweetie?"

"Okay. Where are we going?"

"Somewhere new." Dad smiles at me through the rearview mirror.

"But I don't want somewhere new. I want to be with *Sensei*."

"Stop being a brat, Sebastian!" Mom snaps in an impatient tone.

"I'm not a brat." I pout.

"No, you're not." Daddy gives her a look, then grins at me. "You're our good boy."

"But Mommy called me a brat."

"She doesn't mean it. Right, Julia?"

Mom sighs, then turns around and gives me an open juice box. "You're not, sweetie. I'm sorry."

"That's okay, Mommy." I snatch the bottle of juice and slurp while swinging my legs, bumping against Mommy's seat.

"You'll have friends in the place we'll go to, champ."

I nearly choke on my juice as my eyes bug out. When I speak, I draw the word out, "Really?"

"Really. We'll all start anew. What do you think?"

"Okay!" I bounce in my seat, rocking back and forth.

Mom puts on anime soundtracks and I sing along with them while I drink from my juice.

Sometimes, Daddy sings with me and I giggle because his Japanese is so funny. Mom's, too. I think it's because they're from America and learned Japanese when they were older, unlike me.

I don't know America. Daddy said I don't need to, because we're never going there.

We drive for a long time, passing many people and tall buildings that look like ghosts. After a while, I'm tired of singing.

I think I fall asleep, because when I wake up, Daddy and Mommy are talking quietly, like they usually do when they don't want me to know 'adult' stuff.

But I'm not so little anymore. I'm a big boy and I wanna know grownup stuff, too.

So I peek through my half-closed eyes and pretend I'm still asleep.

Mom is turned in her seat and faces Daddy while he focuses on the road. Beads of sweat cover her forehead and the hairline of her bright-like-the-sun locks. If she gets sweat on her hair, she'll probably tell us she's having a 'bad hair day' later.

Her shaky fingers run through her strands over and over again. "Maybe you should call your father, Nick."

Daddy tightens his hold on the steering wheel. "I'm dead to my parents. I can't just call them."

"But this is a life or death situation. Surely, they'll help their firstborn."

"You were there when they said they'd only attend my funeral. I wouldn't be surprised if they had a hand in quickening the process."

"They wouldn't do that! You're their son."

"A son who not only refused to inherit his father's political legacy but also married a commoner who doesn't fit the Weaver image. Believe me, I'm no longer their son."

Tears shine in Mom's eyes. "So it's my fault?"

"No." Daddy takes her hand and places a kiss on the back of it while still focusing on the road. "I would choose you over all the socialites Mom arranged for me to date a hundred times over if I had to. What we have is real and I'm lucky to have you."

She sniffles. "I'm lucky to have you, too, Nick. I don't know how I would've gotten through this mess without you."

"We'll be okay."

"No one steals from them and gets away with it," she whimpers.

"They'll hunt us down and hurt Sebastian… What if they take away our baby and…and…"

"Hey…we're here. No one will hurt him or us."

"But what if they do? I wish I'd never done it."

"It's useless to think about things that can't be changed, hon."

"I…I don't know what the hell was wrong with me when I decided to take it… I just…just wanted to help pay off our debt. We were working so hard to make ends meet and…Sebastian needs to be in an international school, and…I stupidly thought one item in the midst of twenty others wouldn't be discovered."

Daddy grabs her hand tighter. "We'll be fine. We have each other and our boy. That's all that matters, right?"

"Right." She smiles a little through her tears and I want to smile, too. I love when Mommy is happy after she cries. It means she'll be better and spoil me and Daddy.

She leans over and kisses Daddy on the mouth. "I love you, Nick."

"Love you, too, Julia."

I'm about to open my eyes and say I love them, too, even if I didn't understand most of what they said.

It's okay if I don't have my beautiful teacher anymore. I can just get another one. All that matters is that I'll be with my parents and I'll also have friends.

But before I can say anything, a loud sound of screeching tires pierces through my ears, and the last thing I see is a large truck.

Crash!

There's impact, there's Mom's scream and Dad's curse, and then there's…nothing.

For a while at least. I'm thinking there's nothing.

But then our surroundings burst into my ears all at once and it hurts. There's a long buzz that I can't get rid of.

A mixture of sounds erupt all around me. Sirens. Shrieks. Strangers talking.

Whimpers. I think they're mine.

Mommy…?

Daddy…?

Where are you?

I want to search for them or at least hear their voices, but they're not among all the strangers talking. They're just not there.

Why can't I find them?

And why is everything black?

That's when I realize my eyes are closed, and when I attempt to open them, I can't. Even my body doesn't move.

All I can hear are voices, noises coming at me from all directions, and none of them are my parents.

I'm scared.

Mommy, Daddy. I'm scared.

I strain and my eyes flutter open a little, just a little. Someone is asking me in Japanese if I can hear them and someone else's shadow falls over me.

Another shadow reaches out a black hand and takes the painting from beside me. I want to scream no, that it's ours. It's my mommy's.

But I can't speak. I can't move.

The last thing I see before the world goes black stays with me forever.

The weak are meat. The strong eat.

ONE

Akira

Dear Yuki-Onna,

It has come to my attention that we're toxic.

I know. This should've been evident for the three years we've known each other, but they say you never realize you're in a toxic relationship until it ends.

Is that what this is all about? The ending?

I don't like that. In fact, I hate it so much that I'm contemplating the best way to bring up the toxicity a notch just to keep you here.

So I came up with this idea. Or more like it hit me upside the head when I was gazing at the fucking boring sky the other day.

It was a moment of salvation, and, I swear, I could almost see the angels coming down from heaven and offering me their grace.

Just kidding. There were only demons and they were all sitting with me when I was hit by this thought.

Remember when I told you to never fall for me in my first letter? I said it'd just be tragic, but what I didn't mention is that I will break your fucking heart.

I'll break it so hard, there will be no pieces to pick up and no moving on with your life.

I will slash through your walls so deep, you won't be able to get me out even if you tried.

I will toy with your feelings, to the point that you'll wish you never had them in the first place.

I will conquer your life so thoroughly you will start to think about ending it.

Because that's what toxicity does, my dear Yuki-Onna. It destroys and it does it so savagely, there will be nothing left of you or me.

But you went ahead and fell for me, didn't you?

Even with my warnings, even with all the signs I sent your way, you had to defy logic and think of me as someone other than your faceless, nerdy pen pal from Japan.

You realize that's your mistake, right? And it might as well be your downfall.

Because now that I know your weakness, me, I won't stop until you're begging at my feet. For what, I have no clue, but as long as there's pleading and some crying, I'm sure I will be satisfied.

I can't say the same about you.

Now, I don't like imagining myself in other people's shoes. But if I were you, I'd hide well.

Here's the thing, though.

You're into being chased and I might have developed the appetite for that type of twisted fuckery.

See? You're also corrupting me, which is why we're toxic for each other.

Go ahead and run, Naomi. Go ahead and hide.

If I were you, I would look under your bed and over your shoulder.

I would think twice about every shadow that passes in your peripheral vision.

I would live on your toes.

Because the moment you let your guard down will be the moment everything ends.

You will end, my ghostly Yuki-Onna.
Until that day comes, try to live well.
Believe me, you'll need to savor every moment.

Toxic love,
Akira

TWO

Naomi

Drip.
Drip.
Drip.

Did I forget to turn off the faucet? Or is it coming from outside?

I open my mouth to call for Mom, but no sound comes out.

The dripping continues, escalating in volume and in repetitiveness until it's grating on my nerves.

Drip…drip, drip…drip.

Drip!

Groaning, I slowly open my eyes.

I'm not in my room.

I'm not home.

Or anywhere I recognize.

Dark gray walls surround me from every side. Even the solid ground I'm lying on is dark and hard.

My head is a jumbled mess as I slowly survey my surroundings. I'm in an empty room with no furniture in sight.

There are no windows either, and the only light comes from an old yellow bulb hanging from the middle of the ceiling.

I slowly move my gaze from left to right. There's a door that's as gray as the walls, but it appears to be metal.

In the corner, there's a yellowish toilet and I'd be shocked if it's even functional.

The dripping comes from a small spigot in the wall that's not turned completely off.

Where the hell am I and why does this place appear to be some sort of a prison?

I attempt to sit up and wince when a sting of pain explodes in my neck. I touch it and freeze when my fingers connect with what feels like a puncture in my skin.

Then all the events from earlier rush through the fog in my head.

The dark figures. The chase. The gunshot.

Sebastian.

I gasp, my frantic gaze searching the room. Sebastian was shot. He was shot right in front of me and when I rushed forward, a needle pricked me in the neck.

Then everything went black. The next thing I knew, I woke up in this room.

I pause when my gaze lands on a dark figure huddled in the far corner on my right.

At first, I think it's something ominous, but then I recognize the mass of muscles and the dark blond strands peeking out.

"Sebastian!" I call in a hoarse voice.

I try standing up, but my legs refuse to carry me. I crawl toward him on all fours, ignoring the pressure and discomfort scratching at my knees.

I stop beside him. He's lying on his side, face down. Strands of his hair cover his face. I grab his shoulder and pause when a low, guttural sound escapes him.

Something wet and cold touches my knee and I startle when I stare down.

Dark red.

Blood.

Lots of it.

It forms a small sticky pool beneath his shoulder that's against the ground.

Oh, God.

I wished that his getting shot was a figment of my overactive imagination and that it didn't really happen. That maybe I made it all up due to being pricked by that needle.

But the evidence that it's all real is right in front of me.

Bleeding out of him in a steady stream.

My lips quiver and my heart pounds so hard, I think it'll spill out on the ground.

"Sebastian!" I gently shake his good shoulder so I don't aggravate his injury.

He doesn't even stir. My frantic pulse roars in my ears in sync with the worst-case scenarios that play in my head.

What if he's dying?

What if he never wakes up?

"Sebastian..." my brittle voice echoes around us as I carefully palm his cheek and turn it toward me. His hair falls back from his forehead and I get a view of his ethereally handsome face. The same face that has become such a constant in my dreams.

His skin is pale, making his features less sharp, and his lips are chapped and bluish.

That can't be good.

I slowly flip him over and that's when I get my first view of the wound in his upper shoulder.

The bullet has ripped through his Black Devils jacket, leaving a gash in his skin. Blood soaks the white sleeve, turning it red, and the black stripes look dark brown.

Some of the blood has clotted, but there's an opening from which blood keeps oozing out at a slow, lethal pace.

Shit. Shit!

If he's been bleeding out for long, this will quickly turn fatal.

"Sebastian…" I gently tap his cheeks. "Open your eyes. You have to wake up…please…"

He finally stirs but doesn't respond.

Moisture gathers in my lids, but I don't let the tears loose. Dragging in a sharp inhale of air, I breathe in the stench of blood and the humidity in this place, but there's also a hint of bergamot and amber.

Of Sebastian.

Using his presence as an anchor, I grab his good arm and push him onto his back.

He groans and I pause before I release him. I need to stop the hemorrhage or he'll bleed out.

My gaze strays sideways in search of anything I can use and when I find nothing, I pull my T-shirt over my head and shove it against his wound.

A low, guttural sound leaves his throat as his lips twist in pain. Sweat gathers between his thick brows and on his temple.

I bite my lip and continue.

Cold air seeps through me, forming goosebumps on my bare skin, but I ignore it as I increase the pressure.

"Sebastian…please…please open your eyes."

Goddamnit.

He definitely needs medical attention, not a T-shirt and some pressure. What if this wound kills him? What if I…lose him?

I shake my head at that thought and hold the material with one hand, then search the pocket of my shorts with the other. Sure enough, my phone isn't there. I search Sebastian's pants, but his is missing as well.

It shouldn't be a surprise since whoever brought us here wouldn't have let us keep our phones.

I focus back on the shirt. It's partially soaked, but the bleeding appears to have stopped.

A sigh of relief escapes me.

But even I realize this whole thing is temporary. He needs help and he needs it now.

He grunts and there's movement behind his lids before they slowly open. I've never been so happy to see his tropical light green eyes as I am right now.

They're a bit unfocused, muted, almost as if he's not all here.

But he is. He's not gone. He's with me.

"Sebastian! Can you hear me?"

He stares up at me, slowly, unhurriedly, almost as if he's seeing me for the first time.

I can tell the exact moment he recognizes me. His pupils dilate and fire creeps into his features.

"Nao?" he croaks, his voice hoarse and gritty, as if the act is taking up all his energy.

I nearly break down from the flood of relief while I blurt. "Yeah, it's me."

"What happened…?" He attempts to sit up and groans as he falls on his back.

I keep a gentle but firm hand on his chest so he stays in place. "Don't move. You were shot and the bleeding has just barely stopped."

"Fuck," he grumbles, the rumble of his voice deeper than usual.

Everything is different. His face. His weakness. This whole damn place.

Sebastian looks down at his wound that I'm covering with my T-shirt, then back at me. His inquisitive gaze studies me from top to bottom as if he's relearning my body, then it soon turns frantic. "Are you okay? Are you hurt anywhere?"

I don't know if it's his worried tone or the way that instead of asking about his own injury, he's only focused on my well-being. It could be both of those combined, but I can't control it when big, fat tears cascade down my cheeks.

"Baby…" Sebastian's frown deepens. "Are you hurt?"

"No, you're the one who was shot and nearly bled out. Why the hell are you worried about me?"

"Why wouldn't I be? You're always the first thing I think about. Gotta protect what's mine, baby."

I want to tell him that no, I'm not his and that we're over because of the stupid bet he accepted from Reina. I want to argue and fight him because he thought it was a good idea to be part of a dare where he had to fuck me to impress the campus's queen bee and his football team buddies.

I want to shout at him over all the humiliation I felt when the cheerleaders, led by that bitch Brianna, made me the laughing stock of school.

But that's not important right now.

Not when his life is on the line.

"We need to get out of here."

"Where are we?" he speaks with difficulty, straining with every word.

"I don't know. It seems like some sort of a prison."

"Do you know who did this?"

"I…think so."

He gives me a questioning look, blinking rapidly, probably trying to stay focused.

I lick my lips. "The man who shot you said, *Told you we'd meet again, Hitori-san.* He has the same voice as one of the men who visited me and Mom not too long ago. His name is Ren and I think he's one of my dad's men."

"Your dad's men?"

"Mom warned me that he's dangerous."

"What does he do exactly?"

"I don't know, but Ren is definitely the one behind this."

Static fills the room and we both freeze as a suave voice echoes through the air, "Ding ding ding. That is correct. Now, let the games begin."

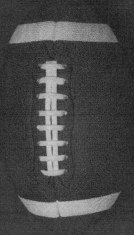

THREE

Sebastian

I THOUGHT I KNEW PAIN.

When I was six years old and was in that accident with my parents, I broke my arm and bruised my ribs.

It hurt like a mother and I couldn't breathe without wanting to cry. There were countless voices floating around me, speaking and arguing in Japanese. When I woke up in the hospital, though, my grandparents were there and told me I'd live with them.

You'll be a 'real' Weaver now. Those were Grandma's actual words. In order to do that, she said I'd have to forget everything my parents had taught me.

They didn't attempt to lessen the blow of a child learning that his parents were dead. That I no longer had a mother or a father.

That the world as I knew it had collapsed with no chance of ever rebuilding again.

I lay there with my casted arm on my chest. My lungs exploded with every breath and my face felt swollen.

But I still didn't feel any pain.

Or maybe I felt so much pain all at once that I blacked out.

I've always used that time in my life as a reference for any discomfort I've felt. Strained muscles? That's nothing. Sprained an ankle? Child's play.

But none of those compare to the pulsing pain in my upper shoulder. It's as if invisible hands are rummaging through my wound, digging and twisting until my breath is stolen.

It might be bearable if I were alone. If Naomi wasn't pressing her shirt against it with a desperation that mutes the color of her dark eyes as moisture clings to her long lashes and forms lines down her flushed cheeks.

Watching her cry is equivalent to digging a shard of glass into my chest.

I don't like seeing her hurt, especially if it's because of me.

Now we're both searching our surroundings to find the voice that filled the room a few seconds ago.

Let the games begin, he said.

Naomi mentioned that she recognized him in the forest and that he could be one of her father's men.

She once said that she was searching for her dad and that her mom didn't want her to connect with him, which is one of the main reasons that her relationship with her mom was strained.

But why do I feel like my grandparents could have a hand in this?

Dad said it fifteen years ago, 'You were there when they said they'd only attend my funeral. I wouldn't be surprised if they had a hand in quickening the process.'

Grandma was obviously against any relationship I had with Naomi, just like she was opposed to my parents' marriage.

Nate always warned me to be careful so that I wouldn't share my father's fate.

Not only that, but he made it his mission to act as some sort of invisible shield between me and the world—my grandparents included. As if he knew exactly what they were capable of.

But they wouldn't have had me shot, right? After all, I'm the future leader of the Weaver clan, as they like to remind me.

Though anything is possible if the goal is to teach me a lesson.

I attempt to sit up again, but Naomi places a soft yet firm hand on my chest to forbid me.

"I'm fine," I strain.

I'm not. The mere act of moving is like lifting weights with my fucking teeth. My head is dizzy and the wound pulses like a motherfucker.

But I can't tell Naomi that or she'll be more scared and hurt than she already is.

The cold concrete floor scrapes against my thigh and palm as I slowly sit up and lean against the wall. Despite her protests.

"You're hurt…" she whines, but gives up trying to stop me and helps me into a comfortable position.

Fresh tears stream down her cheeks as she carefully maneuvers herself so that she's on my injured side. She's still clutching her T-shirt with determination, as if letting go will cause the life to evaporate out of me.

Or allow me to bleed out.

I don't like seeing her cry. Well, I do, but only when I chase and conquer her, because I know she enjoys it, too.

I love her fuck-me tears.

Her 'no, please' that are actually 'yes, please' tears.

But not these.

The pain and desperation in them fucking gut me.

I dislike it when she's sad or hurt. It's even more painful than if they were my own feelings. I can brush those off, treat them efficiently and push them to the background.

I wish I could do the same with Naomi's. I wish I could take away her feelings and treat them as my own so that she's no longer hurting.

Is that…what empathy feels like?

"Hey…" I palm her cheek, thumbing away the moisture gathered there. "I'm really fine."

"You don't seem fine," she murmurs.

"It looks worse than it actually is. Do you want to make it better?"

"Of course."

"Then stop crying, baby. That hurts more than the wound itself."

She sniffles, wiping at her face with the back of her hand.

Static fills the room again and both of us stiffen as the same voice from earlier speaks again, "Very touching. You nearly put me to sleep."

"What do you want from us?" Naomi's gaze searches the room and when I do the same, I spot a few blinking cameras in the corners and a white speaker from which his voice reaches us.

"I already told you. A game."

"Are you one of my father's men?"

"What gave you that idea?"

"Mom said you were."

"Sato-san says a lot of things. It's better not to believe them all. Now, for our game…"

"We're not playing," I grunt out, then wince.

Sick people like him get off on driving others to a point of no return. They like stripping people down to their most primitive forms where they can freely exploit them. There's no way in fuck we'll give him the joy of seeing us spiral out of control.

"Who said you have a choice, Quarterback? Either play or there will be no water and food. Oh, and your wound will get infected and you'll die."

My lips twist and I curse under my breath. I should've known they'd use our basic needs against us.

There must be a way we can thwart his plans…

"If we agree, will you get him help?" Naomi asks.

I shake my head. She's playing right into his hands by revealing that she cares about my well-being. I would've grabbed and kissed the fuck out of her under different circumstances, but right now, we don't know what we're actually dealing with.

This could be a rogue group that's rebelling against her father.

Or maybe her father himself is a sick bastard who doesn't care about putting his own daughter into dire situations.

Until we figure out their angle, we need to be extra careful about our survival, and that means revealing as little as possible about ourselves.

"No promises," the man, Ren, as Naomi called him, says. "Now, the game. We'll start with the rules. No lies. I mean it. We'll know when you lie and if you do, there will be punishment."

"What type of game is this?" I ask.

"I'm glad you asked, Quarterback. We call this survival of the fittest. Just like your tattoo."

I don't miss the smile in his voice as he said the last part.

He knows about my tattoo and he's Japanese.

There's no way in fuck this whole thing is a coincidence.

"Now, let's start. I'll go easy on you the first round. One of you will tell me a deep, dark secret that no one in the world knows about. Do that and you'll get water. Bottled, not whatever filthy shit is dripping from that faucet."

"Don't say anything," I whisper to Naomi.

"We need water," she murmurs back, her hold steady on my shoulder. "Your lips are chapped and dry, and you were bleeding out not so long ago."

"I'll be fine. If you play into his hand, it'll only break us."

"I don't care as long as we survive."

"Not to be a fun-ruiner, but you have ten seconds before your chance is over." Ren pauses. "Seven, six, five…"

"I was molested when I was nine," Naomi blurts, her lips and chin trembling.

My fist clenches at my side, not only because of her state or that she's playing Ren's game, but also because of the reminder of what she's been through.

She's not supposed to divulge that for a sick game.

She's not supposed to rip open her wound and tell a fucking stranger her most intimate secret.

"That's not a deep, dark secret," Ren says.

"It is. No one knows about it and there wasn't a police report."

"Your mother knew, as well as a few therapists and the man who molested you. It doesn't count."

"But—"

"You have five seconds for another try. Four...three..."

"Shit," Naomi mutters under her breath. "Think, Naomi, think..."

"Two..."

"My parents were killed," I whisper low.

Naomi's eyes flit to mine, the dark brown widening with a thousand questions.

"Your parents were in an accident, Quarterback." Ren's provocatively calm voice fills the space.

"It was a premeditated accident. They were running away from someone and the accident was a camouflage to cover up their murder."

Naomi gasps and covers her mouth with the back of her free hand. I can tell she wants to ask me more, but she also recognizes we're being watched.

Her small body snuggles into my side and she doesn't even need to utter a word. Her inquisitive eyes say it all.

I'm sorry you went through that.

I'm here for you.

Maybe if I'd heard those words when I was six years old, things would've been different.

Maybe if I'd known her back then, I would've been able to live another way.

Maybe we wouldn't have ended up here, where she's pressing her shirt to my wound.

"*Sekai,*" Ren says in an amused tone.

Correct.

He knows. The fucker already knows about my parents.

The bad feeling I had when he started this game comes back to haunt me. There's something absolutely nefarious about this. But what?

The sound of screeching metal makes Naomi jump and I stiffen. A small window opens in the door and a bottle of water is thrown inside and then, just like that, the only opening is slammed shut.

She grabs my good hand and places it on top of hers on the wound. "Hold it tightly. I'll be right back."

After I take over the task, she jumps up and hurries to fetch the bottle of water, then runs back with it in hand.

She kneels beside me, opens the bottle, and places it at my lips as she presses on my wound, even when I don't remove my hand.

"You drink first," I say.

"I'm fine. You're the one who's wounded."

"But—"

"Just drink already." She jams it at my lips and helps me take tentative sips. The cold, fresh water soothes my dry throat.

I nearly drink half of it, not realizing just how dehydrated I am. This is bad.

At this rate, I'll get worse real soon.

"Drink more," she urges.

"You drink, baby."

"I'm fine."

"No, you're not. Your lips are also dry." God knows how long we've been here.

Judging by the small pool of blood beside us, it's been some time. I strain sideways, wincing as I study our surroundings.

I try not to be obvious about it, pretending that I'm looking at Naomi as she drinks.

But whether I'm obvious or not doesn't matter. The place has no escape route except for the metal door that they didn't even open to give us water.

"Second round," Ren's loathsome voice echoes from the speaker. "We'll spice it up a little this time and go with a dare. If you do it, we'll give you food. If not, there will be consequences."

A deep, growly sound comes from Naomi's stomach at the

mention of food. She closes the bottle of water that has about half left and stares up. "What is it?"

"Remove the bra."

My jaw clenches as her face reddens. Her gaze flits to mine as she bites her lip slightly, unsure. I sharply shake my head once.

Fuck that and him.

There's no way in hell Naomi will be stripping for the sick bastard.

No way will anyone see her and her gorgeous tits but me.

"Seven...six..." Ren counts leisurely. "This will have a punishment..."

"Let me do it," Naomi whispers. "I don't care."

"Of course you do. You don't even like changing your clothes in front of everyone in the locker room, let alone in front of fucking strangers."

She releases her lips and they form into a stupefied 'Oh.' Is she really surprised that I noticed that about her? I notice everything when it comes to Naomi.

"I'm fine if it'll get us food," she insists.

"Fuck that," I mutter.

"Two...one," Ren finishes with a closed off tone. "Aaaand time for punishment."

Naomi and I watch the door, thinking someone will come in and beat us up or something.

Neither the door nor the small opening moves.

Was he bluffing?

That thought hasn't fully formed yet when the entire room goes black.

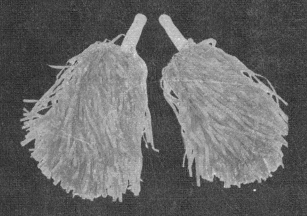

FOUR

Naomi

I BLINK A FEW TIMES AS IF THAT WILL MAGICALLY BRING BACK the light.

It doesn't.

The whole place is black.

It's so dark that I can see nothing. Absolute nada.

I instinctively inch further into Sebastian's side and only release a breath when I feel the warmth of his body against my thigh and my arm.

Our simultaneous breathing echoes through the air. Mine is harsh and fractured. His is deep and unsteady, probably due to the amount of pain he must be in.

He really needs to get some help and at this rate, Ren doesn't seem like he has that in his plans.

I carefully press against his hand that's on his wound. No blood has come out for some time, but it doesn't hurt to prevent it.

"That was foolish." Ren's voice pierces through the dark silence. "Not only will you remain without food, but you'll also stay in the darkness for…let's see… Hmm. Hours? Days? Who knows? The sky is the limit. Sorry, I mean, the ceiling of the cell is."

My throat closes. Sebastian probably can't survive hours in this condition, let alone days. Besides, the lack of food won't only weaken us, it'll also be lethal.

"I'll do it," I blurt. "I'll remove my bra."

"No," Sebastian growls deep in his throat. The sound is equally aggressive and pained.

Considering how possessive he can be, I'm well aware of how much he hates the idea of me being nude in front of other people. I hate it, too, but if it will keep us safe, I don't care.

A low tsking sound comes from Ren. "Your chance has passed. You lost, and per the rules, you'll pay. You might be able to survive for a few days, Naomi. Quarterback, though…"

The static of the speaker disappears and I jolt up. "No… Come back! You said there are many rounds. We can play the next… Come back! Ren!"

"It's useless." Sebastian releases a long breath that I feel with the long rise and broken fall of his chest. "He's gone."

"No. He could be there somewhere. He must be watching us."

"I don't think so. The cameras stopped blinking."

I look around, and sure enough, the red dots have disappeared. Even though that should be a relief, it actually isn't.

They really left us in the dark now.

Maybe we'll be here until we die.

Maybe no one will find our corpses.

"Help!" I scream at the top of my lungs, my voice turning hysterical as the worst-case scenarios flash in my head. "Someone help us! We're trapped!"

"Don't waste your energy, Nao."

"Maybe someone will hear us… Maybe they'll get us out of here."

"You don't really believe that."

I don't. But I choose to hold on to the illusion that there's something more to the hand we've been dealt.

"Let me try to get to the door," I suggest. Maybe I'll be able to open it."

"You saw the door. It's metal."

"Then do you suggest we do nothing? You've been shot!"

"I know. But the best thing we can do under the circumstances is to save our energy. We only have so much water left and once that's gone, it'll only get worse."

I sniffle, then wipe my tears with the back of my hand. I hate being weak, which is why I don't cry in public or show anyone just how soft I am inside.

But that's not the reason I want to stop crying. It's because of what Sebastian said earlier—when he mentioned that seeing me in pain hurts more than his wound.

Besides, crying won't help us solve this situation.

If Sebastian wasn't injured, he could probably break down the door or something. But right now, he's weaker than me.

His godlike body is heavy on the ground and sweat covers his skin, even though it's cold in here.

"I just don't understand why they're doing this. They're my father's people. They shouldn't want to hurt me. Unless…"

"Unless what?"

"Do you think he's taking revenge against my mom? She said she gave him fake DNA tests so he wouldn't know I'm his daughter. Maybe he took that to heart and is now doing this to torment her."

"Why would he hurt you to torment her?"

"Because I'm all she has. She left her family and old friends in Japan and has only had me since she came here."

At the thought of my mom, fresh tears spring to my eyes. I'm supposed to be spending more time with her now that she's in the late stages of cancer. We're supposed to be planning our trip to Japan and spending mother-daughter time together.

"Are you crying, baby?"

"She must be so worried." My voice breaks. "We rarely spend nights apart, even with her busy schedule. I never went on school trips or anything of the sort, because she was always obsessed with my safety. I think I know why now. She said my father is a dangerous man and I didn't believe her. Look where that got me."

"You...didn't know."

"Maybe this is my punishment for being so engrossed in finding my father while neglecting my existing parent. She has cancer, you know. It's late-stage and there's nothing they can do. She only has a few weeks left at best, and I can't even spend that time with her."

"You will." His voice gains a softer edge. "We'll get out of here."

"What if we don't? What if they forget about us and we die and end up on missing person reports? What if they find our remains a few years from now and we're unrecognizable and then they make a true crime show about us?"

A low chuckle escapes him but turns into a wince as it dies out. "That's your overactive imagination coming out to play."

"It could happen."

"It won't. They brought us here for a reason and they haven't accomplished it yet."

I sigh, carefully leaning closer to him. "I'm sorry you're caught up in all this because of me."

"It could be the other way around."

"What?"

"I believe we're both here because they plotted this all along for a specific purpose. It might have to do with my parents or my grandparents."

"Were your parents really killed?"

"I believe so. There was someone who came to collect the painting from the accident site. It was a family treasure Mom bought not long before the accident and insisted on taking with us. Then I think I heard them in the hospital talking about the painting and Mom. There's no way all of that could've been a coincidence."

My heart aches for him, at the horrors he's suffered ever since he was a child. No one should be marked so brutally that way.

"Who do you think killed them?"

He throws his head back against the wall with a grunt. "I don't know. It could have been these people. Or maybe my grandparents had something to do with it."

"Why would your grandparents hurt your father?"

"Because he disobeyed them by choosing Mom."

"Oh." I snuggle into his side, needing to feel his warmth, but when he winces, I pull back.

"It's fine. You don't have to keep holding the shirt."

"But you're bleeding."

"It stopped a while ago. It just hurts like a motherfucker now."

"I'll hold it just in case."

"You really don't have to."

"Just in case…"

"Are you worried about me?" I don't miss the amused edge in his tone. He's always playful, even in dire situations.

"Why wouldn't I be?"

"I thought you hated me with how you insisted that everything ends between us, Tsundere."

"I do hate you for playing with my heart and making a bet to destroy my naive feelings. I hate you for making all my fantasies come true just to shove them down the cliff of harsh reality. But I'll never hate you enough to wish you harm. That's just not me."

I suck in a sharp, fractured breath, surprised at the hot tenor of my words. Maybe that's all I've wanted to say ever since I found out he'd made a fool out of me but never had the right frame of mind to form the words.

Now that they're out, I feel both relieved and stuffed. I want to cry again because of how much it hurt. How much I missed him.

How much I've hated myself for missing him.

"It was never a bet, baby." His voice is quiet, despite the pain interlacing it.

"I was there and clearly heard that it was a bet."

"Technically. In reality, however, I never meant it as such."

"Are you telling me you didn't accept Reina's dare?"

"I did, but not for the reasons you think."

"Then what were your reasons?"

"If I didn't go with it, Reina would've had Josh do it."

"Gee, thanks. I'm honored it was you and not the creeper Josh."

"You're being sarcastic, which means you're on the defensive."

"Am I not allowed to be?"

"Not when you haven't given me a chance to explain my reasons."

"There are many of them?"

"It's one reason, actually. You."

"*Me?*"

"Yes, you. If it were up to me, things wouldn't have started with a bet. But maybe they had to."

"What the hell are you talking about?"

"I couldn't let Josh have you. My reaction was irrational, but I couldn't just allow it to happen."

"You didn't even know I existed before we bumped into each other that time."

"Of course I did."

I frown, staring in his general direction despite the darkness. "No, you didn't."

"Then how do you think I figured out all those tidbits about you? Such as your love for metal music or your sarcastic tendencies?"

"I figured Reina or one of the cheerleaders gave you pointers."

"They didn't need to. I was already watching you."

"You were *what?*" I nearly choke on my own words.

"I watched you, baby. For three years."

FIVE

Sebastian

Three years ago

I**T'S FASCINATING HOW SOMEONE FEELS THEIR BAD DAYS SO** deeply when they don't even notice their good ones.

That someone is me.

Bad days always start with the same thing—the need to hurt.

It pulses inside me like there's a second person attempting to get out but fails to find a way to.

It beats and claws.

It murmurs, then screams.

There's no tuning it out and ignoring it won't help. The only way to placate it is with the promise for violence.

I'm barely focused on Owen and Asher's conversation as we walk from our cars to the school building. Maybe I can beat someone the fuck up at today's practice.

Without breaking any bones.

The last thing I want is to get my grandparents involved. The only reason they like to be called to school is when they're promised to take some honorary awards home.

What's the best way to get rid of excess energy without broaching my grandparents' limits?

There's fucking, but that barely helps. Even when I get rough, it doesn't really satiate that urge for more.

Asher stops walking and I automatically do, too. He's been my friend since we were young. His father owns the firm that represents my grandfather.

After constantly being thrust into each other's presence, we thought, 'Fuck it. We might as well become friends.' Or maybe it's Owen's obnoxious presence that brought us together.

We definitely don't talk as much as when he's the center of attention, making everything about him and his random adventures.

Asher's dark green eyes narrow and a muscle tics in his jaw. He always has a cool mask strapped on his features and only one thing can remove it.

Or rather, one person.

I follow his field of vision, and sure enough, it's Reina.

She stands beside her car, laughing at something one of the soccer players is saying.

A sight that Asher doesn't approve of.

Her eyes meet his and her smile falls for a second before she picks up her conversation again as if her fiancé isn't standing a few feet away.

They started this stupid arranged engagement a few years back and they've only been spiraling out of control since. It got worse after her father died at the beginning of the year and she moved in with her legal guardian—Asher's father. Now that they live together, they're always at each other's throats.

I watch as my friend's body stiffens, his muscles straining against his T-shirt. His face closes off as well and he nearly rips a tendon in his neck from how hard he's gritting his teeth.

"Don't do it, dude." Owen's gaze flits between the scene and Asher's rigid posture. "He's just talking to her."

I lift a shoulder. "He could mean something more."

"Whose side are you on, fucker?" Owen glares at me.

"Asher's, of course." I lean in. "He's putting his hand on her. See? He's touching her arm. Who knows what he'll be touching next?"

That's all it takes for Asher to sprint toward them. Owen flips me off before he runs after him.

It's too late, though.

One second, the soccer player is standing there, and the next, Asher slams his fist straight into his face.

The sound of crunching bones hits my ears and I briefly close my eyes to commit it to memory.

It still doesn't help in chasing away the need for violence and the urge to pummel someone into the ground, but it does sound nice.

It looks nice, too.

The soccer player is on his knees, clutching his bloody nose as he spits profanities at Asher.

Reina's face turns to stone. She's probably used to Asher beating the crap out of anyone who looks at her, let alone talks to her.

He's that possessive and she's that antagonizing. Because, sometimes, she does it on purpose, just to get a reaction out of him.

The player jumps up and lands a punch on Asher's cheek. And then they're punching each other as if it's a boxing match.

Owen tries to interfere while Reina just stands there, her expression tight as she watches the fight. Her arms are crossed over her chest and her nails dig into her skin.

Asher punches harder and gets hit just as hard.

What a nice view.

What's nicer, though, are the drops of blood on the concrete.

If Asher's fist was more powerful, there'd be more blood.

Pity.

I release a bored sigh. I should probably pretend to get them off each other so it doesn't appear as if I'm enjoying the show a bit too much.

There goes my plan to enjoy the fight from a front-row seat.

I'm about to step in when something catches in my peripheral vision.

Actually, it's someone. Overhead.

The parking lot is situated at the bottom of a hill. At the top, there are countless trees that many students use as camouflage to make out.

For a second, I believe the blur of motion is, in fact, a couple fucking first thing in the morning.

But it isn't.

I take a step back so I can get a better view and freeze.

It's a girl.

She transferred to our school this year. I've seen her before because she's on the cheer squad with Reina, Brianna, and the others.

Also, she's so tiny, her size always gives her away in a crowd.

It's not her size that makes me stop and stare, though.

It's her eyes.

Or, more accurately, the tears in them.

Two streaks paint her blushed cheeks as she stares at the bleak sky.

There's something haunting about the look in her eyes, a wretchedness of sorts.

Or maybe it's an urge that couldn't be taken care of, like in my case.

She's not bawling the way the rest of the girls do. She doesn't seem to have red-rimmed eyes either.

Her grief is silent and discreet, as if she, herself, isn't aware that she's doing it.

I've never seen anyone look as heartbreakingly beautiful when they cry as she does right now.

A gust of wind toys with her short black hair and tulle skirt, making them fly in the air behind her. Even her jacket opens, revealing her Metallica T-shirt.

A leaf falls on her nose and she cuts off her staring contest with the sky to clutch it between her delicate fingers.

They're small, just like the rest of her.

Her dark eyes focus on the leaf as if it's the first time she's seen one. And just like that, she smiles.

It's a slow one that builds over time. Her rosebud lips purse and then they curve in the most breathtaking smile I've ever seen.

Her nose twitches and droplets of tears cling to her lips and chin, but she doesn't stop smiling as she fingers the leaf.

An irrational thought takes hold of me, one that I wouldn't ordinarily have under any circumstances. I've never been the irrational type. Not for any reason.

And yet, the need to go up there is stronger than any violent urge I have ever had. I want to ask her why she's crying and why she's smiling.

I want to ask her how it's possible to look like a fucking angel I don't believe in while she's both crying and smiling.

Better yet, I want to be the reason why she has that expression on her face.

Haunted happiness.

As if neither the pain nor the joy could win, so they decided to co-exist.

But I don't go to her.

Because if I do, I'll ruin the perfect image in front of me. One that countless artists could try to emulate but would never manage to.

A piece of fucking art.

"Sebastian!"

My gaze strays away at the sound of my name. It's Owen and he's glaring, pointing at the fight so I'll go and help him break it up.

That's when I realize I completely zoned out from what's going on.

Weird.

My own need for violence is barely there. It's definitely not as strong as it was a few minutes ago.

"Just a sec," I tell Owen and stare up at the hill.

There's nothing.
The angel I made up is no longer there.
Maybe she didn't exist in the first place.
Only, she did.
And I'll make sure to keep an eye on her from now on.
If only to see her cry-smile again. Or maybe just smile.
Or just cry.
As long as I see her.

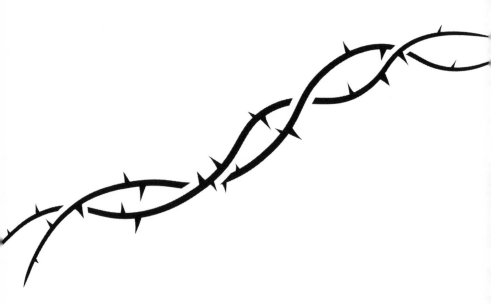

SIX

Naomi

I STARE IN THE DARKNESS, MY LIPS PARTING.

Unable to resist, I reach out blindingly until I touch Sebastian's sleeve. He's no longer retelling the events of the first day he 'met' me, but I'm not done listening.

I'm not done hearing him say that he actually knew I existed all along.

He might not have shown it, but he knew I was there. Maybe for as long as I've known about him.

"Why were you crying that day?" His voice is quiet, almost unsure, which is so unlike him. He's usually bursting with quiet confidence, but right now, he's showing me a side of him he never has before. "I've waited so long to ask that question."

I don't even have to think hard about it. I remember it clearly as if it were a few days ago. "Are you sure you want to know? It's a stupid reason and I hate to shatter your memories."

"Nothing is stupid about you, Nao."

My grip tightens on his sleeve. "It was my birthday. Mom asked me what present she could get me, and I told her I wanted Dad. She didn't like that and we got into a huge fight right before I left for school. That's why I was crying. See? It's a stupid reason."

"It's not. Why did you smile after?"

"I had an angsty teenage moment where I thought, 'Hey, maybe the world would be better off without me.' Then I looked up and asked for a sign to show me that I'm important somehow and that my existence matters. It could have been anything as long as I could feel it. That's when the leaf fell on my nose, and for some reason, that made me so giddy inside. Boring, I know. I've ruined your image of that memory."

Sebastian grabs my arm and tugs me down so that my head lies on his muscled thigh. A muffled wince leaves him and even through the darkness, I can imagine the frown etched deep between his brows.

His lean fingers comb through my hair, stroking gently. It takes everything in me not to moan, and instead, I try to get up so I don't hurt him.

Sebastian locks a steel-like arm over my upper chest, forbidding me from moving. "You didn't ruin anything. You just amplified it, and do you know what that means? You're stuck with me, baby."

The need to cry hits me again, but I sniffle so I don't turn into a crybaby. I have a reputation to keep, dammit. "I still haven't forgiven you."

"Even when I'm dying?"

"You're not dying!" My voice chokes. "We'll get out of here."

"I'm kidding. I was only trying to play on your sympathy."

"Don't do that again." My fingers dig into his pants and I struggle to push the image of him dying out of my head.

That thought chokes me.

It steals my breath and leaves me with muddied, chaotic thoughts.

"I'm just playing with you, Tsundere." His voice lowers and it's almost soothing, despite the tinge of pain in it. "I wouldn't leave you alone after I waited three years."

"You…waited?"

"I think I have."

"What were you waiting for?"

"I don't know. Maybe an opportunity."

I scoff. "You could've made your own opportunity without wait-ing for Reina's bet."

"That's the problem. I didn't know I needed to make a move until that fucker Josh almost took you away. Being threatened made me take action."

"Josh wouldn't have stood a chance. Arrogant football players aren't my type."

"Except for me?"

"I never said that."

"You don't have to, Tsundere. I watched you long enough to recognize your hot and cold attitude."

I bite my lower lip and inhale deeply, taking in his scent mixed with blood and something else. "I can't believe you watched me for three years and I didn't notice anything."

"I'm pretty good. Besides, you tend to be blind to your sur-roundings, especially when you have those headphones on."

"Not to you," I murmur. "You see, I watched you, too."

"You did?"

I nod against his thigh. "Since the first day I got to school. You probably don't remember it, but I do. Clearly."

He's quiet for a beat, and I can only hear the guttural sounds of his breathing in the dark silence. It's haunting and chopped off, a clear indication that he needs help and no matter how much we fool ourselves into believing we'll be okay, we probably won't.

I suck in a sharp breath and choose to remain in the here and now, even if it's only temporary.

The now is all we have.

"It was during my first day at Blackwood High. Once again, I was mad at how Mom kept relocating us from one city to another. Not that I loved San Francisco, but it felt like home for so long. And out of the blue, Mom told me she'd bought a house in some town filled with rich people. We'd lived in small towns before and I'd hated them all. People in those places were mostly racist, narrow-minded assholes, and yet, Mom didn't seem to care.

"I didn't believe her when she said this time would be different. She kept singing different tunes about the wealth of the town or how the crime rate in Blackwood was close to zero or that its residents were the kindest. But she forgot the tiny detail about how I'd be a transfer student in the middle of my senior year and they're always doomed for rejection.

"I missed the tour the principal specifically booked for Mom and me, because we arrived at the last second into town. In addition to being a new face in the middle of the year, I was completely clueless about how to get to Blackwood High, and to make matters worse, it was raining. The GPS got me to the top of a hill, then got so funky that I couldn't tell whether the school was located to the left or the right. So I stopped the car on the side of the road near a football field and got out, assuming it was the school's field. But I couldn't find anyone to direct me to the stupid school. I thought my first day was doomed for failure from the get-go.

"But when I was walking back to my car, someone tapped my shoulder and pointed to the right without really looking at me. He was running in the middle of the pouring rain and he had earbuds in, so he didn't hear me when I thanked him. He didn't notice that I stood there, staring, thinking maybe this town wouldn't be as bad as the others." I gulp down the lump that has formed in the back of my throat. "That someone was you. It was a random show of compassion, but for a newbie in town who knew no one and was clueless, it meant a lot more than you'd think."

He's silent for a second and if it weren't for the irregular rhythm of his breathing, I'd believe he'd fallen asleep or something.

"You probably don't even recall that moment," I blurt. "But... do you know why you did it?"

"Did what?"

"Pointed a stranger in the right direction. You lack empathy, so you shouldn't have stopped to help."

"I didn't stop to help."

"You tapped my shoulder and helped."

"I probably saw something in you."

"Like what?"

"I don't know. Just like I don't know why I stopped and stared at you that day. Maybe all of those things led to how we got together."

"You think?"

"I'm sure. After all, you watched me as much as I watched you. Did you have a crush on me, baby?"

"No!"

"Defensive, Tsundere. How about you be honest for once?"

"It's just that whenever I saw you the other times, I thought of the feelings I'd had on that day. It was oddly relieving and safe."

"Then I came along and crushed those feelings?" There's an exhausted hoarseness in his voice, and while I love the natural edge of it, it's abnormal.

"Not really."

"Do you mean to tell me you still feel relieved and safe?"

"To a degree, yes. The way you came after me with sheer determination scared the shit out of me. Our relationship and depraved chases terrified me, too, but I do feel safe with you. If I didn't, I would've ended it a long time ago."

"Mmm…I…like that…" he trails off, his voice losing its raspiness and turning weak.

I sit up carefully and his hand lies limp on my shoulder, not even attempting to stop me. "Sebastian?"

"Mmm..?"

I gently touch his abdomen, then trace a path up to his cheek. I stiffen when his hot skin meets mine. Holy shit. He's burning up.

Fever is totally bad. He could have an infection or something worse.

I feel up his neck and face that's lolled to the side, his chapped lips slightly parting. "Sebastian, can you hear me?"

He releases an absentminded noise but doesn't stir.

"Sebastian! Open your eyes!"

He remains in the same position. I check under the T-shirt that's against his shoulder and breathe out a sigh of relief when I don't feel any stickiness. Although he's still no longer bleeding, the fever could mean something worse.

Tendrils of malevolent fear snap around my ribcage and worst-case scenarios play in my head.

God, no.

Please don't take him away.

Please. I would do anything.

Fresh tears fill my lids as I feel for the bottle of water, pour some on the shirt, then place it on his forehead.

I continue calling his name, although he's still not moving, and he seems to be getting warmer, not colder.

I drink some water, then brush my lips against his chapped ones, trying to get him to take a sip, even if it's only a little one.

The sound of his swallow is like music to my ears. At least he's staying a little hydrated.

But even I know that if he doesn't get medical help soon, he won't be able to survive.

I continue brushing my lips against his, attempting to get him to drink as much water as possible. When he's no longer swallowing, I pull back and check his pulse in his neck.

Fat tears cascade down my cheeks at the dim pulse beneath my fingers.

I can almost hear the life leaving him, and the most dooming part is that I can't do anything to stop or even slow it down.

Placing both palms on his neck, I lower my head. "Sebastian… please, baby…please open your eyes, please…I can't…I can't live without you anymore. I don't want to imagine it, so please…please stay with me…"

A low grunt leaves his throat and I straighten, sniffling. "Sebastian..?"

"You…called me…baby…"

I smile at the amusement in his voice, allowing the salty tears inside my mouth. "I'll call you anything you want. Just stay with me."

"Baby…" he grunts.

"Yes?"

"Marry…me."

"Huh?"

"When…we get out…of here. Marry…me."

I scoff through my tears.

This is crazy.

We're crazy.

But if there's anything I've learned through this whole thing, it's that nothing lasts forever. Our fates have been connected for three years, even though we've watched each other from afar.

What we have happens once in a lifetime and it's pointless to fight it anymore.

"Okay. I'll marry you."

"You can't change your…mind…once we survive."

"I won't."

"Good…b-because…I won't let you…"

"Sebastian?" I grab his face and shake him gently, but he's out cold again.

This can't go on.

After adjusting the wet T-shirt on his forehead, I jolt up and slowly walk to where I remember the door to be. My steps are careful as I take a stab in the dark.

I bump against a wall and place my hands on it, feeling my way.

Once I touch metal, I bang on the door with both fists. "Open up!! You said you wanted to play a game, so why aren't you playing? Open up, you sick bastards!"

I keep on hitting and calling them names in both English and Japanese. When that doesn't work, I pull, then push at the door, shouting, "If my dad finds out about this, he'll kill you! I'll make sure he fucking kills you!! Open the damn door!"

"Not yet, *Ojou-sama*." The voice that comes from the other side of the door makes me stop in my tracks.

He's speaking in Japanese, but why the hell does he sound so familiar? It's not Ren or the other guy who was with him that day at our house.

This one is calmer, sounds more dangerous. As if he's issuing death sentences to the undead.

Ojou-sama.

He called me princess in the most honorific term possible, and it's not the first time.

Someone called me that before, but who? And when?

"Who are you?" I ask in Japanese.

"The one who will make you worthy of joining our family. In order to do that, you have to suffer a great loss."

SEVEN

Akira

Dear Yuki-Onna,

You're obviously getting two letters back to back, because the moment I sent the previous one, I sat down and wrote another.

Clingy much? Probably. But I blame you for that.

You're the only person I can't kick out of my conscious no matter how hard I try to. It's that toxicity, I swear. You make it addictive in a strange type of way.

But that's not why I'm writing again.

It's your name.

Not Naomi, but Yuki-Onna. You know, I had a daydream just a while ago and in it, Yuki-Onna came through my window.

She was pale as the snow and just as cold. Her lips were like a red rosebud and her huge brown eyes held no light.

It was sad and intriguing at the same time.

You know when a disaster is happening but you realize there's nothing you can do about it so you just stand there and watch?

That's what I did with Yuki-Onna. I just remained still and observed her.

Even when she stretched out her ghostly hands and went for my fucking liver. Even when I felt the frost of her touch deep into my goddamn bones.

I only watched.

Do you know why? Because deep in my mind, she was you.

And somewhere in my head, you came for payback over all the shit I told you. I mean, is there a better cause of death than revenge?

There probably is. Just don't tell me.

I didn't die, obviously, it was all in my head, but when I came to, my heart was beating so fast I thought it'd stop. So I'm writing you this letter so you know I'm alive.

Not that you care.

Or maybe you do.

After all, you do love me in one way or another or you would've stopped talking to me by now.

I guess you're that lonely to think of me as a friend, but then again, if you didn't have me, there would be no one in your life to beat hard truths into your skull.

If you didn't have me, you'd drown in your delusions so deep, you wouldn't even realize when or how to stop.

Not that you do right now.

But at least you know my opinion of your life—that sucks, by the way—but then again, my own life sucks, too.

Isn't that the beauty of it all, Naomi?

Both our lives suck but we're still here anyway. We still go to the post office and send letters.

You still hold on to the hope that I'm the only friend you have and I still like to imagine you as my own Yuki-Onna.

Cold, beautiful, and will one day fucking kill me.

But here's a secret. If you'll be my cause of death, I don't really mind it.

After all, don't they say find something toxic and let it kill you?

Well, that's not exactly the line, but in our case, it counts.

Be safe. Or not. As long as you reply.

And pray that I don't have any other daydreams about Yuki-Onna or I will keep bugging you until you actually show up at my window.

And then I might never let you go.

Akira

EIGHT

Sebastian

I BLACKED OUT.

I must be slipping in and out of consciousness.

Blurred figures appear behind my lids, their gray silhouettes dancing in rhythm with my weak pulse.

Sounds follow. They're hollow, distant, as if coming from an empty underground arena. The figures and the sounds are mixing together and drumming against my skull.

Thud.

Thud.

Thud.

I strain, but tight tentacles of pain keep me confined in place. I try again and a burning sensation shoots through my limbs. The drumming continues, getting louder and more intense, like a musical's crescendo.

And then, right in the middle of the darkness, a shaft of light peeks through. It's slow at first, dim, almost blending with the gray shadows until, all of a sudden, it bursts through, rushing toward me with no pause or deviation.

As if it knows exactly where I am.

As if I'm the only one it sees in the pitch-black.

As if it's well aware I need to get out of the darkness.

A soft hand wraps around my face, warding off the invisible figures that were about to drag me under.

"Sebastian...please...please..."

Naomi.

In my fight against the darkness and its lure, I forgot that she was still here, alone, unprotected.

The thought of anyone touching her while I'm crippled provokes red-hot pain to flare over my skin.

Fucking fuck.

I stir, then groan when my shoulder explodes with fire. Holy shit, they never say in the movies that being shot means hanging on to life by a chapped, faulty straw.

"Sebastian? Can you hear me?"

"Yeah...baby."

"Oh, thank God!" She sobs, fussing over me.

It's still so dark that I can't see my hands. But that's not why I want the light. It's the fact that I can't watch her delicate features and get lost in the darkness of her penetrating gaze.

Not seeing Naomi is no different than living without the sun. I sound cheesy as fuck, even to myself, but I now recognize how much this girl means to me.

She is the meaning.

I lost that meaning somewhere between my parents' deaths and my grandparents' upbringing. I was an image to flaunt around, a makeshift mask of fake emotions.

Then Naomi barged in like a wrecking ball. She didn't care about my outside image and saw straight through it. She didn't want me because of what I am. She wanted me because of *who* I am.

The imperfect, flawed monster.

The beast who woke up in the hospital after he lost everything when he was six.

"You…said you'll marry…me…" I croak, not recognizing my own voice. It's hoarse, exhausted, and on the verge of collapsing.

"Yes…" she snorts between sniffles. "I can't believe that's the only thing you're thinking about right now."

So, it's true.

She said yes to the most horrible proposal ever.

But even if the method was trash, it wasn't impulsive or spur of the moment. I wasn't proposing to her because we're in danger and might never get out of this alive. I proposed because this woman right here is the one I want to spend the rest of my life with.

It's not a hot-blooded moment where two young people make a decision that's seemingly too old for them. It's not about age for me, it's about mentality. I know it for a fact, so what's the point in delaying the inevitable?

Naomi tucks my jacket around my sides so that I'm fully covered. Her hands are cold. She must be freezing without her T-shirt, but she doesn't stop fretting about me.

"You were out for so long. I think it's been more than a day or two. It feels like fucking months." She sniffles. "I got to the toilet and had to use the water to cool you down. I also made you drink some from the bottle. I think it helped bring your fever down, but you're still too hot and I don't think your wound is doing so well. I tried to see if there was a bullet inside, but I didn't find anything and… and I didn't want to hurt you more, so I stopped searching and…"

"Baby…" I attempt to raise my good hand so I can touch her, but my energy fails me and it falls to my side.

Naomi grabs it and places it on her wet cheek. "What is it? Are you in that much pain? What can I do to make it better?"

"Kiss me."

Only a fraction of a second passes before I feel her soft lips against my dry ones. She's gentle, careful, as if she's afraid a kiss will kill me.

Maybe dying while kissing Naomi is the right way to go.

I growl deep in my chest as I attempt to deepen the kiss and taste her properly. But my mouth barely moves. I'm too weak that I can't even kiss my girl the way she deserves.

A groan spills from me, filled with pent-up fucking frustration.

Naomi pulls back and grabs my face with both her small hands as if she can see my expression in the dark. "Did I hurt you?"

My hand drops from her face and I grunt a "No."

There's nothing I hate more than the helplessness. It's fucking insane how the human body can become weak in a fraction of a second.

Right before I went to the forest, I was running over ten miles in an hour and lifting weights like nobody's business, but now, I can't even touch Naomi without help.

This situation could go on until I completely lose consciousness. And then I'll die.

Tap water will keep Naomi alive for a few weeks before she'll follow. That is, if it doesn't give her some sort of infection beforehand.

The only other time I've felt so helpless was after my parents' accident. But I was young back then. It's not the same situation.

"Sebastian? Are you still there?"

"Yeah, baby…"

"Please stay with me…"

"Don't…be…scared…"

"How can I not be? I think they're trying to break me and you're paying the price just because you know me. I'll never forgive myself if something happens to you. I'll just follow you to wherever you go."

Don't.

I want to say that, but even my tongue is heavy and unable to move.

The constant assault of pain from my wound and the pounding in my head don't help in my attempts to stay conscious.

Even Naomi's voice has turned into a low hum.

That's when I know I'll pass out again.

When her voice is clear and she's calling my name, it means I'm back.

I keep slipping in and out of consciousness, and after a while, I think I'm going fucking insane.

The only thing that's keeping me anchored is Naomi and her soft touches and soothing words.

It's the brush of her lips against mine as she makes me drink water. It's the feel of her body snuggled into me.

It's even the low, haunting sound of her weeping when she thinks I'm unconscious.

She doesn't cry when I'm lucid enough to speak a word or two of gibberish. She puts up a strong façade and tends to me, holding on to hope I don't think I have anymore. But when she believes I'm out, she releases her hopeless side, too. She cries silently or sometimes loudly.

Then she bangs on the door and asks them to let us go. She says words in Japanese that I would normally understand, but I don't have full access to my brain and, therefore, can only hear the fear and determination in her tone.

The *fight*.

Maybe she's not as hopeless as I am, after all.

Because, at this point, I do believe they brought us here to kill us. Or to kill one of us.

My grandparents couldn't be involved in this. No matter how much they want to teach me a lesson, they wouldn't put my life in jeopardy.

Does that mean I've been kidnapped? Did they request a ransom?

If they had, my grandparents would've paid it already. This isn't a normal case of kidnapping. If it were, there wouldn't be games of survival.

A hand softly touches my cheek as a cool cloth is placed on my forehead.

"I'll get us out of here, Sebastian. I promise. So please…*please* hang in there."

So many words form at the back of my throat, but the only thing that comes out is a pained moan.

Naomi strokes my cheek as if she knows exactly what I'm trying to say.

She's so fucking strong, my Naomi. She's all alone, and yet, she doesn't break down or give up. She religiously cleans my wound and makes me drink water. She even whispers soothing words to keep me in the present.

If she weren't here, I would've died a long time ago.

Static pierces through my ears, and for a second, I think it's in my head, that all of this is a figment of my imaginary shadows.

But Naomi goes rigid, her chest grazing mine as she leans closer.

The voice I never wanted to hear again fills the room, "Time to resume our game, don't you think, Hitori-san?"

"What do you want?" she snarls, but her voice is weak, weary.

I'm sure she hasn't slept for some time now. Between taking care of me and banging on the walls, she's always up to something.

The lack of food also contributes in altering the human mind. When the body doesn't get its needs, the brain shuts down as well.

Whoever brought us here already planned to make us as weak and as desperate as possible.

Only then will they reveal what they want. Because they know we won't have the chance to refuse whatever ludicrous demand they make.

"I assume you want a doctor to look at the quarterback's wound?" Ren tsks. "It'd be a pity if he loses his arm altogether—or his life."

"What the hell do you want?" she hisses.

"We'll go with a dare again. I'll get Quarterback a doctor. In return…" His voice drops and all humor disappears. "You'll fuck me like you want it."

A roar bubbles at the back of my throat and a loud growl spills out of my lips. "No."

"Oh, you're not unconscious yet." Ren sounds bored. "This is a nice development. You get to watch."

A low grunt spills out of me and my body jolts. Naomi places a shaky hand on my shoulder, steadying me, but when she speaks, her voice is trembling. "It's okay."

"Noooo," I moan. "Don't…"

"You'll die, Sebastian."

"I don't fucking…care… No…"

"Baby…please… If it will help you, I can…" She sucks in a deep breath. "I can do it."

"No…" I sound pained, enraged, and so fucking frustrated. I wish I could cut off my own damn arm instead of letting her go to that scum.

No one, no fucking one other than me will touch her, not even if I have to die for it.

"You have five seconds left." Ren's voice echoes from the speaker. "Four, three…"

"I'll do it," Naomi announces with a broken murmur.

"No…" I shake my head. "She…didn't say that… No…"

"Come to the door, Hitori-san," Ren says.

Naomi releases a shaky breath that bounces off my sweaty skin. She brushes her warm lips against mine. "You'll be fine, Sebastian…"

As she starts to get up, I don't know how I get the superhuman energy to grab her arm. She turns to me at the same time that the light goes on in the room.

I squint before I see her face for the first time in what seems like years, although it's probably only been a few days.

Her lips are chapped and her cheeks have sunken. Her black hair that's usually shiny seems dull and lifeless. Dry streaks of tears line her pale cheeks and her eyes are filled with fresh ones.

She looks so broken, so desolate, and I want to kick myself in the balls for not being able to get her out of this place.

"Oh, God," she whispers as she studies me.

I probably look ten times worse than she does, but I don't even glance at my wound. If I lose feeling in my arm, it would probably be a good thing under the circumstances. That way, I could have them cut it off and she won't have to make any sacrifices for my sake.

"The door, Naomi." Ren's voice is like nails scratching at the interior of my fucking skull.

She gives me an apologetic look, lips drawing downward, and starts to stand again.

But I tighten my hold on her wrist. "Don't…fucking…go…"

"I have to so I can save you."

"Fucking…someone else…is no different…than killing…me, Nao…"

"I don't care as long as you're safe." She mashes her lips to mine, and unlike her other kisses, this one isn't light and careful. It's not soothing either.

She goes all the way in, thrusting her tongue inside and kissing me like it's the last time.

Her hand wraps around my nape and the other sinks in my hair as she gets lost in the kiss. Her tongue twirls with mine and her moans mix with my grunts.

Fuck the pain.

I grab her by the throat, my hold weak as I explore her mouth, kissing her with a desperation that matches hers.

But the spell soon breaks when she pulls away and whispers in my ear, "I'll pretend it's you."

"No…" I moan, the physical and emotional hurt audible in my tone.

"I love you, Sebastian," she murmurs so low, I can barely hear her.

A tear slides down her cheek and clings to her upper lip as she peels my hand off her and stands up.

The door opens and she heads to it without a glance back.

When it closes behind her, I release a roar that reverberates through the silent room.

The image of her with another man cuts me open like a thousand knives. I can't stop picturing his hands on her, touching her, worshipping her body. I'm the only one who's supposed to do that.

The only one who gets to *see* her. Both physically and emotionally. Only me.

But what kills me further is the fact that she's doing this for me. She's letting someone else fuck her so she can save me.

For the first time since my parents' deaths, bitter moisture gathers in the corners of my eyes.

Fuck!

I attempt to sit up. In my mind, I'm running after Naomi and killing every fucker who looks in her direction. In my mind, I'm spilling their blood and kissing her in the midst of it.

I barely move and I'm reared back to the ground as a burn explodes in my shoulder and my lungs suffocate.

Black dots condense in my vision and I gladly surrender to them.

I might as well fucking die now.

Because there's no way in hell I'll ever forgive myself for putting Naomi in this position.

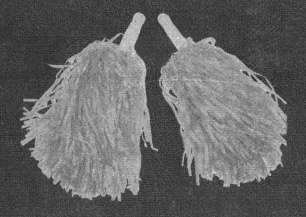

NINE

Naomi

THE LOUD CREAKING SOUND OF THE DOOR CLOSING BEHIND me shakes me to my core.

The courageous façade I put up in front of Sebastian cracks and crumbles all around me.

I lied.

It's not going to be fine.

It's going to be *anything* but fine.

My chin trembles and it takes all of my strength to keep from bawling my eyes out.

I want to get back in there and snuggle into Sebastian's side. I want to hold his hand and take care of him. It doesn't matter if we're locked up or kidnapped or whatever as long as we're together.

But I saw him.

I saw how his wound has turned into angry shades of violet and blue. Not to mention his fever that's gone up, then down, then up again with no clear pattern.

He's lost weight and his proud shoulders have sunken. His

once-mesmerizing eyes have hollowed and dimmed as if he's getting ready for death.

If I didn't agree to this, I'd lose him.

This is only to save him, I tell myself. To save both of us. I meant what I said the other day. If he's gone, I have no interest in life anymore.

Swallowing the onslaught of tears, I stare up and shiver. The hall I'm in is even more freezing than the room I just left. I wrap my arms around myself to ward off the biting lick of cold on my bare skin. I'm still in only my sports bra, despite Sebastian's endless feverish attempts to have me wear his jacket.

I'm weak and hungry. My stomach stopped screaming for food after some time and is just clenching on its emptiness now.

The only thing that's kept me strong and kicking is the need to save Sebastian and get him out of here.

I'll make sure he's safe, even if it's the last thing I do.

Aside from the dimmed light, there's not a soul around.

Hope blossoms at the base of my stomach. Maybe I can find an exit and get some help—

"I wanted Quarterback to watch, but he lost consciousness."

I startle at the sound coming from right behind me and I whirl around, my heartbeat skyrocketing.

Ren stands in the shadows not far from the door and must've been there all along. Or at least, since I came out. A smirk tugs at his lips as he pushes off the wall and strolls over to where I'm standing.

Ren is exactly as I remember him from the first time I met him in our house a few weeks ago. Tall, lean, wears a black suit with no tie and snake tattoos peek from around his neck as a subtle translation of the anger he can possess. His black dot earrings give him a rebellious image that contradicts the rest of him.

Back then, he seemed like a mischievous person out for trouble, like the kids who plot a riot, then hide to watch it unfold.

The same sentiment hits me again. Only, this time, it looks as if he wants to be there to witness the action himself.

He circles around me as if I'm his latest prey. My limbs stiffen and my breathing becomes harsher.

I got off on being treated as prey in the past, but only as part of my games with Sebastian. Only because it was on both of our terms. Not once did I feel I was in danger, no matter how out of control he got or how rough he treated me.

Because he's Sebastian, and deep down, I knew he'd never hurt me.

This situation is entirely different.

Ever since I met Ren, all he's done is hurt me. The fact that I have no clue about his motives and goals is keeping me on my toes.

"Maybe I can douse Quarterback with water so he can watch you bouncing off my dick." He grins. "What do you think?"

I swallow past the lump in my throat and adopt my firm tone. "You said you'd get him a doctor."

"Bossy. Why am I not surprised?" He has a subtle accent when he speaks in English, one that's similar to Mom's. Which probably means that he's originally from Japan.

But that barely tells me anything about him.

I widen my stance and stare him in the eyes. "You promised to get a doctor."

"Only after I fuck you while you moan and scream. Especially the latter."

The sick bastard is smiling at the thought of making me scream.

He reaches a hand out and when he touches a strand of my hair, I flinch back like I've been electrocuted. "Why are you acting so disgusted when we're about to have fun?"

"I'm not doing it unless you get him a doctor."

"That's not the deal."

"It is now." I cross my arms over my chest. "How do I know you won't leave him to die after you get what you want?"

"You don't, which is the entire point." Ren has a subtle grating way of talking. He does it slowly, almost methodically, with a permanent smirk on his lips.

It's like his purpose of existing is to get on people's nerves and provoke their nasty side.

"I won't do it unless he has medical care."

He lifts a shoulder. "Then he'll just rot and die."

Frustration bubbles in my veins and my heart shrinks behind my ribcage. If I don't do it, I have no doubt that Ren will leave Sebastian to die. If I do it, there's no guarantee that he'll get him help.

I suck in a deep breath through my nose and choose the only option I have. "Fine, I agree."

He licks his lips. "Are you sure? I'll make sure Quarterback receives footage at some point in his life. Could be in a week or two. A year or a few. But he'll see you fucking someone else while he's passed out in the adjoining room like a weak, little bitch."

I can't control the moisture that gathers along my lids, but I use that as a strength instead of a weakness. "The only weak, little bitch here is *you*, asshole. You shot him so he'd become defenseless and now you're using manipulation to get your limp dick wet. Do whatever you want, but I'll make sure my dad knows about this. And when he kills you in cold blood, I'll get footage of it and watch it for years to come."

I tremble, my hands balled into fists on either side of me. I fully expect Ren to tackle me to the ground and rape me, then kill me. Or maybe the other way around.

Instead, he bursts out laughing, his head tipping back. The sound is so loud that I jump.

"You're a Hitori, after all," he says once he finishes his psychotic fit of laughter, slightly shaking his head. "Now, come on."

"Come where?"

"You'll see."

I plant my feet on the ground. "I'm not going anywhere with you unless you tell me why and where."

He leans over so fast, I don't have the chance to push back. Then he grabs me by the arm as he peers down at me, his face mere inches from mine. "You don't really have a say in it, now do you? Follow me quietly and without asking questions unless you want to open those legs here and now."

I frown. Does that mean if I follow him, I don't have to open my legs? Or maybe I'm reading too much into things.

Twisting my arm, I attempt to get away from him, but he tightens his hold until he cuts off my circulation.

"Let me go!" I strain.

The sound of a door opening makes me freeze. I stare in the opposite direction and completely forget about Ren and his savage grip.

The man who nonchalantly leans against the doorframe is the last person I expected to see in this place.

Though it all makes sense now.

He's the one who talked to me through the door a few days ago. At the time, I couldn't exactly identify him, because he sounds more aristocratic and composed when he speaks in Japanese than when he does in English.

"You heard the princess," he tells Ren in Japanese. "Let her go."

Ojou-sama.

Again. He's calling me a princess and now I'm even more sure that I met him before this year.

Maybe when I was young...

"She's resisting," Ren says in the same language, sounding bored to death.

"Or you're taking a long time to do a simple task, Ren."

"Are you calling me useless?"

"Your words, not mine."

"K-Kai...?" I stammer, cutting off their back and forth.

The man I thought was a PI slides his gaze to me. Unlike Ren's mocking presence, Kai's is serene, calm, soothing almost.

I always felt some sort of safety with him and even an urge to talk to him about everything and nothing.

That's the type of image he projected, anyway. A big brother of sorts.

A pillar.

A *manipulator*.

Because now I'm even more sure that none of this was a coincidence. Not how I first connected with him, not how I remember him calling me *Ojou-sama* at some point in my life, and definitely not the black van and Ren's involvement.

It all has to do with my father. The same father I never knew and who Mom protected me from because he's dangerous.

Kai smiles and it's warm, inviting. That's what made me fall into his trap in the first place. His damn welcoming smile.

Now, I realize it's no different than the devil when he's on the mission of luring his victims.

"Hello again, princess."

I twist my arm from Ren's hold and he surprisingly lets me go. My entire attention is on Kai. "What is all of this about?"

"I said I'd take you to your father and I always keep my promises."

"You couldn't have done that without kidnapping me?"

He shakes his head once. "I told you, you need to suffer a loss."

I point a finger at Ren. "He promised he'd get Sebastian a doctor."

"That won't work. He has a nasty infection and it must've spread to his lungs, because he's barely able to breathe. He needs a hospital and ICU care, and in order to get them, he has to leave in about…" He stares at his watch. "Five minutes, more or less."

God no.

I knew he was doing horribly, but I'd hoped it wasn't that critical.

"Do it!" I snarl at Ren. "Fuck me and keep your word."

"I'm insulted." He places a hand on his chest. "You really think I'd finish in five minutes? I need at least…thirty?"

"You're a monster."

"More or less." He grins.

"There will be no sex," Kai's voice cuts through our conversation.

My head snaps in his direction. "There won't?"

"No. It was a test and you passed."

I stare back at Ren and he grins again, showing his straight teeth. "You're right. Your father would torture and kill me if I touched you. Though we could always do it behind his back?"

Oh.

So my father is really behind this.

I can't help the taste of betrayal that gathers at the back of my throat. My little girl dreams incinerate, leaving a heap of ashes and slaughtered wishes. All these years, I've held on to a distant fantasy of reuniting with my father. I never thought it would be under such circumstances or that Sebastian could pay the price for it.

"What does he want?" I ask Kai because, for some reason, he seems to be the one in charge.

"It's simple." Kai tips his head in my direction. "You."

"Me?"

"Yes. You see, he's been wanting to reunite with you for as long as you have."

"He could've just shown up instead of pulling this stunt!"

"Not with the way Riko has been poisoning your head about him, no. Everything requires the right timing."

"Like how you pretended to be a damn PI?"

"I couldn't let you go to some stranger when we have in-house intel, *Ojou-sama.*"

"So, now what?"

"You'll agree to our terms and adopt your real name. Naomi Hitori."

I'm sure their terms are equivalent to selling my soul to the devil. Otherwise, they wouldn't have gone as far as kidnapping me, starving me, and shooting Sebastian.

They must know how much I care about him and that I would play right into their hands if his life was threatened.

And that's true.

I don't care what I have to do as long as it keeps him safe. If it means selling my soul for parts, so be it. He's the one who made me well aware of that soul in the first place. It seems fitting to sacrifice it for him.

A part of me fractures and splinters into pieces all around me. I have no idea what awaits me, but something tells me it'll be harder than anything I've ever been through.

The red night included.

I have to stay strong, though all I want to do is curl into Sebastian's embrace and break down and cry in his arms. But I can't do that if he dies.

I can't do anything if he dies.

The decision is crystal clear in my head even as I fight the tears trying to escape. "I agree. But first, get Sebastian the help he needs. If anything happens to him, I'll kill myself and deprive my father of the daughter he wants so much."

TEN

Akira

Dear Yuki-Onna,

It's me again. Your one and only.

Your true friend who doesn't hesitate to call you out on your bullshit because no one else in your life does.

The only person who can actually see through your tough act and miserable life and enables you to smile even when everything crashes and burns around you.

Oh, and your pen pal. You know, someone you actually write letters to?

I didn't receive a reply to my last two letters, in case you haven't noticed, and I'm waiting in case you forgot—and no, you don't get to ignore me.

You should've done that the first time I wrote to you. Now it's a done deal and there's no damn turning back.

I told you I would keep writing to you even if you don't. I told you that my letters will show up at your door even if you hate them.

Is this punishment? Are you rebelling against me because of what I said in the last two letters? It's useless, though. It's not like I can magically get over the toxicity and live my life happily ever after in the city of unicorns and rainbows.

Besides, since when are you such a fragile snowflake who takes everything to heart? Did you develop other nasty habits I'm not aware of? Or maybe you're just being a bitch at this point and living up to the image you painted in my head.

Either way, fuck you very much, Naomi. This isn't how you're supposed to end a toxic relationship. We should talk about it, as toxically as possible, and without sugarcoating.

I thought we were special. As fucked up as that sounds, special relationships don't end just like that.

Special relationships don't end, period.

So how about you pick up your pen and write me back?

It can be as simple as threatening to kill me in the form of Yuki-Onna. Or maybe you can tell me how much you hate me in the best way possible.

Whatever it is, write. You know you want to, even if you somehow followed a spiritual journey and had a million therapists tell you to end your ties with me.

They're lying. It's impossible. This will never end.

Print out those words and hang them in your room, then look at them when you think of me and write me a letter.

I'm waiting.

I'll try to be nice in my reply, although I make no promises.

It'll depend on my mood, I guess.

DON'T FUCKING GHOST ME.
Akira

ELEVEN

Sebastian

I THINK I DIED.

Maybe dying is the best thing that could happen to me.

If I'm dead, I won't be thinking about Naomi with another man. If I'm dead, it'll all be over. I'll join the demons and all their friends and forget about the life I left behind.

But wouldn't that be the easy way out?

Wouldn't that mean I gave up too easily on what I found precious? On the life I finally found?

I don't want to die. Not if it means leaving Naomi unprotected and in danger.

I need to get back and be there for her.

My head throbs and my lids are glued together, refusing to open.

I suck in a sharp breath and cough when the smell of bleach assaults me.

Am I still in the same room?

"Sebastian?"

The voice that calls my name is familiar—too familiar.

Slowly, I force my eyes open, then squint when light bursts through. Fuck.

Who knew that something as harmless as light would hurt as if someone were holding a torch in front of my face?

It takes me a few seconds to adjust, and even then, I don't widen my vision to its fullest.

The first thing I notice is white. Walls. Ceiling. It's different from the gray of the cell where I last saw Naomi.

I'm lying on a soft mattress instead of the cold, merciless floor. I'm in the hospital.

Maybe that's why my shoulder doesn't hurt like a bitch and I don't feel like I'll starve to death.

I should be relieved that I'm getting help, that I'm not, in fact, dying, but I'm not.

The last time I woke up in a hospital, I learned the news of my parents' deaths. Life as I knew it splintered into a million pieces and never really became the same again.

The same damned premonition I had at that time hits me.

Something's wrong.

The fact that I'm not in that cell anymore means Naomi had to pay the price of my exit ticket.

My heartbeat roars in my ears and my dry throat closes. I attempt to get up, but pain explodes in my upper shoulder, knocking me back down.

"Don't move. You're hurt."

I blink twice against the searing pain and make out the contours of my uncle's face. He's wearing his sharp suit that's meant for business, and his expression is just as hard and ruthless as I recall.

But unlike his usual aloof attitude, he stares down at me with a furrowed brow.

"Nate…" I croak in a hoarse, scratchy voice. "I need… I need to find…"

A low groan escapes me when the pain pulses again. It's hard to breathe, let alone talk.

"You're in no condition to find anyone. You're lucky to be alive, Rascal. When the hospital called Mrs. Weaver and told her you were in critical condition, they meant it. You were apparently dropped off near the emergency room by masked men."

"They kidnapped us…" I cough, then wince when it triggers the pain. "Fuck…"

"Don't talk." He adjusts me back into a reclining position. "And we know you were taken."

"They…called you?"

"No. But you're not the type who would disappear for three days without a word. Your car and phone were found near the forest. Mr. and Mrs. Weaver flipped the whole town upside down to find you. They even used their connections and money, but it produced nothing. We thought we'd lost you for a second."

But they didn't.

And it's not a fucking miracle.

If my influential grandparents, who are more powerful than anyone I know, couldn't find me, then this is a lot more fucking serious than I thought.

"Nate…" I grunt.

"Don't push it. You need to rest. Mrs. Weaver went to get the doctor. You spent three days in a medically induced coma to help you recuperate and she thinks there's something odd going on, because you weren't waking up. You know how demanding she is of everyone's time. Mr. Weaver is talking to the police and calling them useless because they still haven't found who did this. Want a bet that he'll use this incident in his upcoming campaign? His chosen vocabulary will be all about the turmoil and family bond and so on and so forth."

I don't give a fuck about my grandparents right now. The fire inside me only burns for one person.

Her.

My Naomi.

The thought of her safety precedes my own. I've been

suffocating ever since she kissed me, told me she loved me, then walked out of that door.

I won't be able to breathe properly unless I make sure she's safe and sound.

"There was someone else, Nate..."

"Someone else?"

"My girl."

"Naomi?"

"She...she was with me."

The crease between his brows deepens. "You're the only one they dropped off."

"She's there... They have her... Fuck! They have her, Nate..." I try to straighten up again. "L-let me talk to the police so they can find her..."

"Stay fucking still." He easily pushes me back against the mattress. "I'll get them here. You need to rest now."

My uncle's twin appears by his side and it's then that I realize I'm seeing double. I grab on to his jacket sleeve, my tongue feeling heavy against the roof of my mouth. "Naomi...I need to find her..."

"We will. Just calm down."

"Nao..." I murmur in my haze, blinking, and just like magic, she appears right beside me.

She's wearing the shorts and sports bra from the cell. Her black hair that resembles the most beautiful nights sticks to the sides of her face and her eyes shine with unshed tears.

"Baby..." I reach a hand for her, but she flinches back as if disgusted with me.

She shakes her head once and stares down. I follow her line of vision and freeze.

Blood trickles between her legs, splashing her thighs in a deep red.

"Nao...?"

"It's over, Sebastian." Her voice is low, haunted.

Fucking *wrong*.

"No…no…"

"It's done."

"I don't fucking care, baby. I'll be there. I'll fucking kill them all."

"It's over…it's over…" she repeats in a chant as more blood slides down her legs, soaking her white shoes red.

I reach out for her, wanting to hug her close, even though pain slashes through me. The blood leaving her body feels like my own. I'm bleeding out, holding on to life by a mere fucking thread.

The moment my skin meets hers, she turns into smoke.

Thick.

Foggy.

Untouchable.

And just like that, my world is painted black.

TWELVE

Akira

Dear Yuki-Onna,

   I think we're at a point in our relationship where we just cut to the chase without any introductions.

   So here it goes.

   I told you not to ghost me.

   I made sure to type it in big letters so you'd understand there's no damn point in ghosting me, and yet, that's exactly what you did.

   You fucking ghosted me.

   You stopped writing to me as if that was your right, as if you have the full liberty in our relationship, friendship, toxic-ship, or whatever-the-fuck-ship.

   But that's not how it's supposed to go, my dear Yuki-Onna. You don't have a say in how far we go or when it ends.

   You don't have the right to disappear on me after I put up with your selfishness and bad decision-making. You put up with my asshole dickish behavior too, so it's not like you happened to have a wake-up call all of a sudden.

   But now that I think about it, maybe that's exactly what happened.

Maybe you stopped replying to my letters because you were finally hit by other hard truths. Who did the hitting?

Maybe I should be friends with them. I'm in the market for a different pen pal since my current one is ignoring me.

You do realize it's a dick move, right? And here I thought I was the asshole in this whole thing.

We should go back to the drawing board and create a different division of roles.

Also, it's so unfair that I listened to you for three years, and just when I dropped the mask and started getting comfortable in this unorthodox setting, you up and disappeared.

And then you deny that you're selfish.

And then, you call me the asshole for not being your yes-man.

How hypocritical is that?

Spoiler alert. Very.

Also, I'm not doing well, thank you for not asking. I kind of hit the rock bottom in my life for the first time in a long time.

I'm at a phase where I hate everything and everyone, and wish I could be the only person on earth just because it's better if everyone else died instead of me.

Yes, it's destructive thinking, but I've always been that way. Generally cynical and absolutely fucking pessimistic.

It balances out the fake pessimism that you use as a façade to hide your natural optimism.

But I'm a true pessimist who doesn't think twice before offing his damn good vibes.

I think I should call it what it is: I'm having an existential crisis. It's so strong that I don't even know who or what I am anymore.

Maybe I'm a nobody.

Or maybe I'm just an asshole.

Either way, my reason for existing is fracturing and I can't keep it in one piece.

You must be laughing at my expense. Go ahead. You have every right to after everything I said.

But that means you have to stop fucking ghosting me and actually write back.

Don't even believe for a second that this is the end. I might be having a crisis, but I'll still be the Akira you love to hate.

Write back.

Even a word would do.

Your other half you had no idea existed until now,

Akira

THIRTEEN

Sebastian

WHEN I WAKE UP NEXT, I'M BOMBARDED BY EVERYONE.
The doctors. My grandparents.
The police.

They're the only ones I want to talk to. I didn't blink twice when the attending physician told me that the infection in my shoulder had spread and I might not be able to play football anymore.

While football is what's helped me cope through the years, it's not what's made me feel alive.

It's not the reason I'm still unable to fucking breathe.

So no, I don't give a fuck about football right now.

My grandparents are on either side of me as I talk to the detective in charge of my case. His name is Wyatt and he has a thick blond moustache that covers most of his mouth.

He and another officer stand by my bed as I relay how I was shot in the forest and then taken with Naomi. I tell them about the cell and that fucker Ren.

I tell them that Naomi suspects it has something to do with her father, but when he asks me his name, I'm lost.

She's never mentioned it. I suspect she doesn't even know it.

"You need to find her," I insist. "She's been in there for three fucking days since I left and we only survived on water for three days before that."

She could be trapped. Or worse.

Maybe the hallucination I had before losing consciousness earlier was true and she's ruined beyond repair.

But even if that's the case, I'll stand by her side until the end.

Even if she pushes me away.

Even if she calls me names.

Even if she fucking hates me.

"Now, that's the problem." The detective shares a look with his colleague, then focuses back on me. "Miss Naomi Chester was never reported missing."

"What?"

He flips through his notepad. "Her mother, Ms. Riko Chester, never reported her missing."

That can't be possible considering how protective she is of her daughter. "She could've been looking for her on her own, or maybe she's been in contact with Naomi's father."

"That isn't the case, Mr. Weaver. Ms. Riko confirmed to the police that she was getting ready to go on a trip with her daughter. They left yesterday."

"They couldn't have. Naomi was with me the whole fucking time."

"They did, though. A day after you were dropped off at the emergency room."

I stare between him and my grandmother as if that will somehow help me make sense of his words. Mrs. Weaver's lips twist in disapproval, probably because I insisted on talking to the police and kept asking about Naomi's safety.

She still doesn't like me involved with her, but fuck her opinion.

Fuck anyone who thinks that I can't be with Naomi.

"You must've gotten the wrong person, detective," I grind out through my teeth, which puts a strain on my wound.

"No. We did, in fact, talk to Ms. Naomi Chester before she and her mother left for the airport. She said she hadn't seen you since the day you disappeared."

The airport.

Naomi lied to the police and then left the country?

What the fuck is that supposed to mean?

"That can't be true," I murmur more to myself than anyone else.

"It is," Grandma says in her haughty tone. "I personally paid that seamstress a visit as soon as you disappeared and she said that you hadn't shown up at her house for a long time."

"But did you see Naomi?" I ask.

"No, but I didn't have to. She was in her room."

"No, she wasn't. She was with me," I tell the detectives.

"The doctor said that your facts could be hazy due to the infection you suffered."

"I'm not making things up. She was there and fucking took care of me."

Detective Wyatt nods with feigned understanding and I want to reach out and strangle him. I want him to go out there and search for her, find her and have them tell me where I can talk to her.

But it's useless.

Judging from the way everyone is watching me, they definitely think I'm hallucinating.

The detective tells my grandfather that he will keep us updated about their findings, but I already know there will be none.

Those guys were professionals and fooled the police into thinking that Naomi wasn't even abducted.

The only trace they left behind is me and my memories that automatically became faulty due to my fever.

It was all calculated.

But they don't know me. Or my Naomi.

No matter what they do, there's no way in fuck they can separate us.

My grandfather walks out with the police. As soon as they

leave, Grandma fixes me with a glare. "Stop making us look like fools. It's enough that you've gotten yourself in trouble, don't start acting like an idiot now."

"She was there," I say point-blank.

"I don't care. The only thing that matters now is that she's gone and stopped muddying your logic. This isn't the Sebastian I raised."

"The Sebastian you raised is a mere image, Grandma. He was never real."

"Even better. That's the only Sebastian that should be shown in public. The seamstress's daughter isn't on your level, do you understand?"

I say nothing, because if I do, I'll be screaming like a lunatic.

Wanting to get rid of her, I pretend to be sleepy. Soon after, she leaves, because Grandma isn't the type who stays around and takes care of a patient. She pays people to do that.

Now that she's made sure her precious heir won't die, she'll just move on as if nothing happened.

Stifling a groan of pain, I reach for my phone on the edge of the table. Nate brought it over earlier before he headed out to attend to one of his cases.

I turn on the Wi-Fi and a thousand pings accumulate all at once. Messages from Owen, Asher, and even Reina. Other friends. Other people.

Just when I'm about to clear all the notifications, I notice something. *Someone.*

A message from Naomi and it's a day old.

Straightening, I ignore the pain as I click on it faster than anything I've done in my entire life.

Naomi: I'm fine. I survived. Barely. But I lost something in there, Sebastian. I lost a part of me that I don't think I'll ever find again. I'm just going through the motions so I can be there for Mom. She decided to spend her last days in Japan and I tagged along. This place has grown on me and I don't think I'll want to leave, even after Mom's gone. Don't try to find me, because the moment you do, I'll run again. I can't look at your face anymore without recalling what happened to me. I keep wondering if saving you was worth the sacrifice and if maybe you should've been the one who sacrificed instead. I'll never know the answers to those questions, but I do know that whatever I felt for you vanished the moment I took the blow for you. I can never be with you again without feeling pain, and, therefore, I'm ending whatever we had. Live well.

The more times I read it, the stronger my grip around the phone becomes until my knuckles turn white.

My nightmare wasn't wrong, after all.

They did rape her.

"Fuck…" I murmur with a pained groan as my chest tightens so hard, it's impossible to breathe.

I grab a fistful of my hospital gown in the place where my heart lies and suck in shaky breaths.

The ugliness of the situation is like a weight slamming over my chest, but I don't let the circumstances rule me.

I hit the call button and place the phone to my ear. I'm surprised when it rings. I don't know why I thought she would've turned off her phone.

My pulse rate heightens with every ring. Just when I think it'll go to voicemail, she picks up. "Hello?"

My heart jolts against my rib cage and some of the asphyxiation withers away.

I've thought of so many things to tell her since I woke up, but now that she's on the other end, I don't know what to say.

Sucking in a sharp breath, I speak the only words I feel deep in my bones. "Baby…I'm sorry."

"You're the one who said to never apologize for something you never had a hand in." Her voice is apathetic, toneless, and I fucking hate it.

I hate that she feels far away—both physically and emotionally.

"But I couldn't protect you and you blame me for it. I totally understand."

"You understand nothing. You weren't there."

"But I'm here now and I *will* be there for you."

"I don't need you."

"But I need *you*."

"That's your problem, not mine."

"It was the anger talking in that text. I know you care."

"No. I realized that I don't."

"You said you loved me, Nao."

"I thought I did, but it was all smoke and mirrors."

"You promised to fucking marry me."

"You didn't really think I meant it, did you? I was exhausted and at my physical limit and would've said anything at the time."

"Baby…listen to me…"

"No, it's time you listen to me. I'm done with you, Sebastian."

"But I'm not done with you," I growl into the phone. "I'll never be done with you, do you hear me? You can escape to the other side of the globe and I'll follow and make you mine again. I'll chase you over and over until you know you can't escape me. I meant it when I said you're mine and I don't plan to let it end."

"It's over." Her voice lowers, losing its apathetic tone for the first time as she murmurs, "Reality."

The phone goes dead. The beep that indicates the end of a call echoes in my ear like a raging thunderstorm.

My hand flexes around the device and I stare at it, as if holding it tighter will conjure her voice again.

But I know it won't, not when the last thing she said is reverberating in my ear.

Reality.

Naomi just used her safe word and completely erased me from her world as if I never fucking existed.

FOURTEEN

Akira

Dear Yuki-Onna,

I don't know why I keep writing to you at this point.

Not only have you erased me from your life as if I've never been there, but you also treated our relationship as nonexistent.

Is that what you do to people you know? Act as if they mean nothing?

Because I have a gash in the middle of my black heart and it's kind of bleeding dark ink onto the keyboard. I blame you for it, by the way.

I blame you for a lot of things. What started it all is when you wrote back to me that day. You shouldn't have. You didn't need to. Not when you knew nothing about the stranger who sent you a letter from overseas.

I also blame you for responding religiously every week and making me wait for mail like in an old nineties movie with horrible colors.

But what I blame you for the most is how fucking easy it is to talk to you. To know that there's someone who waits for my black fucked up letters and opens them every damn week. That there's a person who thinks of me, reads my words, and considers them important enough to write back immediately.

And it all goes back to the first fucking time.

Why did you reply if you planned to never do it again? Why lead me on when you didn't think of keeping up with it?

It's your nasty selfishness, isn't it?

Ever since the beginning, you only ever cared about yourself, your thoughts, and your damn problems. I put up with it and your character, but I should've seen the potential narcissist in you.

It should've been easy considering I'm probably one myself.

But narcissists are supposed to stick around, you know. They're supposed to use people to their benefit and keep telling them boring tales about their fucking lives to feel a sense of grandiose shit.

So why the fuck aren't you doing it anymore, Naomi?

And why the fuck am I writing this letter I will never send to you anyway?

Because you changed your address and I won't be able to find your new one.

I guess my existential crisis is turning into a nihilistic one, and I don't even believe in that fucking shit.

If one day you see this, know that I will never, and I mean never, forgive you.

Don't live well,
Akira

FIFTEEN

Sebastian

Seven years later

"SMILE, MOTHERFUCKER."

I roll my eyes but can't help smiling as I fasten my cuffs. Daniel takes the shot and grins like a fucking idiot on steroids, showcasing his dimples.

He taps his phone with a satisfied expression. When he speaks, it's in his signature British accent that gets all the girls to drop their panties for him. "Now this, my mate, is what I call front-page newsworthy. Though you'll never steal my title as the hottest bachelor of the year."

I stare at the mirror and fix my tie as he circles me, snapping pictures and releasing satisfied sounds.

Daniel is about my height, but he's leaner and has the type of blue eyes that make you want to stab them because they're always on the lookout for trouble—like right now.

"Are you done?" I ask in a bored tone, managing to ignore him for the most part.

Mastering the art of observing one's surroundings doesn't mean I have to pay attention to everything that happens. It's more about being aware of my environment and only reacting to what directly threatens me. Everything else is white noise.

"Nah. Possessing pictures of Prince Weaver is as rare as witnessing a bloody shooting star. I need to sell these babies to magazines—or fangirls. Whoever offers the best fuck first."

"If you can handle an infringement of privacy suit, sure. I'll be happy to steal some of your shares."

"Oh, fuck you. As if you'd ever win against me in court."

I raise a brow. "Want to try? I'm taking a pro bono case next month, so how about you take a similar one and we'll see who wins first?"

"I would in a heartbeat if your uncle wouldn't chop off my head for not doing my own pro bono cases."

"It could be a good promotional opportunity. At least one of us will win. Me."

He narrows his eyes as a smirk tugs on his lips. "You know what, fuck it. I'm taking more pro bono cases just to have a better record than yours."

"We'll see about that."

He steps in front of me and clutches me by the shoulder. "I'll win with flying colors. By the time I'm finished, you might have PTSD from standing in court and consider quitting law. Are you okay with that?"

"As long as you're okay with me actually winning while you're dragged in court by the prosecutor."

"Oh, you're fucking on. Don't go crying to your uncle when I invade the magazines' front pages again as the 'Dream Lawyer of Every Woman.'"

I scoff.

He runs his fingers through his brown hair. "Don't be jealous of my looks and skills, Bastian. It shows."

"Fuck, and here I thought my complete disregard of your whoring habits wasn't visible on my face. My bad."

"You and your arrogance can sod the fuck off."

"See you in court, Danny. Make sure you invite all the associates so they can watch your ass getting whipped."

"You're speaking to the student who graduated at the top of his class at Harvard Law. You merely took the two-year program and passed the bar. Show some respect, peasant."

"Maybe you should take your own advice. I barely went to law school and still passed the bar with a score better than yours."

"Nate helped you cheat."

"Hearsay."

Daniel shoves himself off me with distaste, but he still snaps a picture here and another one there.

I have no doubt that he'll actually try to sell them. Unlike him, I keep my public appearances to a minimum and specialize in corporate law so I don't have to take on cases that get too much public attention.

If I'd wanted to be in the limelight, I wouldn't have metaphorically cut ties with my grandparents, and instead, I would have just followed in Grandfather's footsteps.

Mrs. Weaver about had a stroke when I announced I was joining Nate in law and she threatened to take away my trust fund, apartment, car, and everything I've ever owned.

So I left them with her and slept on Nate's couch for months while I took an intensive law course, apprenticed at his firm, and then studied for the bar.

My grandparents still actively try to ruin me and Nate for turning our backs on them, but I couldn't give a fuck about them and their legacy.

If there's anything I learned after being at the brink of death, it's that I don't have time to play other people's games.

I have my own.

Before, I always saw my grandparents as my saviors and I

accepted that I had to pay my dues by being the perfect Weaver. But I was wrong.

They only ever cared about themselves. They're the reason Dad ended up in Japan, broke and with nothing to fall back on. They're the reason we were poor and Mom had to steal from dangerous people, which is what got her and my father killed.

My grandparents might not have had a hand in it, but they indirectly participated in their deaths.

I was only fooling myself by thinking I wouldn't meet the same fate.

So I had two options. Either I became their puppet or I got out of their shadows.

I chose the latter.

We still see each other at her banquets, because they like to brag about my and Nate's accomplishments, even when they're privately against them.

The door opens and Daniel stops his photo session when Knox walks in, dressed in a white tuxedo. Seriously, he looks like some Italian businessman from the sixties, but surprisingly, he pulls the look off with his build.

He pauses in the entrance and stares at the ceiling as he forms an *L* with his thumb and forefinger. "Take a picture, Dan. Make sure the line of my jaw is visible."

Daniel complies, circling him like he did me. "Give me your best poses, my muse. Yes, more brooding…more handsome but still less than me. That's it, give me the mystery, the thrill…"

They spend a few minutes taking pictures and feeding each other's egos.

Daniel and Knox are both English and came to the States after they graduated high school. They studied law at Harvard, fucked half the female population, and are currently plotting to conquer the other half.

They're also Asher's acquaintances through Aiden King,

a mutual friend from England from when my childhood friend studied in Oxford.

Daniel specializes in international law because it gets him on the cover of countless magazines around the globe. Knox has made criminal law his bitch because, as he said, he has 'tendencies to satiate.'

We met after I joined Weaver & Shaw, Nate's law firm that he founded with his best friend/ex-rival, Kingsley Shaw.

At the start, we competed so hard and made each other's lives hell. They hated me because I'm Nate's nephew and then ganged up on me. But over the years, that rivalry has become our favorite pastime. We enjoy digging holes for each other and waiting to see if the other will take the bait.

We give Nate a headache, but it's worth it.

We all recently made junior partner, but it's far from being the end of our weird-as-fuck rivalry.

Daniel and Knox finish their photo shoot and force me to take a selfie with them that they'll probably blast all over their social media pages.

"Are we ready to go or does your ego need more stroking?" I ask in my bored tone.

I almost always sound that way now.

Dull.

Hollow.

Down.

I lost a part of my soul seven years ago and I've never managed to get it back. Which is strange as fuck since I thought I didn't have a soul in the first place.

Finding out I actually do, then losing it cost more than I can afford.

"Someone take this grumpy fucker and toss him somewhere that I can't see," Daniel jokes.

"Or hear," Knox adds.

"Or even think of."

"Nate would kill us, though." Knox taps my head. "You know how protective he is of his little prince."

I flip them off and head to the door. They follow after me and fall in step on either side of me. The organizers gave us a special room we can retreat to whenever we wish, which definitely has to do with the amount of money Nate donates.

The moment we step out, a myriad of sounds and colors explode in front of us.

Low classical music fills the space and staff members dressed in formalwear offer us glasses of champagne.

We each take one and Daniel smiles, making sure his dimples are on full display as he winks at the waitress who blushes and scurries away.

The attendees are wearing either tuxedos or cocktail dresses, and the women have their best pieces of jewelry on exhibit. Chatter fills the air as everyone mingles.

Nate sent us to this charity event to give away some of his money and snatch clients from other firms.

So our mission is to basically help the poor and take from the rich.

Nate being Nate will probably show his face later on like he's making some sort of a surprise appearance.

For now, his three 'show-offs,' as he likes to call us, will bear the weight of attending this gathering until his majesty is here.

Many women bat their eyelashes at us as we pass them by. We attract that type of attention when we're in public, and being the focus of these kinds of events is Daniel's kink.

Knox's, too, when he's in the right mood. And he seems to be tonight.

Both of them smile at the passing ladies and Daniel is still making sure they notice his dimples. The fucker uses them as a magnet any chance he gets.

"I'll take the west wing," he announces. "Lots of beautiful ladies."

"East for me." Knox pats my shoulder. "You don't mind taking one for the team and going to the old folks' area, do you, Bastian? They love you."

"All the pure people do. Not my fault you're rotten."

"Oh, fuck you," Daniel whispers, and Knox flips me off.

I leave their side with a smirk and head toward a small gathering of businessmen. I recognize them from the days I used to play the good grandson.

They come from old money and know how to manage it—their money, that is. They're now represented by one of our rival firms, Carson & Carson, which is owned by the father of my friend, Asher, who currently works for them.

Although he specializes in international law, he'll have my balls if he knows I'm gunning for their clients.

But then again, if the roles were reversed, he would do the same. Both of us still like the challenge, just like when we first chose to play football back in middle school.

I summon my showtime smile. It's harder to do that these days. Smiling. Whether it's real or fake.

In fact, I've forgotten the last time I genuinely smiled. It was robbed from me the same day I lost the meaning of living and started to simply exist.

Working is the only thing that keeps my mind functioning and alert. And that's why I intend to have more cases than I can handle.

Maybe that will manage to shut off whatever feelings try to rise to the surface.

Maybe that will help me get my soul back.

My feet come to a halt not far from the small group as tingling erupts at my nape.

At first, I think it's just a figment of my imagination.

An untasteful fucking joke from my brain.

Otherwise, I wouldn't be having the sensation that the world is being set on fucking fire and the only thing I can do is to stand there and watch.

I search my surroundings, because I know, I just know that she's somewhere here.

She has to be.

My frantic gaze scans all the faces and attendees even as I remain in place. I survey the people at the bar and everyone coming inside, searching for those inquisitive dark eyes and rosy lips.

Searching for the face I've never been able to forget.

The face that I picture when I take shooting fucking lessons.

I pause when my eyes land on her brown ones. She's standing near the corner with a champagne flute in her hand.

Her posture is erect, accentuated by a long black gown that skims the floor, and her hair, the color of the night, is gathered in a twist.

I've dreamed about this moment a million fucking times, but nothing, absolutely nothing could've prepared me for the view in front of me.

Her face is almost the same—petite, delicate, with soft lines contouring it. But it seems mature, touched by the hands of time. Her lips are a deep shade of red as they part the slightest bit.

Lips that I've feasted on and whose taste I still remember. It's turned fucking bitter over time, but it's still there all the same.

A diamond necklace that must've cost a company's budget wraps around her delicate throat.

The same throat that I've grabbed countless times and have marked just as many.

Her arm is looped around an Asian man's who is wearing frameless glasses.

Her lips part when my eyes connect with hers. They're also the same, dark, haunting, but they're now a little bit strange, a little bit changed.

A little bit far away.

She inhales a breath, which from this distance, I can almost hear, then feel trickling against my fucking skin.

It's her.

Naomi.

The one who broke me.

Broke us.

Now, it's time I do the same.

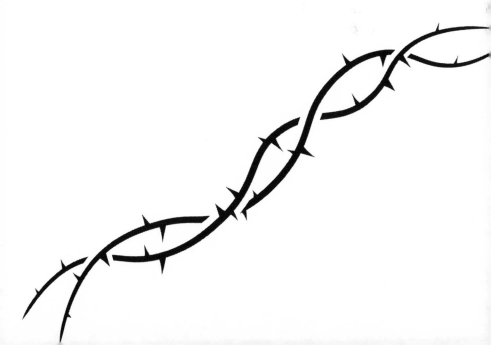

SIXTEEN

Naomi

HOW IS IT POSSIBLE FOR YEARS TO BLUR TOGETHER AS IF they never existed?

A single moment.

A single glance.

A single second of eye contact.

And it all bursts back in as if it were never gone. All the details are still the same but somehow not.

The tropical green color of his eyes has darkened, almost dulled. His sharp features have lost all playfulness and they're now gloomier, more serious.

More lethal.

Any boyishness has disappeared and he's all man now. Masculinity drips from every part of him, whether it's the cut of his jaw, the dip in his heavy brows, or the thick veins covering the back of his hand as he grips the glass of champagne.

Unlike his haphazard look in the past, his hair is styled. The tuxedo is fitted to his developed body. He's still as tall and muscular as in my memories, although he's no longer an athlete.

There are a lot of things that he no longer possesses. Like the gleam in his eyes.

Maybe that part of him died.

Just like many parts of me did.

I've always thought about the time I'd meet Sebastian again. In my mind, I was sure that our paths would cross.

Maybe in Blackwood if I summoned the courage to go back. Or in New York, where he currently lives. Or in Japan, if he ever came over for business.

I subconsciously created all sorts of scenarios in my head about how I'd react. I trained myself to be unaffected, to only show a façade. I even practiced it in front of the mirror so I wouldn't make mistakes.

So I would act like I'm supposed to.

But I should've known better.

Nothing could have prepared me for the moment when I'm face-to-face with him.

His eyes peering into mine, even from a distance, feel like lava on my skin, burning it and melting into my soul.

The effect is a lot stronger than I could've ever anticipated and I find myself gripping Akira's arm harder, needing some sort of an anchor against the storm that's ripping me apart and dragging me under.

It's silent, but I can hear the slow rise in volume within me until the explosion fills my head.

Don't come here. I say with my eyes. *Just go away.*

But again, I should've known better.

Sebastian only does what Sebastian wants and fuck everyone else. One trait that apparently hasn't changed.

His blank expression darkens as he moves in our direction. His sure strides eat up the distance and what remains of my nerves in a few seconds.

Judging by the powerful way he moves, I expect that he'll scoop me up in his arms and take me away. Or maybe he'll grab me by the throat and back me against the wall.

The base of my stomach tightens at the image and it takes everything in me not to squirm.

He does neither, of course, and I don't know if the lump that's blocking my breathing is due to relief or something entirely different.

Sebastian stops right in front of us and I suck in a sharp breath, praying that my emotions aren't painted on my face for everyone to see.

For *him* to see.

His intense gaze falls on me exclusively, as if I'm the only one here. There's no warmth in it, no welcoming smile. Only dark depths and a harsh interior that he wraps so well in a groomed, just-out-of-a-photo-shoot look.

"Long time no see, Naomi."

Oh, fuck.

The sound of my name in his deep, slightly raspy voice is making me weaker than I ever imagined it could.

His voice is manlier, too. He's aged like Nate—elegantly, sharply.

Coldly.

"Sebastian," I greet back, using the professional tone I reserve for business, then tug on Akira's arm. "This is my husband, Akira Mori."

Sebastian's focus goes to my finger, and for an irrational second, I want to rip the ring off of it. Then his gaze flits to Akira's matching ring and I expect his expression to darken, but his eyes remain the same.

In fact, the void in them deepens. If I somehow stared into them hard enough, I'd be dragged into a bottomless abyss.

"Akira…" I continue with a smile. "This is Sebastian. We went to the same college. The one I told you about in Blackwood."

"Right, yes." Akira offers his hand, speaking with a subtle accent. "It's always nice to meet Naomi's friends."

We were anything but friends, I want to say, but soon realize just how wrong that statement is.

At one point, Sebastian was my closest friend as well as the person who set my world ablaze.

After him, everything is…ashes.

Sebastian takes Akira's hand and I can tell the shake is firm as both men stare at each other with pure contemplation.

My husband isn't the type who shows his emotions openly—or at all, really. But I can sense the way he's openly watching Sebastian as if trying to read him.

Or intimidate him.

His brown eyes light up beneath his glasses and he seems up for a challenge. I internally shake my head. Why am I not surprised?

"The pleasure is mine," Sebastian says, his gaze sliding back to me for a fraction of a second as he releases Akira's hand.

"What do you do, Sebastian?" my husband asks.

"I'm a partner at Weaver & Shaw."

Law.

Even though I already know it, I'm still in awe to hear that he chose to be a lawyer.

I was well aware of his resentment of politics, but who would've thought this was the path Sebastian wanted to follow?

"That's impressive," Akira says. "I've heard making partner at a young age is an accomplishment."

"Some might say so." Sebastian focuses back on me and I feel like a mouse trapped with a cat. "What do you do now, Naomi?"

"I manage Mom's couture house," I say in a voice that I'm thankful doesn't break.

"She's being humble," Akira says with a note of pride. "My Naomi is the CEO that no one can keep up with. Not even me."

Sebastian is quiet for a second and I think I see a muscle tic in his jaw, but then he says, "Do you work together?"

"Not really. I specialize in imports and exports. It's why we came to the States. I needed to take care of our branch in New York and open a new subsidiary." Akira pauses. "Speaking of which, I've been looking into some law firms to represent me here, and Weaver & Shaw was among the files. Maybe it's fate that brought you my way." He lifts my hand and kisses my knuckles. "Or my Naomi."

"Maybe." Sebastian reaches into his jacket and produces a business card. "Call me whenever you're ready and I'll be happy to discuss this further."

Akira takes the card, studies it for a bit, then nods. "Sounds good."

I want to step between them and tell them to cut it out.

That this shouldn't happen.

But something stops me.

The dark look in Sebastian's eyes and the hidden promise in them.

He's doing this on purpose, isn't he? This whole thing is only an excuse so he can insert himself back into my life.

And something tells me it's not because he's missed me.

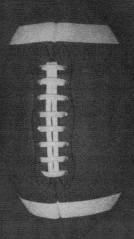

SEVENTEEN

Sebastian

SHE'S MARRIED.

Naomi is fucking married.

I try repeating that in my head over and over so I can stop myself from grabbing her and backing her against the fucking wall.

I tell myself that we're in public, that her husband is right beside her and I can't possibly yank her back by the hair and let my body talk to hers.

I remind myself of the days and nights I spent wondering why and hating my thoughts and her. I recall the years that went by in radio fucking silence and how I learned to survive after her.

None of those thoughts help in pushing my head in a different direction. Not when I'm barely stopping myself from barging forward and causing a scene neither of us needs.

Do I *have* to stop myself, though?

I could carry her petite body in my arms and kidnap her the fuck out of here. I could punish her, fuck her up, and leave her on the side of the road.

Just like she fucking left me.

She smiles at something her husband, Akira fucking Mori, says. It's as soft as I remember, but it's lost one quality that makes Naomi who she is—honesty. There's nothing real about it. Yet she fakes it so well, she's able to fool the tool standing by her side.

But not me.

She'll never be able to fool me. Not in this lifetime, anyway.

Being in her vicinity again is filling me with more emotions than my chest can contain.

I want to get close to her.

Touch her.

Fucking hurt her.

But even I recognize how dangerous that would be. Just being near her is chipping at the steel-like control I've cultivated over the years.

After I chose a new path in life, I had to be in a strong state of mind so I could make it happen. For that, I built solid walls around my head and body. I adopted a disciplined lifestyle and have stuck to it.

The reason I avoid the limelight isn't only because of the needless fuss it creates. It's also because it doesn't allow anyone a chance to dig their claws into me.

Seeing Naomi again is testing all my efforts.

And all of it translates into one need—to hurt her.

Maybe then, the fucking weight I've been carrying for years will finally be lifted.

Maybe then, I'll get back the fucking colors I lost.

For now, I need to leave to gather my cards and, most importantly, to keep from doing something I'll regret later on.

I plaster on my most plastic smile. "It was nice meeting you, Mr. Mori."

"Please, Akira is fine." His eyes glint and I want to break his glasses and gouge them the fuck off. "My Naomi's friends are mine as well."

My Naomi.

It's the third time he's called her that in my presence.

My. Naomi.

I was the one who said that first. How fucking dare he take something of mine and turn it into his?

Burning sparks of hostility rush to the surface in need of release. It's been a long time since I've thought about inflicting violence, but Akira's prim and proper face seems like the right place to relapse into old habits. Because fuck this guy.

Instead, I nod, my eyes meeting Naomi's again. She digs her fingers into her husband's arm for the second time tonight as her dark gaze stays on mine.

Her pupils are slightly dilated, her lips parted, and there's a pink blush on her cheeks. She probably doesn't even realize her reaction is visible to me.

Time hasn't erased what I already know.

"Naomi. Good to see you again." I take her hand in mine and kiss the back of it. My lips linger on her skin that still smells like lily and peaches. It smells like that fall from seven years ago and its memories.

My eyes never leave hers as my mouth rests on the back of her hand. I want her to see that she made a mistake by coming back.

That I'll ruin her as much as she ruined me.

Ruined us.

She sucks in a breath through her teeth and her hand slightly trembles in mine.

The message got through. Good.

I release her hand and nod at her husband, who's been watching us with a critical gaze. "I hope to see you around soon."

His lips tilt at the side. "Oh, you will."

I pause at his antagonizing tone, but then I turn around and leave.

An itch starts under my skin. One that urges me to turn and take another look at her, to see the fucker touching her.

But I don't.

I already got the message through. Now, all I have to do is wait for her to fall into my trap.

Because that's what Naomi does. She willingly walks over the land, even while knowing it's full of mines.

I stop by the bar, abandon my untouched glass of champagne, and order a glass of Macallan 18. I ignore the brunette bartender with a lip piercing who's batting her lashes at me.

As soon as she brings me my order, I take a long gulp. The burn of the alcohol quenches the burn in my chest, but that only lasts for a second before the flames turn hotter.

Daniel slides to the stool beside me and winks at the bartender. "Same as him, love."

"Right away, handsome. Your accent is so dreamy."

He shows her his dimples. "You have a good eye and ear."

She laughs in a flirtatious way and slides his drink over with a napkin beneath it. "Call me sometime if you want to see what else I'm good at."

"I wouldn't miss it, love." He brushes his hand against hers as he takes the drink.

She gives him an apologetic glance when she's called to the other end of the bar.

"A brunette with curves." He tilts his head and checks her out. "My fucking type."

"What are you doing here?" I grumble.

"What the fuck is wrong with you, mate? Beautiful girls are surrounding you from everywhere and you're sulking like an old cat lady who just heard that the judge won't allow her cats to inherit her fortune, because her children are countersuing."

"Then go have fun with all the girls. Why are you stuck with an old cat lady?"

"Hello? Obviously, because I love cats." He takes a sip of his drink. "Now, back to business. Who was that?"

I stare at the bottom of my glass and how the ice swirls. "Who was who?"

"The one who got your knickers in a twist and gave you cat lady syndrome?"

"Are you stalking me?"

"Nah. Just noticed you were more rigid than usual. Do we need to bring in the big guns for Akira Mori?"

I break eye contact with my drink and face Daniel. "You know him?"

"Of course I do." He throws up a dismissive hand. "International law, hello? That's me, by the way."

"Have you worked with him before?"

"No, but I dealt with an associate in England who did. Eh, you know him actually. Knox's foster father."

"Ethan Steel?"

"That's the one. Knox and I went to Japan a few years back to provide legal advice to his father about signing with Akira's company. Ethan wanted an extra opinion outside of the law firm that represented him for international affairs, and we were there to serve—and fuck hot ladies, of course."

"What do you know about him?"

"Ethan or Akira?"

"Akira."

"He's successful. He works with different conglomerates around the globe and is their entryway into Japan and many other Asian countries. He recently financed a South African man with no background or business ventures under his name. But guess who that man is?"

"Who?"

"Friedrich Jacobs."

"The man who discovered a diamond mine?" I read about that once in the news.

"Yup, that's the one. And he didn't discover just any diamond mine. It's one of the few in the world that produces black diamonds. Akira is now the sole exporter of those goodies worldwide."

"So he's rich. Anything else you know about him?"

"He comes from a powerful traditional family in Japan. He never invites people who aren't close family members to his house, from what I've heard."

"How about his wife?" The words burn in my throat.

His wife.

She shouldn't be his damn wife. Fuck that guy again.

"This is the first time I've seen her. I think she has her own business ventures that are separate from her husband's. Both of them are private, that's for sure."

Private.

Of course she would be fucking private.

After all, I couldn't find her, no matter how much I looked in the beginning. I hired a PI in Japan and begged Nate to use his connections to search for her, but it was like she'd never existed.

Turns out, she's been under her husband's private umbrella all this time.

"You know her, though." Daniel's voice brings me out of my thoughts.

"What makes you think that?"

"I don't know, your stiffened posture and chatty self, maybe?" He pauses, his eyes widening. "Wait a minute. Is she the girl who broke your heart and stole your soul, leaving a grumpy asshole behind?"

"Fuck off."

"She is!" He taps the bar table, grinning. "How does it feel to see her again? Please share your thoughts with your invisible fans."

"I don't feel anything."

"Fucking liar. Forget cat lady syndrome. Your face is turning into a serious case of granite. Are you in a mood because she's married to a man who's richer than sin?"

"It's because she came back," the words leave me in a low whisper, forcing me to taste bitter acid.

"What?"

"She should've stayed away."

"I don't understand what that means, and no thanks, I don't need an explanation. What I do need, however, is deets." He slides closer and wraps an arm around my shoulder. "Tell me some deep, dark secrets I can use to make her husband my client."

"He'll be *my* client."

"Wait, and I mean this in the most sodding way, *what?*"

I take a long drink. "I'm making Akira Mori my client."

"But you don't do international law."

"I do corporate. That's enough." I stare at him. "Besides, no offense, but you can't handle him."

"And you can, motherfucker?"

"I will."

Daniel opens his mouth, probably to curse me, but Knox cuts him off, grabbing us both by the shoulder and jamming himself between us. "Are you having a moment without me? Do I need to sabotage you and ruin your careers?"

"Vindictive bitch suits you, Knox." Daniel jabs him.

"What can I say? I love digging graves."

I stare at him. "Help me dig one then."

His mouth moves into a Cheshire cat grin. "I like that. I'm in."

"Don't be." Daniel tsks. "It's a bad idea."

"I love bad ideas." Knox squeezes my shoulder. "What did you have in mind?"

I stare back at where I left Naomi and Akira. She still has an arm wrapped around his as they mingle with the attendees.

She's still fake-smiling and putting on a show.

The Naomi I knew would never fake anything, but that's the thing.

I don't know this Naomi.

And I sure as fuck have no clue why she married Akira. It couldn't be the money since she must have plenty of her own.

Was it by chance? Did she meet him and not feel suffocated? Did he save her when I fucking couldn't?

One thing's for sure, she chose him and I'll make her unchoose him, even if it's the last thing I do.

I tip my chin toward them and speak to Knox, "Get me all the dirt on the Mori couple."

As if feeling my gaze on her, Naomi turns her head in my direction.

Her smile falters and her dark eyes glint, but it's only due to the lights, not the life that used to spark through her every movement.

Maybe this whole thing wasn't a coincidence, after all.

Maybe I'm meant to yank that part of her to the surface **again**.

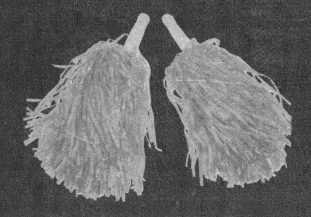

EIGHTEEN

Naomi

I THOUGHT THE NIGHT WOULD NEVER END.

I imagined myself stuck in a loop, stumbling and tumbling out of my depth until my mind cracked.

Whenever I looked at Sebastian, my body shook. Whenever my eyes met his, I could feel my soul being sucked from my body.

Or what remains of it, anyway.

I had to tell Akira I was tired so we could cut the night short. He didn't mind since we were having guests come over for a late dinner.

If I'd stayed in Sebastian's vicinity any longer, I have no doubt that my nerves would've gotten the better of me.

If I'd watched him any closer, I would've lost the control I've perfected over the years.

But as we leave, I steal one last look at him.

He's at the bar, drinking with two other men. I recognize them from the magazines as Daniel and Knox. Both of them are British and probably the closest people to Sebastian nowadays.

From what I read, he's still friends with Asher and Owen, too.

Daniel and Knox are laughing, but Sebastian isn't. I doubt he's even hearing what they're saying.

The three of them attract the entire hall's attention and women keep approaching them or trying to make as much eye contact as possible. Something hot and fiery erupts inside me and I squash it before it's able to burn me alive.

Sebastian lifts his head and I lower mine before he makes eye contact. I really don't think I can handle it again. Not that I did the first time—or the second. If I keep getting caught in the maze his eyes create, I'll most definitely never find a way out.

I let Akira lead me outside and breathe the icy air into my lungs before we get into the back of the car.

Our driver takes us to the outskirts of Brooklyn. Akira owns a house here, although we don't visit it much.

I don't, at least.

Akira often has business in the States and comes alone. I prefer to stay in Japan.

Ever since I moved there seven years ago, I've made it my mission to stay away. I've focused on keeping Mom's legacy alive and have just played my role so the system can go on.

The car stops in front of the mansion, which has modern architecture mixed with a traditional Japanese style. The entrance to the house has a large black gate, but the inside is laid out in a square way. Wooden panels are situated on every side, and one has to remove their shoes before going in. The large space in the middle has a few rare plants that Akira personally takes care of. There's even an enormous pond full of goldfish, koi, and other types of fish.

He feeds them himself and takes pride in everything that connects him with his roots.

Akira comes from a noble family with samurai blood that goes back several centuries.

His upbringing was strict and disciplined, and as a result, he's a conservative Confucianist with a great appreciation for anything traditional, whether it's plants or green tea done the authentic Japanese way.

However, he rose beyond that and opened himself to the world, which is the reason behind his success as a businessman. He's achieved things no one else in his family was able to.

They let their traditional ways shackle them, but he didn't. While he loves his origins and takes pride in them, he doesn't let them pull him down and can become a chameleon if need be.

He's in an internal war with his brother, who's waiting for any mistake so he can turn the tables and become the leader of the Mori empire.

Of course, my jerk husband didn't tell me anything about his origins or fortune when we used to be pen pals back when I was eighteen and he was twenty-one. Because the sucker totally lied. He was in college when he first wrote to me, not in high school. He's thirty-one now.

Akira gets out of the car first, without waiting for the driver to open his door, then strides to mine as I'm about to step out. My husband offers me his hand and I take it before we walk inside together.

His steps are moderate, never too rushed, and never too slow. Everything he does is previously calculated to the smallest details. He's like a mountain sometimes, I swear. No one can tell what's inside its sturdy silence.

We take in the view of the garden that's lit by dim yellow light coming from lamp poles between the trees.

"It's a beautiful night, don't you think?" he asks.

"It is."

"Even the charity event was nice."

"Uh-huh."

"I had a few memorable impressions of a couple of people."

I wet my suddenly-dry lips. I've known Akira for long enough to recognize that he doesn't take note of everyone he meets. He might act polite and welcoming to each person he talks to, but he's always filtering them in his mind.

He only recalls those he'll work with.

Or those he'll destroy.

"Like who?" I ask in a tone that I hope to hell doesn't betray my emotions.

"Knox Van Doren and Daniel Sterling, for one."

Sebastian's colleagues. They came over and said their hellos to us after we talked to Sebastian since, apparently, they were previously acquainted with Akira.

"I thought you'd met them before."

"Yes. But tonight, I met them under different circumstances. Let's say, *new* ones."

"I see."

"Then there's your college friend. What was his name again?"

He's playing a game, wanting me to say his name myself, because no matter how much I tried to control my body language, Akira is a master at reading people's reactions and he must've sensed all the stiffening going on whenever Sebastian was in sight.

But if I choose confrontation, he'll just deflate and make it appear as if I'm being defensive.

So I smile. "Sebastian. His name is Sebastian Weaver."

"Right. Weaver. I heard his grandfather is a senator again."

"Could be."

"His uncle owns the firm in which he, Daniel, and Knox work. I heard he passed the bar after taking an accelerated course."

"Nice." When the hell did he manage to get his hands on this information? I knew Akira's line of intel worked fast, but I didn't know it was this fast.

"Do you have any secrets to tell me about him?"

"Why do you ask?"

"Because I'm considering working with him."

Fuck. *Shit.*

When he expressed his intentions earlier, I thought they were mere empty promises. I didn't think he'd really want to work with Sebastian.

"Wouldn't it make more sense if you worked with Knox or Daniel since you're already acquainted with them?" I'm thankful my tone is casual.

"Logically, it does, but where's the challenge in that?" He smiles in that mysterious way that still gets under my skin.

Akira always appears like a blank canvas who only shows people what they want to see. He does have his hidden tendencies, though, and presents them through that infuriating smile.

I don't even trust anything he told me over the years when we used to write letters back and forth to each other. At the time, I thought they were genuine, but that could've been another way for him to manipulate me so I'd end up in this position.

Because no matter what Kai and Ren say, I don't believe this whole thing hasn't been plotted for years. Maybe since I was born.

"So?" Akira insists.

"So what?"

"Any weaknesses I can hold over him?"

"Why would I know his weaknesses? We only studied at the same college. Our classes weren't even in the same department, so it's not like we were close."

"Interesting. I don't know why I got the impression that you were, in fact, close. Maybe it was my imagination."

"Could be."

Akira pats my hand. "No worries. Although you didn't help me, I'll find his weakness in no time. It'll be a fun challenge."

My spine jerks upright and I force myself to relax so he doesn't read my reaction.

If there's anything I've learned about Akira after all these years, it's that he makes it his mission to find other people's weaknesses. It's how he manages to step over them and get what he wants.

No one gets under Akira's radar and escapes unscathed. He's so similar to my father that way.

But I can't try to persuade him out of it, because if he senses my interest in the matter, he'll latch on to it.

"Good luck."

He lowers his head and kisses my cheek as we reach the entrance. "Go ahead and change before our guests arrive."

"You, too." I smile as we go in separate directions. His room is on the eastern end and mine is on the west.

My room is simple with a king-sized bed in the middle and tall lamps on either side of it. The only personal item here is the sketchpad on the bedside table that I use whenever I need a breathing outlet.

I lean against the door and close my eyes the slightest bit, catching my breath.

It feels as if I haven't been breathing properly since the moment my eyes fell on those tropical green ones. For a second, the past flashes before my eyes, but all I can think about is the last time I saw him.

Bleeding, feverish, and dying.

Slowly opening my eyes, I lift my hand, the same hand that Sebastian kissed, and stare at it in the light.

It still tingles, still feels as hot as his lips. I can imagine them on my skin, kissing, lingering as he holds me prisoner with his savage gaze.

I walk to the bed on unsteady legs and unzip my dress on the way, my breasts spilling free from the built-in bra as the material pools on the floor.

My skin feels so warm and sensitive that even the sensation of the air hitting it manages to cause discomfort.

I lie on the soft mattress and slip my tingling, hot hand that Sebastian kissed inside my panties.

My back arches off the bed as I rub my clit in slow circles.

I'm so wet that I soak my fingers in a second. It's been such a long time since I got so aroused this fast. It feels foreign. New, even.

Or maybe I'm just projecting the past onto the present.

My pussy throbs as I slide my fingers through my folds while still stimulating my clit. Sparks of pleasure flood my starved core and I dig my teeth into the cushion of my bottom lip.

My nipples peak and I cup one with my free hand as I stare at the ceiling.

But it's still not enough.

I close my eyes and let my imagination loose. Rough, calloused fingers pull on the tight peaks of my nipples, painfully twisting them.

A moan spills from my lips as he grabs both nipples and squeezes one between his lean fingers. Then he bites on the other one, trapping it between his teeth before he sucks it into his hot, wet mouth.

My moans and whimpers echo in the air, rising to a crescendo. It's like I haven't been this turned on in my entire life.

No.

I haven't been this turned on in seven years.

And it's all because of *him*.

The shadow I feel perching over me, his large, hard body squashing mine beneath him. He's so huge, so much bigger than me.

He can hurt me.

Can *ruin* me.

My sticky inner thighs clench together at the thought and I thrust two fingers inside me, but in my fantasy, it doesn't feel like them.

Not even close.

His huge cock pounds into me, stretching me until I'm whimpering and tears sting my lids. His harsh, unforgiving eyes peer into mine as he fucks me without mercy. As if he's punishing me.

As if he wants to teach me a lesson.

I want him to kiss me, but I don't think he'll do it. So I just lie there, taking his punishment and the rough thrusts.

In my mind, my hand rests on his chest, feeling the stiff muscles rippling under my touch and the strong heartbeat beneath it.

He ups his rhythm until I'm gasping, holding on by a thread to the carnal pleasure that he's ripping out of me.

"Sebastian…" I moan, and my heart jolts as the name hangs in the air, but I don't get to think on it long as a wave of pleasure drags me under.

He doesn't speak, though. The Sebastian from my hallucinations never does.

Usually, I don't speak either, but today, lust takes complete hold of me until I can't think past it.

I imagine his hand around my throat as he drives into me harder and faster. I slide off the mattress due to the power of his cock forcing its way into my pussy over and over until I'm screaming.

My orgasm goes on and on and I think I'm going to pass out from the strength of it.

I ride the pleasure, murmuring his name like a chant. I don't want to open my eyes, don't want to leave the fantasy and return to the world of the living.

But I do.

No matter how high I float, I always eventually crash down.

I slowly open my eyes, and just like that, the spell is broken. The scent of sex lingers in the air, but the only thing touching me is my own fingers.

I'm all alone.

A tear slides down my cheek and slips into my mouth.

It doesn't matter how many times the scene repeats, it still hurts like a fresh wound.

I think it always will.

But today, the hurt is stronger, deeper, as if someone dug a knife into that wound.

Because when I saw him again, I couldn't help thinking about where we might be right now if those black days in the cell had never happened.

If he hadn't been shot and we weren't taken.

If I hadn't dug my nose in where it didn't belong.

But it's useless to think of that, isn't it?

Not when our story has already been written.

I wipe my cheek with the back of my hand and stand up. I need to put on my steel armor to meet our guests.

As in, my fucking family.

NINETEEN

Naomi

AFTER I CHANGE INTO A PANTSUIT AND RELEASE MY HAIR so it falls to my shoulders, I head to the hall.

Akira is already waiting at the entrance of my wing.

He's wearing a yukata with a men's kimono that has his family's crest embroidered on either side of his chest on top of it. This type of fine-quality traditional wear costs a small fortune, but he's more comfortable in these clothes indoors. I think it has something to do with how he was raised in Kyoto.

Another thing he lied to me about in the letters. Akira isn't from Tokyo.

"Ready?" He offers me his hand.

I take it. "Are they already here?"

"Yes, they've been waiting. Good to keep them on their toes, don't you think?"

"You're the only one who believes keeping a Yakuza leader on his toes is a good thing."

"Not the only one since you're right there with me, my dear wife."

I scoff and he smiles as we go into the dining room. It has an ancient design where everyone is seated on the floor and has a small table in front of them full of premium side dishes.

Sure enough, our guests for the night are seated and waiting.

Kai, Ren, and my father.

The same father that I spent my stupid childhood and teenage years fantasizing about finding.

The same father I had countless fights with my mom about.

Abe Hitori.

Aka the leader of the New York City branch of the Yakuza and a man even more dangerous than Mom could have ever warned me about.

The man who can blow the only thread keeping me alive to bloody pieces.

"Sorry to have kept you waiting," Akira says in Japanese as we bow in greeting and take our seats opposite them.

Akira and I speak only in Japanese when we're around each other.

"It's okay. We haven't waited long." My father pours himself a drink and watches me from above the rim of his glass.

He's not tall, but he has a piercing stare that's meant to bring those who oppose him to their knees. My father is the epitome of a charismatic man who knows what he wants and how to get it.

Even if it means crushing his own family in the process.

"May I compliment the way you look, Mrs. Mori?" Kai's calm attention is on me and I wish I could throw a glass at his face.

That man is not only Dad's second-in-command/trustee/strategist, but he's also the one who metaphorically twisted my arm.

He acts silently and without drawing much attention to himself or his beloved boss.

Kai and I share a dark past, though, which is part of the reason why I thought he was familiar.

"No, you can't," I say coyly, then take a drink.

Ren scoffs, laughing silently, and while I hate everyone in

my father's organization, Ren might be the one at the top of the pyramid.

He's cunning and puts different masks on throughout the day. Sometimes, he tries to be friendly whenever we meet, calling what he did 'a job,' but I'll never forgive him for what happened seven years ago.

At the sound of his scoffing, something my husband considers juvenile and tasteless, he stares at Ren. Instead of just lowering his head like Akira expects of people, the younger man glares back. It's a full-on glare, as if he doesn't like Akira to tell him when to scoff and when not to.

They've always had some sort of weird communication, even though they don't really work together.

Kai tips his glass of *sake* in my direction as if drinking to me. He likes acting in that mighty way, as if he's better than everyone else and doesn't hold grudges. As if he's too old for such nonsense. He recently turned thirty-five, but he seems as old as Father sometimes.

"How's business?" My father asks Akira, to which my husband nods.

"Good. It's growing."

"Will you be staying in the States for a bit?"

"Yes. We need to stay here until I get the new branch up and running and Naomi takes care of her own business."

"I can't work from Japan forever," I say. "Unfortunately."

"Yes, yes." My father pretends to act nonchalant as he takes a bite of his favorite fish. "Let Kai know if you need anything, Mori-san. We're here for you."

I resist the urge to roll my eyes. Of course they're there for him. Because he's also there for my father.

After all, he married me off to Akira because it fits his business ventures. It was either that or not get the chance to say goodbye to my mom.

That, among other things he shackled me with until I couldn't move anymore.

While I was having naive thoughts about reuniting with my father, he was plotting to sell me off to the highest bidder.

Akira wanted to marry me 'for reasons,' as he likes to say, which are basically our secret. And Father had to make that union happen.

Becoming in-laws with the Mori clan is an honor that can't be accomplished by just anyone, let alone someone with a criminal background, such as my father.

Akira's family hates me and refuses to meet me for those reasons, but Father couldn't care less as long as his business is up and running, thanks to Akira's help.

My husband takes a leisurely sip of his *sake.* "Instead of Kai, I want Ren."

The latter freezes with his chopsticks halfway to his mouth. Ren, who I eventually discovered is around my age, loves his freedom more than anything.

So the thought of working with a control freak like Akira must be blasphemous to him.

"Kai is my most efficient man," my father points out the obvious.

"No offense, but that makes him boring. Ren, however, is reckless and could use some *discipline.*" There's a smirk on Akira's lips as he speaks.

Father laughs, a deep-bellied one. "As you wish."

Ren places his chopsticks down. "No."

"Did you just tell me no?" my father hisses.

His younger lieutenant faces him on his knees. "I want to stay with you, Boss."

"If Mori-san wants you, he'll get you."

Ren glares at Akira, who smirks. "It's decided then. Let me go get the present I brought for you from Japan, Hitori-san."

"You didn't have to," Father says in a fake way.

"Of course I did." Akira stands with the graciousness of a warrior and beckons Ren. "Come help me."

"Don't you have servants?"

Before Father can reprimand him for talking back, Akira's voice hardens. "What's the need for servants when there's you? Get up."

Ren grinds his teeth and curses under his breath before he jerks up and follows Akira out of the room.

As soon as the door slides closed behind them, I speak to Father without looking at him, "He's getting you premium ginseng herbals. Act surprised."

"That is very generous."

"You don't deserve it," I mutter.

"What did you just say, Naomi?"

I lift my head and meet his gaze. "That you don't deserve it."

His lips twist. "You're being ungrateful."

"For what exactly? For making me into a mafia princess, forcing me to get married or else you would've sold off my half-sister when we're your own fucking flesh and blood, or threatening me with never allowing me to see my mom on her deathbed? Or maybe it's making me believe that you were a father worth waiting for all these years?"

Kai shakes his head at me as he keeps eating. Screw him and his boss.

My father slams his chopsticks on the table. "Stop being a little American bitch and lose that tone."

"What tone? The one that tells the truth?"

"The one that disrespects me. Remember, Naomi, you need me."

"As much as you need *me*. My marriage is bringing you more profit than you could've ever dreamed. Don't forget that."

"And don't forget that you have a duty toward me."

"Duty?" I scoff. "You don't even know the meaning of that word. You lured my mom, knocked her up, and neglected her so you could marry for money and status. Not only did you find me for the sole reason of using me in your schemes, but even your legitimate daughter isn't safe from your tyranny."

"Riko is the one who chose to escape me, not the other way around."

"Because she realized how much of a dangerous person you are. She didn't want me to be raised in your world."

"But you ended up in it anyway, so keep your head down, clamp those lips shut, and follow the rules."

I open my mouth, about to give him a piece of my mind, but Akira and Ren return, carrying the box of ginseng. My father puts on a perfect show, acting flattered and happy.

After dinner, Akira suggests taking us on a tour of his pond. My father readily agrees and I take my time finishing my tea before I get up.

My husband, Dad, and Ren go out first, and I'm about to follow with Kai, but he touches my arm. I halt when he communicates with his eyes that I should stay.

He still has his hair long and tied at his nape. The sharp lines of his jaw have turned more callous, and his eyes no longer appear human. Probably due to the number of killings Father makes him do.

Oh, and his last name is Takeda, not Collins like when he impersonated being a PI seven years ago.

"What is it?" I murmur.

Kai might have thrust me into this life, but he's been more my ally than my enemy in the last seven years.

After all, he was the one who came to save me during that red night. He was only sixteen when Dad put him there to watch me from the shadows.

Back then, when he saw Sam—my mother's boyfriend at the time—coming at me, he didn't hesitate to barge in and kill the bastard. It was his first kill, he told me, and it was bloody and gory and so damn messy.

According to Kai, Mom stabbed the asshole's corpse a few times when she found me in shock with blood covering me.

Sam's blood.

That's why it was always the red night in my head.

It's also when I met Father and some of his men, but I don't remember it, because I blocked those memories out of my head.

But the moment he called me *Ojou-sama* again, I knew that we go way back. The familiarity struck me harder than I would have imagined.

I guess that's why Kai and I have some sort of a hate-love relationship.

He's an absolute dick for what happened seven years ago, but sometimes, it feels like he's looking out for me in his own screwed-up way. I know not to take it for granted from someone as detached as he is.

"It's about Mio."

My breath hitches at the mention of my much younger half-sister.

I learned about her existence when my mom was dying, and I felt like I was given a chance to have another family member and do better. I've tried to meet with her on the rare occasion she goes to Japan, but we're mostly on different continents and Father keeps her under a strict guard.

"What about Mio?" I ask Kai.

"He's marrying her off to the Russian mafia."

"What?"

"Lower your voice. You're not supposed to find out about this."

"He can't marry her off. I got married so she'd stay safe."

"His thoughts and yours are different. Both of you are assets of power that he'll use to its fullest potential."

"If she gets married into the Russian mafia, she'll be eaten alive."

"There's that, but the bigger issue is that she's agreeing to it."

"She's *what?*"

"You know Mio. Dutiful to a fault."

"God. This is a disaster."

"I agree."

"Then tell him that."

"He believes this to be the most logical choice to strengthen his ties with the Bratva and, therefore, won't listen to me."

"And you think he'll listen to me?"

"No. Which is why you need to be careful, *Ojou-sama*. Don't antagonize him."

"If he marries her off, I won't stand still for it."

"Don't tell me any details. I'm not your accomplice."

"You've been my accomplice since the day you saved me, Kai."

"Unfortunately. Maybe."

I lean against the wall, catching my breath from all the things that have happened in the span of a day. Japan feels so much safer now. At the beginning, working from there was a challenge since Chester Couture is based in the States; I managed it well and even opened a branch in Japan so I could have something to focus on.

But now that I'm back in the States, I'm not so sure if it was a wise decision at all. Ever since I married Akira soon after Mom's death, I've never thought about coming back here.

That's a lie. But lying is better than the truth sometimes.

I straighten and face Kai. "Let's go outside before they notice we're gone."

"*Ojou-sama*."

"Yeah?"

"You spoke with him tonight?"

My heart skips a beat and a painful thud I thought would disappear claws its way to the surface. I don't have to play dumb and ask who, so I nod instead.

"You survived then. You have to keep surviving by staying away from him."

Kai thinks it's that easy.

He believes surviving is a convenient thing that I can simply attach my mind to and it'll follow my command.

I release a sigh. "I have to meet with him."

"And make Akira suspicious?"

"That's the main reason I need to do it. Akira wants to work with him and I have to prevent it."

"I'll take care of it."

"No! The last time you took care of something, he almost died."

"But he didn't die."

"Kai…"

"Fine. Do it your way. But are you sure you can talk to him without sacrificing something in return? The man he is today is different from the quarterback you knew back then."

I suck in a sharp breath. "I can handle him."

Or so I like to believe.

TWENTY

Akira

Dear Yuki-Onna,

    I'm only writing these letters for self-records now.

    I lost hope that you'll ever reply to my previous ones, let alone read this, but I guess old habits die hard.

    Every week, I sit in front of my computer and type these things, not because I want to, but because something feels fucking missing if I don't do it.

    insert shrug here

    My life is going downhill. I thought I hit rock bottom before but, apparently, there are fucking levels for that shit and I'm now in the middle.

    Or maybe I'm barely scratching the surface.

    I lost my soul. Yeah, funny, I know. The soulless guy actually lost his nonexistent soul.

    My crisis is book-worthy, I swear.

    But maybe it's not a crisis, after all, and I'm only imagining things. Maybe my soul is indeed missing and I'm just being a dramatic asshole who needs attention.

    I don't, usually. I'm not you, after all.

Whatever it is, something is missing. And before your head grows in size, no, it's not you. It's something in me. I felt it before, but now it's just empty and soundless.

Maybe it passed away during my sleep.

Maybe Yuki-Onna came through my window, after all, and is now confiscating whatever I have to offer.

Maybe you're the one who put her up to it. Or maybe she's you.

Either way, it's working. My sins are finally catching up to me.

I pray that you're living a shitty life.
Amen,
Akira

TWENTY-ONE

Sebastian

"**M**R. WEAVER IS ASKING FOR YOU."

I stop near the door of my office at my assistant's voice. I peek at her from around the glass door that separates her space from mine.

She's juggling a phone between her shoulder and ear, fussing with countless case files with one hand, and typing away at her keyboard with the other.

"Do you need another assistant, Candice?"

She gives me the stink eye.

Candice is a middle-aged black woman with a big figure and a sharp tongue. She's been with Nate and Kingsley since they opened Weaver & Shaw, and I stole her away with my negotiating skills. She soon hated me due to the workload she has to take care of.

"What do you think, young Weaver?" She tips her chin in the direction of her desk. "This won't sort itself."

"I'll get you one of the interns."

"Daniel and Knox have them all in their pockets. They love the charming ones, you know."

"Rude, Candice. Do you mean I'm not charming?"

"Not intentionally, you aren't."

"Fine. I'll smile more and be good to them."

"Not at all of them. I don't need starstruck trainees walking around here, giving you heart eyes and not getting things done."

"I can never win with you."

"At least you recognize that." She motions down the hall. "Go and see what he wants. Seemed urgent."

"First thing in the morning?"

She lifts a shoulder and answers the phone, "Weaver & Shaw, Sebastian Weaver's office..."

I wave at her with two fingers, drop my briefcase in my office, then head down the hall to Nate's lair, as Dan likes to call it.

If this is another one of his boring strategic meetings, I'm out. Uncle is the only person I consider family anymore, but he's too strict and stoic for his own good.

Though everyone else would argue I'm no different.

No one would've accused me of that seven years ago, but at some point, I got tired of pretending and stopped putting on a façade unless it's absolutely necessary.

So I dropped one of my masks—or a few.

I knock on Nate's office door, ready to tell him that I have work to do and cases to review.

But most of all, I have some plotting to take care of.

It's been two days since the charity event where Naomi waltzed back into my life, following her husband around.

I expected said fucking husband to get in touch, but he hasn't. He hasn't even called Daniel or Knox. I know because I've been pestering them like a needy cat lady, as Dan called me, and nearly confiscated their phones.

If Akira isn't going to make the first move, I'll have no choice but to do it myself. But I can't look desperate or he'll be suspicious of my reasons.

"Come in," Uncle's voice floats from the inside.

I step inside, making a show of my exasperated sigh.

Nate's office is the biggest in the firm and he's even having construction done on the upper floors. Weaver & Shaw is expanding, and the numbers over the years indicate increasing profits.

It's all thanks to Nate. Not his senator father or his influential mother. Just him.

And part of it is because he doesn't let just anyone join. In the law circuit, his interviewing process for associates is infamous as being absolutely ruthless and scrutinizing. He's the type who knows your deepest, darkest secrets before even you do.

In a way, my uncle inherited the Weaver quality of only wanting the best.

Nate sits behind his glass desk in an erect position. He's older now, close to hitting forty, and could be mistaken for a fucking vampire due to how little he's aged.

"What is it?" I ask, stepping into the office.

I pause when my eyes land on the woman across from him.

The same woman I pictured underneath me with my hand around her throat as I jacked off against the shower wall last night.

The same woman I had a dream about and woke up with my hand around my hard dick.

She looks different than she did at the party, less put together but more guarded.

Her black hair is loose, falling to her shoulders. It's longer than it was when we were in college, making her look more like her mom. She's wearing a smart blue suit and black high heels, and the combination of the three give her a mature edge.

Her lips are painted a bright red and the urge to smear it across her fucking face with my fingers, then with my dick is all I can think about.

Maybe I should make all of her skin red.

Her expression is closed off, strained, even, like some of the businessmen who have a take-no-nonsense personality.

For some reason, this is closer to how I imagined she would

evolve. A beautiful woman with a no-bullshit attitude. Not a fucking side piece on an influential man's arm.

I hide my surprise. Seeing her in Nate's office is the last thing I expected.

Yes, I'd planned to meet with her again, but on my terms and definitely not where I work.

"What is this?" I say in the cold, professional tone everyone but Candice is used to from me.

"Sit, Sebastian." Nate motions at the seat across from her. "Naomi came here with a request."

I unbutton my jacket and lower myself into the chair. The small coffee table is the only thing separating us, and another urge grips me.

This time, I want to grab her by the nape and jam her against the table, maybe punish her. Maybe toy with her.

Maybe hurt her.

At any rate, I'd fucking have her.

"He's here. You can talk," Nate speaks in his unaffected tone, ignoring the fact that a ghost from our past just jumped back into our lives.

He didn't even see her that night at the charity event since she left before he made his brief appearance.

Though I'm sure the two fuckers, Daniel and Knox, tattled after all the jokes they made at my expense.

Naomi lifts the cup of coffee that's on the table and takes a sip, slowly savoring it before her eyes meet mine.

I keep the contact, even when she slides her attention to Nate. "My husband will make an offer to Sebastian to become his acting attorney for the new branch he's opening in New York and I'd like for you to deny that offer."

Well, well.

Akira does want us to work together, after all, and Naomi hates the idea.

Good. This will be my perfect fucking opening.

"Why would I refuse such an important work opportunity?" I ask nonchalantly.

Her gaze slides back to mine, slightly widened. "Why would you want to work with him?"

"Why wouldn't I?"

"I don't know. The past, maybe?"

"You said it yourself. It's in the past. We shouldn't let personal affairs get in the way."

She purses those blood-red lips, and for some reason, it brings back memories of that fucking cell when she pressed her T-shirt on my wound in a desperate attempt to save me.

Only so she could stab me in the back afterward.

Her attention returns to Nate. "You need to stop him."

"I don't really interfere with how he or anyone else takes on clients unless there's a strong reason to do so."

"There is a reason. I don't want to mix the past with the present."

"But you won't. Sebastian will be working with your husband, not with you, Mrs. Mori."

A muscle clenches in my jaw when Nate calls her by her husband's last name. I thought I'd never hate anything as much as the way she fucking disappeared, but here it is.

Her name attached to another man.

Her name with another fucker.

It's almost as bad as the pain I felt after she broke up with me via phone.

Almost.

"Does that mean you won't stop him?" she asks Nate with a note of impatience.

"I'm afraid not. I have no compelling reason to interfere. Take it up with him and convince him yourself."

Her glare falls on me and I give her a smile, a genuine one, with an edge of darkness. Because there's no way in fuck I'm letting this golden opportunity slide.

I like the way she glares. How her lips still twitch at the corners and how a pink hue covers her pale cheeks.

Some things never change, after all.

"You'll both regret this." She jerks up and snatches her handbag, then storms out of the office.

I relax in my seat to stop myself from standing and going after her. Maybe grabbing her and pushing her into a dark corner. Maybe touching her and imprisoning her.

Nate raises a dark brow, forming a steeple at his chin with his fingers. "Do I need to know what that was all about?"

"She's back in town."

"I'm not blind. I can see that. She's married, too."

"I know that."

"Apparently, you don't, because your eyes are shining with that impulsiveness again, Rascal."

"Don't worry about it."

"The last time you said that, I had to write checks and settle with random people at bars."

"I'm not young and reckless anymore. I'll be fine."

"You better be. We don't want Mr. and Mrs. Weaver to say I told you so. And I definitely don't want my nephew to get caught up in the wrong crowd."

"Wrong crowd?"

"Akira Mori is known to deal with criminal organizations. He has no morals when it comes to business, and that means he also has no boundaries with interpersonal relationships."

"I wouldn't call myself someone with morals either. So this should be fun."

He leans over in his seat, interlacing his fingers at his chin. "I'm not a fool. I'm well aware you're doing this for her, not for the challenge or work-related reasons. I was there and saw you at your worst, Rascal. So you can't tell me this whole thing is just a business venture for you."

"But you can believe it is. That way, you get the profits and a clear conscience."

He sighs and relaxes back. "I warned you, but I can't hold your hand and stop you, so suit yourself. You're not a kid anymore."

"Thanks, Nate." I stand.

"Put the firm in jeopardy and I'll kick you while you're down. I'll even get Daniel and Knox to help."

I roll my eyes as I leave his office and head back to mine.

My mind is crowding with options of how to go about destroying Akira Mori and Naomi through business ventures.

If she already knows he'll make an offer, then the opportunity will present itself soon enough.

I stop by Candice's office for today's schedule, but instead of finding her multitasking a thousand things at once, she's bringing a glass of water to someone sitting at her desk.

"You have a guest," Candice tells me as I step through her doorway. "She doesn't have an appointment, but she says she's a personal acquaintance."

Naomi stands and turns toward me, her stance wide and her face still closed off. "We need to talk."

"I already gave you my opinion in Nate's office. My answer won't change a few minutes later."

She purses her lips. If it were old times, she would've cursed me by now. But maybe she's reined that part of herself in.

Or maybe she's just disappeared.

"Hear me out," she says, her voice softer, but I can tell she's pushing herself to sound like that.

"No."

"Sebastian…"

"You didn't hear me out seven years ago. Why should I do it now?"

Her face pales, lips parting, but she says nothing.

Good.

Now she understands a sliver of what I fucking felt.

"Email me my schedule, Candice." I leave her standing there and step into my office.

The door opens behind me and Naomi enters, her breathing harsh as she shuts the door.

I face her with an intentionally exasperated sigh. "What is it now?"

"You can't just ignore me and pretend I'm not here."

"Believe me, I can."

"Fine, you're right to be aloof and apathetic. The past was bloody and wrong, but we're not there anymore. We're here and you need to hear me out."

"Maybe I'm always there. Maybe I didn't wake up in the hospital. Maybe I remained in that fucking cell for seven years."

Her mouth drops open.

"I see you still have the habit of going speechless when hard facts are thrown your way, Naomi. Or should I call you Mrs. Mori now?"

Saying the name is like swallowing fucking acid down my throat. It's like stabbing my own goddamn eyes and floundering in the dark with no exit in sight.

But I continue with my taunting look and tone. I continue to roll in the lie until it consumes me.

"Akira is dangerous," she says in a low voice. "Don't be fooled by his outer businessman appearance. He's ruthless and callous and has not one bone of mercy in his body, especially since he's approaching you for reasons other than work. He wants to dig into my past through you and he won't stop unless he gets what he's after, even if it means ruining you and Nate's firm in the process. So walk away now while you can."

"You forget one minor detail. He wants to work with me."

"He'll eventually give up."

"You just said he won't stop until he gets what he wants. Which happens to be me."

"Just don't accept his offer."

"Why do you care whether I accept it or not?"

"Because it'll impact me."

I take a step toward her without realizing, because this fucking pull we have is apparently not something that can be eradicated with time.

The scent of lilies mixed with peaches and the past fills my nostrils when I stop a few inches away from her, and my voice drops. "Impact you how?"

She sucks in an audible breath, her pupils dilating. When she speaks, it's with effort. "I don't want Akira to know about my past."

My jaw clenches at her insinuation that our past is some sort of a dirty secret she wants to hide from her hotshot husband.

"Why should I care about what you want?"

"You don't want him to know either."

"Maybe I do. Maybe I'll have a drink with him and tell him about all the ways I chased his pretty wife and fucked her in all her holes while she screamed for more. He could use some pointers."

That pink hue explodes on her cheeks again and she raises her hand to slap me, but I'm faster. I grab it in mine before she has the chance to act.

Maybe it's the fact that I'm touching her again or it could be the anger shining in her dark eyes that she's not allowed to have. But in a fraction of a second, my mood goes from gray to black.

All the bottled-up emotions rush to the fucking surface, eradicating any sliver of control I possess.

Using my hold on her, I back her up, slam her against the door, and imprison her wrist above her head. She gasps as I crush my front against hers, my lips meeting the shell of her ear. "You have two options, Naomi. One, turn around, leave my office, and never fucking show your face here again. Don't talk to me about your husband or your concerns, and don't ever fucking ask me to hear you out. Two, stay and bear the consequences."

She blinks rapidly, her delicate throat working with a swallow. My hand itches to wrap around that throat and squeeze until she's lightheaded and gasping for air. Until she's hazy and dizzy but not fighting me, because she trusts me to allow her oxygen.

Fuck.

Now that the image has formed in my head, I can't chase it away.

She doesn't make a move to leave either. Doesn't attempt to pull herself from me.

"Your time is up, Naomi."

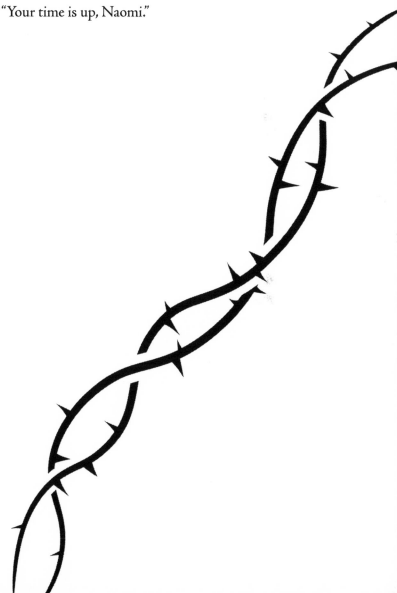

TWENTY-TWO

Naomi

I'M FROZEN.

Unable to move.

Unable to blink.

Unable to even breathe.

My heart hammers so loud, my ears buzz with its rhythm. The air feels like sharp needles pricking at my skin and hooking against my bones.

Your time is up, Naomi.

I heard Sebastian say it, yet my brain doesn't fully process it. But then I recall why I made the risky move of coming into his office in the first place.

I had to make him change his mind about working with Akira. That's the sole reason I'm talking to him.

But it blurred along the way when he touched me, grabbed my wrist, and slammed me against the wall as if he's been waiting years to do it.

Maybe I've been waiting years for him to do it as well.

No.

I can't allow myself down that rabbit hole again. This time, there really won't be any way out.

Snapping out of my stupor, I attempt to pull my hand from his, but he tightens his lean fingers on my wrist until I wince in pain.

His hard chest is flat against my heaving one. A flash of heat shoots through me as my body's memory kicks back to seven years ago when he used to trap me.

When his bergamot and amber scent filled me with a burst of both thrill and fear.

When having him close meant my life would be turned upside down.

Seven years later, it's still the same.

No matter how much I've meditated and trained my mind to rise above my bodily needs, one encounter is enough for my effort to crumble.

All my hopes of holding everything in vanish.

Like an addict, I relapse to the phase of my life when it had no meaning because he was no longer in it.

When I fought myself from booking the next flight back to America just so I could see him one more time.

Even from the shadows.

But I was only fooling myself.

In what world would seeing him one last time be enough? It's been only two days since I bumped into him again and I've been in a constant state of hyperawareness that I can't explain.

My nights are spent tossing and turning and touching myself more than I'm used to and still getting no satisfaction.

This feeling has been mounting for so long and it's now exploding in my face.

"What…" I trail off at the sound of my breathy voice and clear my throat. "What are you doing?"

"I gave you a choice and you didn't leave." He's speaking close. So close that his hot breaths, mixed with coffee and mint, toy with my skin. His proximity is messing with my head more than I'd ever admit.

"Let me go, Sebastian."

"I told you there would be consequences to bear and you didn't move to leave."

"I did."

"Not fast enough." His free hand wraps around my throat.

A shock load of sensations shoot through me and my heart nearly stops beating.

Holy Jesus.

My whole body goes limp as his thumb grazes the pulse point, then presses on it hard enough to make me completely aware of his presence.

It's been such a long time since someone touched me with un-apologetic control. And even though I don't want to be affected, I can't help the burst of tingles that cover my skin.

"Talk then. You were saying something about how I should stay away from your husband," he whispers in a tone that gets past the confinements of my ears and flows in my blood.

"You have to." My tone is so low, I barely recognize it as my own.

"Why?"

"I told you. Because he's dangerous."

"What if I'm dangerous, too, but in a completely different way? What if I want to see which one of us is more immoral?"

"Don't…"

He thrusts his knee between my legs and I gasp when his thigh brushes against my core. Our clothes separate us, but it's like we're flesh to flesh.

Pulse to pulse.

Body to body.

"Sebastian…stop…"

"You know that word doesn't stop me."

"We're not kids anymore. This isn't a game."

"Maybe it is. Maybe we should pick up where we left off."

His lips brush against the shell of my ear and I shudder both at their heat and at how he rubs his thigh against my pussy.

Stop is on the tip of my tongue, but it doesn't come out.

And knowing Sebastian, it probably wouldn't work, as he said. It doesn't matter that the ring of another man is on my finger or that he saw me with said man not too long ago. He'll see whatever he wants to see and ignore the rest.

That part has never changed about him.

He glides the tip of his tongue from the shell of my ear to my cheek. I shudder, my hand flying to his side, to stop him, to push him away, but I don't.

My fingers remain there, frozen, unable to move as his hot wet mouth trails a path to where his hand is grabbing my throat.

"Fuck. You still taste the same."

And you still feel the same.

But I don't say that aloud as I let myself drown in the moment. I've been on guard for so many years that I've forgotten what it means to let go.

To feel.

To just be alive.

And right now, I'm that and more. I'm bubbling with life and I can feel it pouring in and out of me.

"This is wrong," I murmur.

"So?" He speaks against my chin, his skin setting mine on fire.

"We shouldn't do this…"

"And yet we are."

"I…I'm married."

"That means fuck all to me."

"We're over."

"I never agreed to that."

I place both palms on his chest and push back as hard as I can, breathing harshly. His lips leave my face, but his steel hold remains around my neck.

"We've been over for seven years, Sebastian."

"To you, obviously, since you got married."

"You said it yourself. *Married.* You don't have the right to touch a married woman this way."

"Says who?"

"Common decency."

"I don't have that."

I see it then. The apathy in his mesmerizing eyes. At first, I thought it was his way of expressing the coldness he felt toward me, but maybe that's what he's become now.

An apathetic person with not a sliver of warmth inside him.

Maybe common decency isn't the only thing he doesn't have anymore. Maybe he's lost other parts of him, too.

Maybe he's corrupted beyond repair.

What happened to you? I want to ask, but I'm too afraid of the answer.

"Then you should at least have a sense of self-preservation and do as I say."

"You mean, staying away from your husband?"

"Yes."

"What do I get in return?"

"Your safety!"

"Pass."

"What do you mean by pass?"

"You need to give me something."

"Something like...what?" I sound spooked, even to my own ears.

"Agree first."

"Not until I know the catch."

"Your loss." He releases me and steps back.

A gust of cold air covers my skin and it takes all my will to remain planted in place and not seek some sort of friction.

"The door is right behind you, Mrs. Mori."

I want to go back a few seconds in time and shove that name back down his throat so he can't say it again.

Or maybe I could go back seven years and prevent all the hell that broke loose.

Or maybe if I hadn't been born as Abe Hitori's daughter, I wouldn't be standing here in the first place.

But all those options are impossible, so all I can do is focus on the now.

My shoulders straighten. "What do you want?"

"You're not ready for what I want."

"Tell me and I'll decide."

"Give me your new phone number."

"Why?"

"I'll text you a location. If you're ready to find out what I really want, be there. If you're not, I'll move on."

I'm still shaking from my meeting with Sebastian.

It got so bad that I had to spend a few minutes in the bathroom so I could sober up and get my shit together.

Then I drove to my father's house, which is located in a well-secured neighborhood in Brooklyn. Thankfully, it's far enough from our house that I don't feel like Akira's breathing down my neck.

I made it clear to Akira that I wouldn't be moving around with his men following me and he surprisingly complied. I thought I'd have to fight to the death so he'd remove the bodyguards.

But then again, he's a practical person and doesn't mind losing a battle or two in order to win the war.

The security in my father's house, however, is on another level. My car is searched thoroughly by his guards before I'm allowed through the gate.

I don't have to drive up to the house, though. The only person I'm here for doesn't spend much time indoors.

After parking the car near the back garden, I remove my heels and leave them beside my car, then step onto the grass barefoot.

The cold sensation is soothing against my hot, aching skin. It's been that way since Sebastian touched me and spoke against my ear, awakening memories he had no damn business awakening.

And what's with the whole, *be there if you want to find out what I want?*

Does he really think I'd start an affair or something?

Though I was about to when he had me by the throat against the door.

My thoughts scatter when a rustle of movement catches my attention.

A petite woman dressed in kendo gear is holding a bamboo sword and training by hitting a tree.

Her sharp, precise movements and erect posture are part of the discipline she's been maintaining for over a decade.

My baby sister might only be twenty-one, but she has the aura of a thousand-year-old wise monk.

"Mio," I call out gently.

She turns around, her sword held high and her dark eyes gleaming beneath her helmet. "*Onee-chan!*"

Older sister.

I never thought I'd like being called that until Mio said it shyly the first time.

Can I call you Onee-chan? She asked in a low voice while hiding behind Kai and that fucker Ren. Back then, she had her hair braided and wore a cute white and pink dress with matching flats. A blush covered her cheeks as she stared up at me for long moments.

I don't think I've ever fallen in love with someone faster than I did then.

Mio was just another innocent soul trapped in the middle of bloody madness.

She quickens her steps toward me and stops a few steps away. "I'm sweaty."

"Come here." I pull her into a hug and she giggles against me, her helmet nuzzling into my chest.

We didn't use to be so touchy when we first met. Mio was raised in the strict, traditionalist way and is usually against any type of touching. Sort of like Akira, who likes physical contact only when he initiates it and on his terms.

But my sister and I have become close enough to hug whenever we see each other.

She removes her helmet and grabs a towel from a tree, then wipes her neck and the sides of her face.

Her dark brown hair is tied in a bun. If it were loose, it'd reach the small of her back, but she never actually lets it down.

Her almond-shaped eyes give her round face a softer edge that fits with her tiny voice. Sometimes, I have to lean close to hear her talk.

"Papa told me you were coming back, but he didn't tell me more, and Kai isn't cooperative." She speaks in a sophisticated American accent, thanks to all the homeschooling and prim and proper private teachers she's had since she was born here.

"When is Kai ever cooperative?"

"You're right." She smiles. "I'm glad I can speak to you face-to-face and not through a phone."

"Me, too, Mio."

We talk about Japan and the cherry blossoms that she loves so much. Then Mio tells me about her studies and her kendo training that she's obviously obsessed with.

When she's done, I clear my throat. "Do you have something else to tell me?"

She traps her bamboo sword between her legs as she picks at the grass. "Like what?"

"Kai was actually cooperative for once and told me what's going on."

She frowns. "That fox. He promised not to get you involved."

"You think he promised, but he probably manipulated you into thinking that, Mio."

"Probably."

"So?"

"So what?" She's still gripping grass in her fists.

"Are you going to tell me about agreeing to marry some Russian mobster?"

"Papa said it's to help our family."

"Your *papa* only cares about himself, Mio. You should know that by now."

"But…I don't want him or you in danger."

"Me? Why would I be in danger?"

"Papa said you and Mori-san could be targeted because of Mori-san's new business endeavors. He's having problems setting up his new company because of all the customs bureaucracy, no? If I marry into the Russians, they won't only help, but they'll also provide you protection."

That bastard.

He knew exactly which cards to play to make Mio agree. Father and I are her world, and she'd agree to hell if it means protecting us.

"Akira and I aren't in danger. And even if we were, we can protect ourselves."

"You don't know that."

"Mio…"

"I'll play my part, too, *Onee-chan.*"

"But the Russian mafia is dangerous."

"Mori-san is also dangerous, and you're doing just fine."

"That's different. Akira was my friend before and he's not a mobster. The Russian mafia is notorious for its ruthlessness, and Dad plans to marry you off to one of their leaders. They're known for their violence and could hurt you, Mio."

She jumps up, holding her sword in a defense position. "I can protect myself."

I shake my head but don't press it. Instead, I choose to spend a peaceful day with her.

We have lunch together and talk about everything and nothing. We're basically each other's only friend. Being with her brings back memories of college days when I didn't really have friends.

Except for Lucy and Reina at the end.

Sometimes, I consider calling them and getting together, but the thought of putting them in danger has always stopped me. Except for that one time I got drunk and texted Reina and nearly poured my heart out to her.

Mio is pouting when I have to leave at the end of the evening. So I promise to spend more time with her now that I'm back. Something that makes her smile and wave me off.

I drive home, my head still filled with endless thoughts and theories.

Spending time with Mio, no matter how fun, didn't purge away what happened this morning.

I can't purge away the image of Sebastian's hand, lips, and words.

Hell. I can't even forget the sound of his voice.

I didn't leave him my phone number before I stormed out of his office, but I keep checking my messages anyway, as if he'd magically get the number.

It wouldn't be the first time he's gotten my number behind my back.

Stopping the car in the driveway, I take a moment to gather myself, then I make a few work calls and schedule some meetings. I take the legacy Mom left behind seriously, even if only from the administrative side. Amanda, who was Mom's assistant and is now mine, takes care of diva designers and all that jazz.

Work keeps me busy enough to not think about other things, but that was before.

I have a feeling it will no longer apply now that my world has collided with Sebastian's again.

After finishing my check-in calls with Amanda, I step into the house.

I pause at the sound of arguing coming from Akira's office. This late?

For the seven years I've been married to him, Akira has always been as meticulous as fuck about his working hours versus his resting ones.

Any time after seven is his 'me time' that no one dares to interfere with.

Also, arguing?

The occurrence is so rare that I stop and listen outside his office, but I can't really hear the words. Just a male voice.

And it's not Akira's.

I knew my husband wouldn't be arguing. The man doesn't raise his voice and still accomplishes whatever he sets out to do.

Sometimes, it feels like he's a samurai in modern times. Or maybe a lethal ninja.

I'm about to continue on my way when the door of Akira's office swings open and Ren storms out, slamming it shut behind him.

He comes to a screeching halt upon seeing me, his face contorted as he bows in greeting.

I don't bow back. "Ah, I should've known the arguing would be all you."

"Are you happy?"

I smile. "About your misery? *Very.*"

"That doesn't erase yours, *Ojou-sama,*" He mocks.

"No, but it's good to have a companion."

"Who says I'm miserable?"

"You clearly are. Akira is effectively getting on your nerves. Finally met your match, huh?"

"You wish. No one gets to me, not you and not your psycho husband."

I pat his shoulder, pretending to dust something off, then whisper, "Watch your back. He already has you in his sights."

Ren stiffens as I pull away, his smaller eyes narrowing on mine before he strides off. I watch him with a satisfied smile. That rattled him enough to make him paranoid for a while.

"Aren't you a little daredevil?"

I turn around at Akira's voice. He stands in his doorway, leaning against the frame, and is wearing his yukata, which means it's definitely his 'me time.'

"That makes two of us," I mock.

He adjusts his glasses. "How was Mio-chan? That is, if you really spent all day with her."

"She's fine, and whether or not I spent my day with her is none of your concern. You don't tell me what to do, last time I checked."

"Hmm. It's back."

"What's back?"

"That fighting spirit. You lost it for a while. I wonder what triggered it, my dear wife."

Shit. I should've known he'd focus on that. This is Akira, after all.

From now on, I need to be more careful.

TWENTY-THREE

Akira

Dear Yuki-Onna,

I had my first dream about you in years last night.

It was as dirty as you are.

You came through my window like your ghostly self while I was sleeping, and then you slipped under the covers.

A shiver ran down my spine and I felt freezing through my bones, but instead of pulling away or trying to close the window, I remained still.

What? Don't judge. I needed to feel the moment Yuki-Onna finally took my life.

But that's not what you did.

Your hands slid up my thighs and you pulled my pants down. Your small hand wrapped around my dick and I became hard like a priest after abstaining for fucking years.

Again, don't judge. I didn't have a hold on my reaction.

In my defense, I never thought you'd attempt to seduce me or view me inappropriately like in some scenario of your favorite hardcore porn.

Anyway, my dick was definitely not having an existential crisis when *your tiny hands wrapped around its length, and I might have been on the verge of coming when you struggled to fist your palms around my huge cock.*

I could tell you're not really that experienced despite all the kinky scenarios you told me about, and that might have turned me on harder until my abdomen contracted and I had to grit my teeth.

But then you put me in your mouth, and, fuck me, it was like touching a piece of heaven as I was plummeting into hell. Your little tongue licked the side and you swallowed the precum like you waited your entire life to do it.

And fuck, I almost came down your sweet throat like a pubescent kid who was touched for the first time.

I couldn't stop watching the up and down of your head as you took me all the way to the back of your throat, using your tongue, lips, hands, and every fucking part of your body. Even the swish of your dark hair against my thighs was a stimulation I didn't think I needed.

And the worst part? Even when you struggled and seemed to be choking on my dick, you didn't stop. Not even close, not even a little. You kept going and going, swallowing my dick like a champ who was chasing her next trophy.

And just when I thought you did succeed in sucking my soul through my dick like a succubus, you looked at me.

Your eyes were droopy and your cheeks were flushed, and you had this look of challenge mixed with seductiveness.

And you bet your fucking ass that I rose up to it and hit the back of your throat until you spluttered and made these sounds that shoved me all the way down to my designated spot in fucking hell.

I came all the way down your little throat and you swallowed as much as you could, but my cum still dripped down your chin and coated those beautiful lips, smudging the red lipstick all over your face.

You marked by my cum as you gulped it down is a sight I will never forget.

Best imaginary blowjob I've ever had.

But like any dream, I woke up and you weren't there. I couldn't be a dick and torture you to orgasm.

I couldn't even imagine touching you.

Funny, right? We used to talk about porn like two boys who stole their dads' dirty magazines, but we never really talked about it between each other.

But you went ahead, appeared in my dreams, and blew me as if you had every right to.

You don't, Yuki-Onna.

Next time, just stick with sucking my soul.

Thanks, but not really,
Akira

TWENTY-FOUR

Sebastian

I FALL INTO A BLACK FUCKING HOLE.

No. That's not supposed to happen.

Yes. I was doing perfectly well pretending that the world wasn't burning down around me.

For seven years, I've managed so well to stay away. Although I had a nasty habit of googling her name at the beginning.

Of pestering Lucy, Naomi's friend from college, to find out where she was.

I spent sleepless nights going through every portal and profile with the name Naomi or Naomi Sato because I sure as shit couldn't find her with her old surname. Her social media accounts were gone as if they never existed.

She never paid much attention to those, anyway, so I didn't hold up much hope in finding her through them.

For months, I searched.

For months, I fucking obsessed.

My violent tendencies took the front seat and drove my life up the wall. I lost count of the number of times Nate had to stop me from punching someone to death and then got them to settle before they sued me.

After months in that state, I realized I was slowly killing myself and I needed to stop or I'd end up giving my grandparents the satisfaction of saying 'I told you so.'

And in order to move past the asshole I was at the time, I deleted my search history and let the bloody knife fester inside me with its blood.

I didn't search for her again. Didn't google her name. Didn't even talk to Lucy except on the rare occasion when we bumped into each other for the games we attend for Owen's sake—who's now a hotshot NFL player.

So why the fuck am I staring at a thousand tabs with her name on them again?

Why the fuck can't I step on the brakes?

Maybe because I saw her face again and I sure as fuck know her last name now.

Naomi Mori. The wife of Akira Mori.

I want to jam my fist through my laptop screen and somehow yank his last name from hers.

The more I read about them, the thicker the red mist that covers my vision gets, and I can feel myself relapsing into old fucking habits.

The Mori couple is known to be private, classy, and have a general regal presence that rivals my grandparents.

She's smiling with her hand on his arm in all the pictures of them together. There's a shot of them at a temple in the New Year's festivities in Japan. She's wearing a white kimono with dark blue flower motifs and he's in a yukata that matches the color of her motifs.

Her favorite fucking color.

Naomi laughs, tipping her head back as he whispers something in her ear with a smirk. I jam my laptop shut so I don't throw it against the wall.

I run a hand over my face and take a few deep breaths. But nothing I do is able to chase away the haze.

Nothing is able to dispel the fucking curse. Except for maybe beating Akira Mori to death and bathing in his blood.

There's a knock on the door and I grunt, "Come in."

Candice appears in the doorway and jams a hand on her hip. "You need to see this."

I stand because I'm ready to indulge in any type of distraction.

My assistant walks beside me as we head to the open office area that's designated for interns and junior associates.

Daniel and Knox are gathering all the interns and standing on a small pedestal. The females look at them with awe and the males regard them as if they're role models and they want to follow in their footsteps.

"Beautiful ladies and honored gents." Daniel grabs an imaginary microphone. "We're gathered here today to pay tribute to my legendary looks. And, ladies, I know my accent is irresistible, but don't faint just yet. Because, unfortunately, my Adonis appearance and killer dimples are not, in fact, why we're here. Disappointing, I know."

Many interns giggle and the others smile, playing straight into his manwhorish hands. Some would call that charming.

I was that once. Charming.

Now, interns are just as scared of me as they are of Nate.

Knox places an arm around Daniel's shoulder. "What's more disappointing is that it's time we split you guys up. Those who want to be on Dan's side, raise a hand. Those who prefer me, raise two. No pushing, please. As much as I want to, I can't accept everyone."

Chaos ensues as interns split themselves up between Daniel and Knox.

"Do something," Candice chastises in her stern voice. "They'll leave you scraps again."

I check my watch since it's close to my lunch appointment with a judge. "And we care because...?"

"The load of work on your desk, maybe? My going home to my family at a reasonable hour, maybe? Also, maybe not settling for the choices those two make anymore. They gloat about it in front of the other partners and make a drama out of it."

"I don't care about any of that."

"Well, I care about my reasonable working hours and you promised to get me some help. It's perfect timing for that."

"Fine. Who are the best interns?"

She points at a tall girl and a lean guy who aren't making as much of a fuss as the others but are veering more toward Knox. His twisted obsession with high-profile criminal cases makes many interns flock to him.

"Kate Bukowski and Omar Taylor, Jr. Both top of their class," Candice tells me.

"Grades only mean they spent all-nighters studying or cheating. I need them to be smart."

"They're the best interns we have. Now, do something."

Sighing, I approach the scene. The chaos halts for a bit and the interns watch me with eyes wide and mouths agape.

They aren't used to me getting involved in things like this.

"What are you doing here?" Daniel jumps down from his pedestal.

"Aren't we picking interns?" I ask, casually running my gaze over the interns, who've suddenly grown silent.

"We'll send yours later." Knox waves me away. "No need to waste your time."

"I'm going to personally pick mine." I stare at the two interns Candice pointed out to me. "Kate and Omar. Follow me."

They both startle, but it's not in a bad way. More like their eyes get wider and they stare at each other in an 'is this happening?' type of way.

I might not hunt down high-profile cases like Knox, but I get a lot of work that will look good on their resumes.

"What? No." Daniel slides in front of me with the grace of a panther. "That's not how it works!"

"It is now." I turn around and leave. The two interns hesitate for a second before they follow without a word.

"This is called preferential treatment, because you're Nate's prince," Knox whispers as I pass him by.

"Take it up with him then."

"Why the hell are you even here?" Daniel calls after me.

"Take that up with Candice," I motion at her and she gives him a gloating smile as she guides the interns to my office.

I tell them what's expected of them, efficiency without headaches, then grab my briefcase and leave.

Daniel and Knox are still making a show out of dividing the interns and I ignore them as I head to the exit.

"They're at it again." Aspen, the only senior female partner at the firm, falls in step beside me and we get in the elevator.

She's in her early thirties and one of the founders of Weaver & Shaw. They would never admit it, but Aspen is the line that kept Nate and Kingsley Shaw from killing each other and actually doing something productive with their destructive energy.

In a way, she's Nate's strategist and close friend, but she can turn into a fireball that matches her hair color in court.

"I know." I release a sigh as I hit the button for the parking garage.

"How have you been?"

I raise a brow and she raises a perfect one back.

"Let me guess. Nate tattled and now, I have to deal with his enforcer arm and secret weapon of mass destruction."

"I'm anything but a secret, Sebastian. And you forget that I was there when you hit rock bottom. I'm going to be the bearer of bad news and inform you that it won't happen again, not only for the sake of Nate and the firm, but also for your sake."

"I'm going to be fine."

"You better be. I don't want to start using what I know to keep you in line."

The elevator pings open and we step into the parking garage, then stop. "What are you talking about, Aspen?"

"Everything isn't what it seems in your family."

"That doesn't tell me anything."

"It's not supposed to. If I give you all the answers, how are you going to figure it out on your own? But here's a hint, your grandparents and even Nate are hiding something from you." She waves at me and strides to her car.

What the fuck was she getting at? I know for certain that Aspen wouldn't have brought it up if she didn't think it was of vital importance, but I'm also in no mood to play her mental games.

I'm not in the mood for anything. Fuck moods.

Shaking my head, I get into my own car and go to my meeting.

My mind isn't focused on work or forming interpersonal relationships, though. Usually, I'm the best at this—using my grandparents' name whenever I see fit.

Nate doesn't, because he wants a clean break from them, but I don't see why we shouldn't. After all, we've put up with their snobby, stifling behavior for long enough and we should be able to reap the rewards.

But today, all I want is to leave.

And once I'm able to, I drive back to my apartment. It's located in a quiet building on the outskirts of Brooklyn. Not only is it spacious and soundproof, with a great view of the city, but it's also a place where I can be myself.

Not a lawyer, not a Weaver, and not Nate's nephew.

Not even Sebastian sometimes.

Just…me.

The interior is vast and the wood flooring shines under the late afternoon sun coming through the floor-to-ceiling windows. The only furniture is a TV that I've only turned on a few times.

There's no sofa or rugs. No decorative things or sacred belongings.

I have a bed in the bedroom, a desk and a library in my home office, some utensils in the kitchen, and that's it.

It's been a few years since I moved here, but I've never felt the need to make it a home.

Which is another reason why I don't invite people over.

This is where I get to be alone with myself. Where I can drop whatever mask I wore for the day and just exist.

It's my haven that I don't want anyone else in.

But I invited someone over.

Naomi.

I stare back at the text I sent her a few days ago. She read it, but she sent no reply to either deny it or confirm.

When I made that offer in my office, I didn't expect her to take it. She wouldn't actually do whatever I want just so I'll stay away from her husband.

Because if she did, that would be no different than agreeing to an affair.

However, she must realize that I won't let it go with merely groping and licking her. Even after all this time, she has to know that putting my hand around her throat wasn't enough.

The mere recollection of that day still gets me fucking hard.

Naomi must've seen the sadism and need for more in my eyes, which is why she bolted out while she was still able to.

She might not have told me her number, but she left it with Nate when she gave him her card.

Last night was the date I specified in the text.

She didn't show up.

I don't know why that made me fucking livid and drove me to googling her name.

Could be because if she did show up, I would get her, but she's only doing it to keep her husband clueless about us.

Or maybe because her no-show means that she loves her husband enough not to cheat on him.

Fuck.

I'm backpedaling into the bitter asshole I was right after she left, and that jerk and I don't get along. At all.

After I place my briefcase in my office, I get undressed and step in the shower.

I tip my head back, letting the scorching hot water cascade over me.

My mind is buzzing with strategies for Akira. I need to get close to him, which would force Naomi back into my vicinity.

She refused to come? Fine. I'll make the choice for her. Or, more like, take it away so she realizes she should've never fucked with my newfound life.

Yes, it wasn't perfect. Yes, it was all jaded and sometimes forced, but it was all mine. It was what I built for myself to escape her fucking ghost.

The doorbell rings and I roll my eyes. It must be Nate. Not only did he put Aspen on my case, but he keeps bugging me as well.

Stepping out of the shower, I wrap a towel around my waist and head to the door.

I look through the peephole to make sure it's not the talkative old lady from next door. While she's friendly and gives me homemade food sometimes, she can chat for hours on end.

It's not Nate or even the talkative lady.

It's…her.

The fucking nightmare.

The twisted dream.

Naomi.

She's wearing an elegant dark blue dress, her hair is styled, and her lips are painted the color of blood.

Her gaze shifts to the side and she gulps, which means she's nervous and out of her depth.

Naomi is here. Even if it's a day late.

Seeing her in front of my door all pretty and done up awakens something inside me.

The beast that's been dormant since she left.

The beast that I thought would someday rip his way out of my chest.

That someday is today.

The longer I stand here not opening the door, the more she fidgets, watching her surroundings.

The new Naomi doesn't get anxious or show her vulnerabilities. She doesn't have her lips parted or allow her eyes to widen.

She's a blank, respectable slate—like her husband.

Not this Naomi.

This is different. She's different from the person at the charity event or even in my office.

That version was for the public, this one's for me.

And because she came to me on her own accord, there's no way in fuck I'm letting her slip between my fingers.

I don't open the door right away, though. She needs to have to wait like I did for seven years.

By the end of tonight, she'll remember why the fuck she's mine.

She's not Akira's or anyone else's.

She's fucking mine. Always has been and always will be.

TWENTY-FIVE

Naomi

THIS IS A TERRIBLE IDEA.

    The worst I've had in years.

    Or ever.

And yet, I can't make my feet cooperate and take me away from here.

I can't listen to the voice of reason ringing at the back of my head.

I steal a glance sideways to make sure no one is watching me. Sebastian's building is vast and sophisticated, but it's, thankfully, not full of people. So far, I've only seen a lovely old lady who was more than happy to let me in when the security outside asked who I was.

The thing is, I didn't plan to come over.

I had an all-nighter at the office yesterday, approving designs and plotting Chester Couture's next show.

In my mind, if I stayed busy, I'd forget all about where I really wanted to be.

I'd forget about the star quarterback from my past.

But I was only fooling myself.

All I could think about was him. Sebastian fucking Weaver.

I typed and retyped a dozen messages but deleted them and kept obsessing all night long. My brain couldn't stop for one second and the more time passed, the more questions filled it.

Was Sebastian mad that I stood him up? What if he goes to Akira?

That's what brought me to his doorstep today. Or, at least, that's what I tried to convince myself when I drove here.

I push the doorbell again, my finger trembling.

Am I too late? What if he *really* went to Akira? If it gets ugly— and it will—I have no clue how the hell I'm going to react.

My shifty gaze flits to my surroundings as the seconds tick by. They echo in my head like time bombs, increasing in volume the longer I stare at the closed door.

I reach into my clutch bag to retrieve my phone. I should've called him first. But I wasn't exactly thinking when I drove all the way here.

The door clicks open and I startle, my hand pausing halfway in my purse. I straighten, my spine jerking upright as I wait for Sebastian to appear in the doorway.

One second passes.

Ten...

Twenty...

He doesn't show up.

I push the door with a careful hand. "Sebastian?"

No answer.

Something malevolent pulls at the base of my stomach and my lips part as I slowly walk inside.

Is it even okay for me to go in when I wasn't invited?

As soon as I step a foot into the apartment, pitch darkness greets me. I can't even see my hands, let alone where I'm going.

My heartbeat thunders, rattling through my whole body as I take a tentative step and then stop. My toes curl in my high heels and my nails dig into the strap of my bag.

"Sebastian?" My voice is low, haunted.

I have no idea what this is, but it's obviously not going to end well for me. I wonder if I should turn around and leave, but then another more urgent thought hits me.

What if he's injured and needs help?

The door clicks shut behind me and I jump with a small yelp.

Shit.

I'm so hyperaware that I can hear the sound of my breathing and can feel the cold air licking at my skin.

It's been a long time since I've been in a state of sensory overload. It's like my own body is unable to contain me.

"Sebastian…" I try again, my voice so breathy, I barely recognize it.

A blur of movement comes from behind me, and when I quickly spin around, I stumble forward.

I don't have time to scream as a hand wraps around my throat and shoves me back so hard, I shriek.

The piercing sound slashes through the silent air like sharp knives. My back hits something solid with a loud thud that knocks the breath out of my lungs.

A foreign sense of energy shoots through me and I start to swing. It's a blind sense of survival that's fueled by primal necessity.

I kick at the solid wall of muscle, nails digging into big hands with a steel-like grip.

I scream, or I attempt to, considering his solid hold around my throat.

Hot, threatening breaths assault my ears. "Shut the fuck up, slut."

Sebastian.

I'd recognize that low baritone anywhere. I could handpick his beast from a thousand others, even if I were blind.

We come from the same darkness that no one else in the world belongs to.

And right now, we're in that phase again, shedding our façades and slipping back into our primal, animalistic selves.

My struggle slowly subsides, my nails no longer scratching him, even though I don't release his wrist. My body goes slack against what I assume is the wall.

In letting go of my blind fight, the outside world starts to filter back in. His bergamot and amber scent seeps inside my nostrils.

His harsh breaths match my hopeless, rugged ones as we stand there for a fraction of a second. We're two screwed-up souls who recognize each other in the darkness.

My eyes have somehow adjusted to my surroundings and I can just about make out his wide shoulders, his tapered waist, and the silhouette of his sharp-edged face. The hardness of it. The fucking depravity that I'd expect to see written all over it if his features were visible.

He's naked. At least from the waist up.

I don't know why I reach a hand for his face. Don't know why I want to touch him, feel him. Maybe it's to make sure this isn't another one of my cruel nightmares, or to confirm that he's indeed alive.

I've never had the chance to personally check before.

He pulls back before my skin meets his and I flinch, my hand falling limply to my side.

Right. We're in no position for me to touch him. Not after the ugly way everything ended.

His other hand pulls at the strap of my dress and I gasp at the sound of tearing cloth.

My instincts kick back in and a roar of energy pulses inside me. The decision to fight comes to me in a fraction of a second.

I kick, claw, and try to cause as much damage as possible.

The adrenaline makes me feel stronger, but no matter how invincible I think I am, I'm unable to move him, let alone peel him off me.

If anything, with each of my wiggles and kicks, he tears the dress further until it falls off me and pools around my feet. Cold air swallows me in a cocoon and forms goosebumps on my skin, but I don't stop.

I lift my leg to kick, but I stumble. Sebastian tightens his hold on my throat, slamming me against the wall again.

"Ahhh!" I cry out in pain.

He uses the chance to rip at the straps holding my bra together and yanks it down my flailing arms.

I arch off the wall, but he grabs one breast in a harsh hand and pinches my aching nipple, then twists it in the opposite direction. My teeth sink into the cushion of my lower lip, but I'm unable to stifle a whimper.

His mouth finds the other nipple and he sucks, then bites until I'm crying out. My nerve endings swell, sending signals in all different directions.

He does it again, twisting and sucking, giving me a safe relief, then bites down harder than the first time. His pinching gets more violent and out of control until all the lines blur. Pain is too similar to pleasure. Wrong is too close to right.

"Ahhh…oh, God…"

"No one will save you, my slut. Not even him." The masculine edge of his voice veils sadism so deep, it shakes me to my core.

He bites down on the tight bud again and I swear he's going to draw blood.

"Jesus…" I whimper.

"He won't be doing any rescuing either." He releases a nipple and the sound his wet mouth creates makes my toes curl. "Praying is the last thing you should be doing, my slut. Go ahead and fight me like you want to."

I do.

Not only because he told me to, but because the harder I kick, the harsher he gets. The more I claw and squirm, the closer I am to him.

But both of us know I'll never be able to overpower him or

turn his strength against him. I have no doubt that he'd squash my rebellion in a second if he chose to, that he's only using the bare minimum of his strength to subdue me.

The thought of how easily he could overpower me shoots a myriad of twisted emotions through me.

"Fight more, kick me harder, claw deeper. The more you hit me, the rougher I'm going to take your cunt, my dirty little slut."

I give it my all, his words fueling me with an alien sense of energy. It's been so long since I felt the need to fight as if my life depended on it.

Sebastian pulls me from the wall by the throat and shoves me forward. I squeal as I land on solid ground with a thud.

I try to crawl away, but he grabs me by the ankle and drags me back. My aching nipples tighten as they rub against the floor. I dig my nails into what feels like wood, but I don't get away and only manage to break a few. No matter how much I fight, I'm no match for his savage strength.

It's different from before. He used to feel emotionally closer then, like he might stop any second. But now, he's a true monster with no Off button.

Except for maybe the safe word.

But that's not what's pulsing in my head with increasing speed. At the moment, all I want is him.

Just more of him.

Of this.

Of us.

Or what remained of us.

"Where do you think you're going?" He yanks down my panties, despite my flailing. Then his chest covers my slick back.

The hard ridges of his muscles are damp with sweat, too. We're both breathing harshly, my breaths more shattered than his.

I'm sprawled on the ground, completely naked, being crushed down by Sebastian's weight. I attempt to slip from underneath him, but he shoves my face into the wood with his merciless grip on the back of my neck. His weight eases off me and he slips a hand against my stomach, then pushes me up so that I'm on my shaky elbows, my cheek still pressed to the ground.

He's always handled me unapologetically and without second thoughts, never treated me like someone breakable and fragile.

He's treated me like a man taking from a woman, knowing full well she wants him to.

That hasn't changed, even after seven years. In fact, he's become even more unapologetic about his claiming. Circumstances be damned.

Something hard nudges against my ass and I pause, my heart hammering.

I never thought I'd ever feel his desire again.

To know that he wants me as desperately as I want him.

Even if he wants to punish me for it first.

Sebastian grabs a fistful of my hair and hauls me to my knees. I shriek when pain explodes at the roots along my skull.

His dark silhouette appears in front of me as he grips his hard cock with one hand and tightens his hold around my hair with the other.

My pupils must be dilating with how much my needy eyes try to take in as much of him as possible.

Sebastian slaps my mouth with his dick, ripping a strange strangled sound out of me.

"Open that fucking mouth."

My lips part and my tongue tentatively sticks out. He thrusts all the way in and uses his grip on my hair to forbid me from moving.

My gag reflex kicks in and I slap at his thighs, my broken nails digging in his thighs so he'd give me some air.

He doesn't.

Sebastian chokes me with his huge cock until my lungs burn and my eyes sting. A hollow sputtering sound tears from my throat and my spit douses his thickness and my chin.

"That's it, slut. Make my dick nice and wet so I will fuck your cunt so hard, you'll be dripping with my cum."

I whimper, but the sound is barely audible. He pulls out, then thrust back in, deeper, rougher. I gurgle on my own drool.

"Hmm. Hear that? That's the sound of you choking on my dick like the dirty slut you are."

Just when I think he'll suffocate me to death, he pulls back. I splutter, coughing and tasting the distinctive saltiness of his precum.

He only allows me a fraction of a second, or what feels like it, before he pounds in again, hitting the back of my throat.

Sebastian has my hair in a vice grip as he thrusts his hips with increasing force. There's no catching my breath—or air at all.

The maddening rhythm of in, out, deeper, rougher repeats over and over again in a twisted dance of dominance.

The small rush of oxygen after the lack of it leaves me light-headed and levitating. My core tingles and my heart aches and I have no idea if it's because of this situation or because I haven't had this for such a long time.

Sebastian pulls out of my mouth and wrenches my hair back at the same time. I cry out as I lose balance and fall backward, hitting the ground.

He's on me in no time, his hand parting my thighs and his thumb finding my clit, twisting and rubbing.

A muffled cry echoes in the air and I realize it's mine as the orgasm hits me.

I come in a few seconds. Just like that. He didn't even try hard and I'm already riding a wave I didn't think I'd experience again.

"Such a dirty slut." The lust and satisfaction in his voice is my aphrodisiac.

I keep coming and coming until I think I'll black out.

Until I'm existing someplace different from here.

Sebastian mounts me, his large body like a shadow over me as his hand loops around my neck.

Being in this position is like coming home.

Like finally finding that missing piece and sliding it back in place.

I've done everything to try to fill the gap inside me. I tried every trick under the sun and talked to more therapists than I can count. But none of them helped me alleviate the chronic emptiness.

None of them told me the only way to erase the hollowness is to recharge. To go back to him.

My beast.

My monster.

My twisted enigma.

He thrusts inside me so violently, I sob. Not because it hurts, though it does, or because he's huge, even though his cock feels like it's ruining something inside me, but because of all of this.

The fight.

The chase.

The fantasy.

It's the raw and primitive way he touches me. As if he never stopped touching me.

As if we've been beast and prey for as long as we've lived and we're just finally finding our way back to each other again.

Even if it's only for this moment.

I arch my back, taking more of him in. I'm not fighting anymore as my body recognizes his and we fall into a magical synergy.

Or maybe it's twisted.

"Fuck…such a good slut…" he groans as his thrusts turn deeper, longer. Rougher.

My slick back slides off the wood with each of his merciless pounds. Only his grip on my neck keeps me anchored in place as he takes and takes.

In return, he gives me the missing piece of my soul.

He gives me what I haven't had in a long time.

It builds with a fast, ruthless force that doesn't allow me to catch my breath. By the time it slams against me, I'm screaming, my hands reaching out for him.

I don't care which part I touch, as long as I touch him, as long as I make sure he's here.

He's alive.

My palms find the sweaty muscles of his chest and I dig my nails in as I tremble through my orgasm.

Sebastian lowers his head and sucks on the flesh of my collarbone, then bites down. Hot fiery pain explodes on my skin and detonates another orgasm in the wake of the first.

His movements turn out of control as he drives inside me with a violent type of carnal desire.

Then he stills on top of me before his cum warms my insides.

I pant, mewling in the after-effects of my orgasm. Sebastian's guttural inhales and exhales mix with mine as he continues biting on my collarbone, my breasts, my throat.

Everywhere.

A tear slides down my cheek, but it's different from how I sobbed and screamed through my orgasm.

This is my first tear of joy in seven years.

And it's all because of him. My heartbreakingly beautiful monster.

My beast has made me feel wanted.

Important.

Alive.

TWENTY-SIX

Naomi

I don't know how long I lie there sprawled out on the ground.

But it's long enough that the sweat has started to get cold and goosebumps erupt on my skin.

Sebastian disappeared from on top of me soon after he was done, but I haven't heard his footsteps around me.

For some reason, it feels as if he's watching me from the darkness, biding his time before he jumps me again.

Or maybe he's giving me an opening so I can get the hell up and leave his apartment.

The reality of what's happened hits me hard and fast and I jerk up into a sitting position. A slight ache erupts between my legs and I wince as I lean on my palm to catch my breath.

I can't stay here.

When Sebastian said he'd tell me what he wanted in exchange for staying away from Akira, I knew it would be something sexual.

But I never thought we'd pick up right where we left off as if nothing had happened. I never thought the mere touch of his skin on mine would set my world ablaze. It's even more intense than when we were college kids.

His touch has become more firm and unapologetic.

Control oozes from each of his movements, turning me into a bundle of shriveling nerves.

The thought of him doing that to anyone else boils acid in my stomach. It brings out the angsty, stabby part of me I thought I left in Blackwood.

Not that I have the right to be jealous.

Anyway, I need to get out of here so I can pull myself—or what remains of myself—together.

I attempt to stand when Sebastian's heavy footsteps echo around me. I still, holding my rugged breaths in. It's so hard to breathe with him around and I find myself counting each inhale and exhale.

Blinding white light bathes the room. I was so used to the darkness that the brightness assaults my sticky lids.

My eyes slowly widen when I make out Sebastian. I knew he was naked earlier, but feeling it and seeing it are entirely different.

He's leaning against the wall, crossing his developed arms over his chest and crossing his legs at his ankles. The two tattooed lines are the only break in his perfect abs and they look so aesthetically pleasing.

Despite quitting football, he hasn't lost much weight. He's now muscular in a lean type of way that fits the man he grew up into.

I try not to ogle his cock, but it's impossible, considering the way I can still feel its impact inside me.

It's long and thick, even when half-erect, and I can't help the shiver that goes through me when I think about the pleasure and pain that part of his anatomy can bring me.

Sebastian's light eyes fixate on me, staring at my body the same way I'm observing his.

That's when I realize I'm sitting naked on the floor. I scramble for my dress. Or what's left of it. The scraps of material barely hide my nakedness, despite my attempts to fold into myself.

"It's nothing I haven't seen before," he says ever so casually, his voice regaining that cold edge he's been using ever since we reconnected.

My chest squeezes, but I ignore it, holding a piece of my dress against it. "I did my part. Now, you have to do yours."

"And what might that be?"

"You said you'd stay away from Akira if I showed up at the address you sent."

"I said I'd think about it. Besides, the date we agreed upon was yesterday, not today."

"What are you saying?"

"Exactly what you're thinking." A cruel smirk paints his lips. "It was all for nothing."

I jerk up, letting the ruined dress fall to the ground as I walk over to him. "You can't do that!"

"Just did."

"Sebastian, don't test me or I swear..."

"What? What will you do, Naomi?" His eyes heat as he dips them to my bruised nipples. "It's not wise to threaten me when your tits are tempting me with something entirely different."

My libido awakens again at his attention. I've been starved for so long and now that I've had a taste of what I truly craved, my body is unable to abide by my frustration.

But I hold on to my barely existent cool. "Why are you so insistent on working with Akira?"

"Because you don't want me to."

"You can hate me as much as you want, but don't destroy yourself in the process."

He pauses, his mystical gaze sliding back to me. "I can't destroy what's already been destroyed."

A lump lodges in my throat and I can't get rid of it, no matter how much I swallow. "Sebastian..."

"Why did you come here?"

"Because you asked me to."

"You could've not shown up like yesterday, but you chose otherwise. Why?"

"You said you wouldn't work with—"

"Don't say his fucking name in my presence again and don't use him as an excuse, because you and I know you're not here because of that."

My shoulders hunch and a strange cold sensation settles at the bottom of my stomach. "If you already figured it out, why are you asking?"

"I want to hear you say it. I want to hear you admit that you're a slut who'd rather be fucked against the ground by me instead of your husband."

"Don't call me that outside of whatever fucked-up shit that just happened." I raise my chin. "It was just sex. People have it all the time."

His jaw tightens and a haze of darkness falls on his features. "Do you make fucking people outside of marriage a habit?"

"I don't see why that concerns you."

"I just fucked you without a condom. Who knows what type of shit you just gave me."

"It should be the other way around."

He says nothing, his expression easing a little, but he continues to openly stare at my nakedness.

I step backward and gather my scattered underwear, which is also ruined.

That's when I notice that his living room is empty. As in, there's no furniture whatsoever.

From what I know, he didn't recently move here, so why is it so…vacant?

"Can you lend me some clothes?"

"Why?"

I spin around, showing him my ripped underwear and tip my chin at the dress. "It's the least you can do after you ruined my clothes."

"Say please."

"I'm not going to beg for clothes."

"Then you can stay naked."

I purse my lips, staring him down. "You're such a dick."

"Calling me names will diminish your chances, not strengthen them, Tsundere."

I jolt, swallowing thickly at the sound of that nickname coming out of his mouth. Black butterflies take flight in my stomach and it takes everything in me not to grin like an idiot.

"Do you make a sport out of being an asshole or is it just your personality?" I pretend I'm not affected, even though I'm internally flying.

"A little bit of both."

"Just give me some clothes so we can get out of each other's hair."

"I don't hear a please in there, do you?"

I grit my teeth. "Please."

"I didn't hear that."

"Please!"

"Much better." He pushes off the wall and heads into a room.

I fidget, observing his apartment and wondering why it's cold and impersonal. Almost like there isn't a person living here.

A few moments later, Sebastian returns with sweatpants and a hoodie that will definitely swallow my petite frame.

Our hands brush when he gives them to me. Instead of backing away, he remains there, unmoving.

I clear my throat. "Can I use your bathroom to wash up?"

"No."

"No?"

He grabs my wrist and I yelp when he pulls me forward and whispers in my ear, "You'll go back to your husband with my cum dried in your cunt and between your legs so he knows you were fucked like he'll never be able to fuck you."

TWENTY-SEVEN

Sebastian

"**F**ocus."

Aspen's no-nonsense tone drags me back to the present.

We're representing the firm at a charity event being thrown by my grandparents in their mansion.

Nate is a no-show, and unlike other events where he comes late, he'll probably pull a dick move and skip this one. Grandma will clutch her pearls and Grandpa will make a hundred excuses as to why his 'hotshot' son hates him.

Of course, no one knows all the strings they pulled to try to stop him from starting Weaver & Shaw. To this day, they still have hopes that my uncle and I will carry on the family legacy and go into politics.

But while Nate avoids Mr. and Mrs. Weaver, Aspen and I think differently. Since they're using my and Nate's success as a chance to brag anyway, we should milk them for our own sake, regardless of our personal relationship.

Just earlier, my grandparents made a show of introducing me

to their friends and other party members, but they'd curse me if we were all alone.

Not that I care.

I'm only showing my face here so Aspen can get what she wants—connections—and I can get what I want—judge files. If it were up to me, I'd be chasing my little prey.

My Naomi.

What happened last night wasn't supposed to go down like that. I did plan to claim her and take all she had to offer. When I saw her standing in front of my apartment, my mind whirled with a thousand scenarios and all of them included fucking her until she couldn't move.

But I didn't count on her reaction.

I didn't think she'd be so into it, that it'd touch something inside me.

No idea what that something is, but it was there with every moan from her throat, every wrestle, and every claw. Even with the way she tried to touch me.

She wanted to fucking touch me.

That's what triggered it all for me. The moment she reached out a hand for me, I wanted to slam her against the wall and ask her why the fuck she thought she had the right to touch me.

I needed to punish her for making me want her, but I ended up losing myself in her.

My beast found the perfect prey in her and there was no stopping or holding back.

There was no logic.

There was only me and her. As if no time had passed since the last time I touched her.

As if I'd just been inside her yesterday.

But that's the thing. Time *has* passed and that can't simply be written the fuck off.

I can't pick up the pieces when she never gave them back.

In the beginning, I thought I'd feel triumph at making her a cheater and ruining her picturesque fucking marriage. I thought the mere act of destroying a part of her carefully built life would make me feel victorious.

It didn't.

Or maybe it did for a while, until she changed clothes and went back to her husband.

The fact that he could've fucked her after I did, that he tasted her lips and pounded into her cunt like I did has been blackening my vision all day.

I contemplated going to Akira and painting her as a cheater. I wanted to see the look on his stoic face when he realized the wife he had on his arm and whispered things to while she laughed had my dick inside her.

The only thing that stopped me is the unpredictability Akira Mori is known for.

From what Knox and Daniel told me, he has secret webs to criminal organizations, namely the Yakuza, and he doesn't hesitate to chop off the heads of whoever opposes him.

Coupling that with how Naomi wants me to stay away from him, I'm sure he's no normal businessman.

He doesn't scare me, but the fact that he could hurt Naomi does.

Fuck.

That's why I didn't barge in front of him and yank Naomi to my side.

I shouldn't care whether she's safe or not after what she did to me, but fuck, I do.

In a twisted, fucked-up way, I want to be the only one who hurts her. Not that fucker Akira or anyone else.

And for that, I need another way to make her pay other than involving him.

Aspen digs her nails into my arm and paints a bright smile on her face as she leans in to whisper in hissed words, "Did you leave your brains somewhere today?"

Probably on the wood floor of my apartment.

"Relax." I whisk two glasses of champagne from the tray of a passing waiter and give her one. "If we pretend we're having fun on our own, the others will flock to us."

She flips her fiery hair over her bare shoulder, showcasing her golden dress. "Let me guess. Nate taught you that?"

"Nope. The senator himself did." I lift my glass in Grandpa's direction and smile.

He's in the midst of his high-profile friends and has no choice but to lift his glass back and give me his political bullshit smile.

"There." I focus back on Aspen. "That will give us the attention you're here for. You don't have to try so hard at these types of events, Aspen. It's not the courthouse."

"Yeah, sure thing, rich boy."

"Watch and learn."

Sure enough, some of Grandpa's associates start toward us. I plaster on a smile and pull her hand in mine. "It's showtime. Give it your all."

"You, too." She jabs me.

"I don't need to. I'm the senator's grandson."

She laughs as a few businessmen join us. We put on our show, talking about nonsensical things that only serve to help us play the social game.

Being the Weaver's good grandson isn't exactly what I'd rather be doing, but it's better than being lost in my own mind loop.

Aspen gives the performance of the century, laughing and flirting, even when she's grabbing my arm.

"Why do you do that?" I ask when we leave the group of people we were with. "We both know you're not interested in relationships."

She fixes my already impeccable collar, running her red-painted nails down the lapel of my jacket. "Maybe I'm interested in baiting. Men covet what's not theirs, call it a primitive type of characteristic. Seeing me on your arm is a sure way to pique their interest."

I pause at her words.

Is that what this is all about with Naomi? The fact that she belongs to someone else?

"How would they differentiate between genuine interest and a need to conquer?"

"Simple. They can't. At least not until it's over."

"The flirting or the fucking?"

"Neither. They wouldn't know it's genuine interest until whatever I have with you is over. They'll most likely lose interest if they find out I'm single and theirs for the taking. That's why I always come to these things escorted."

"So I'm your victim of the night?"

"You could say that." She tips her head in the opposite direction. "Isn't that Asher?"

I smile when my eyes meet my childhood friend. He's in a sharp suit like mine, but his body has become way leaner than mine, probably because he quit football three years before me.

"Well, if it isn't Carson & Carson." I approach him with Aspen in tow and he smiles as we greet each other in a bro hug.

I move in to kiss his wife, Reina, on the cheek, but he pushes me back with a calm yet firm hand on my chest.

"Back off if you don't want a brawl tonight," he whispers so only I can hear.

I laugh. "I see some things never change."

"And never will." He gives me a warning stare as he pulls Reina to his side by an arm around her waist.

"You're lucky Owen isn't here. He'd be demanding things from Rei." I waggle my brows.

"Not if he wants to keep his football career, he wouldn't." Asher draws circles on Reina's side with his finger.

She rolls her eyes. "You're over the top, Ash."

"But you already knew that, prom queen." He kisses her forehead.

"Do I need to go?" I taunt. "Get you a key to a room, maybe?"

Asher gives me his signature blank look while Reina laughs. Then her smile turns mechanical when she directs it at Aspen.

I can tell she's measuring her up and probably weighing her in that critical way she used to be famous for in the past. "And... you are?"

"Aspen Le Blanc." She offers her hand. "Senior partner at Weaver & Shaw."

Reina seems impressed, but her lips twist as she struggles to keep up her façade. "Aren't you too young to be a partner?"

"So is Sebastian, but because of his gender, no one asks him that."

"I didn't mean it that way." Reina sighs. "I'm just...surprised is all."

"Don't be. We're unicorns, but we exist." Aspen smiles at Asher. "Isn't that right, Mr. Carson?"

Asher makes an absentminded sound, but doesn't confirm or deny.

"I'll be right back," Aspen leans in to whisper, then kisses my cheek. "I'll go steal their clients. Stall for me or I'll be naughty when I come back."

Great. Now she's taking what Reina said as a serious offense. And since she noticed Reina was bothered by our closeness, she's taking advantage of it.

"Who the hell is she?" Reina hisses as soon as Aspen disappears.

"I should be asking you why the fuck you were out to insult her."

While Reina and I aren't that close, we have Asher in common, and that makes us see each other more than either of us prefer.

"She seems annoying."

"You don't even know her, Reina."

"He's right." Asher strokes her arm. "You were aggressive to a woman you just met."

"Unnecessarily so," I shoot back.

"She had a reason," Asher tells me without breaking eye contact with his wife. "Didn't you, prom queen?"

Only he would be patient enough to read behind her apparent bitchiness and actually discern why she's acting the way she is.

Reina sighs. "She annoys me because she seems to have eyes for you, and I don't like seeing you with anyone but Naomi."

My jaw clenches. "But it's okay to see Naomi fucking married?"

"I didn't know that until she came back, and only through her photos in social columns. We don't exactly keep in touch, except for a random text she sent from a number I couldn't reach afterward."

I narrow my eyes. "She sent you a text?"

"It was about two years ago. I think she was drunk. She said she didn't think she'd miss her bitchy captain and then she begged me not to tell you because you guys are complicated."

I should feel something other than bitter rage, but that's the only emotion crowding in my veins and ripping into my bones.

Reina softens her tone. "And to answer your question, yes, it feels weird to see her with anyone else, too. I know it's irrational, but I can't digest the idea of you two being with different people."

Asher strokes her hand as if in approval. Ever since they got back together, he always makes sure he's touching her in some way. "That's your opinion, but it's not theirs, prom queen."

"I know that. But I can't help it."

Fuck this.

Just when I'm attempting to get my mind off her, she comes back in uninvited.

Reina's eyes widen as she stares behind me. I think Aspen has returned, but Reina's lips move in a barely audible murmur, "Naomi."

My body bursts back to life and it takes everything in me not to turn around and face her.

I don't have to, though.

Naomi comes into view on the arm of her fucking husband and they appear to be headed our way. Her silver and black dress molds against her slim curves and hugs her perky breasts. A small amount of cleavage is visible, but there's no trace of the hickeys I left the last time I saw her.

I made sure they were all over her tits so she must've used something to conceal them.

Naomi smiles at Reina and Asher, but subtly ignores me when she addresses them, "Hey, you two. It's been a long time."

"That's an understatement!" Reina pulls her in for a hug, and that breaks Akira's hold on her arm. Temporarily.

He greets Asher in his seemingly welcoming but actually stoic nature, then focuses on me. His dark eyes gleam as a slight smirk tips his lips. "We meet again, Weaver."

"Seems Brooklyn is a lot smaller than one would think."

"Indeed." His smirk deepens. "Maybe even tiny for some people."

"Could be."

Once Naomi straightens, he pulls her back to his side and a red mist covers my eyes. The need to break his fucking arm pulses through me.

It's even worse than my violent tendencies. I learned to control those, but now I'm on the verge of reaching out and poking his fucking eyes out.

"My Naomi didn't tell me you were the senator's grandson. That's impressive."

My Naomi.

Again.

The fire flaming inside me turns hotter and brighter. I take a deep breath to maintain my façade and stop my lips from snarling.

"He's the senator, not me," I say in a calm voice I don't recognize. "Naomi and I weren't that close, so she doesn't know everything about me."

Her eyes meet mine for the first time since she joined our circle. It's brief and barely noticeable, but it's enough to spill her deepest, darkest secrets.

The ones she's probably been hiding since she left my apartment last night.

Lust.

Pure, raw lust.

Even when she's on her husband's arm, her fuck-me eyes are directed toward me, not him.

Her cry for the beast is only meant for me, not Akira or any other fucking man.

Only me.

She breaks eye contact, focusing on Reina instead. But it's useless. Her cheeks have already turned a deep shade of pink and her throat bobs with a thick swallow.

Naomi just gave me a signal for more.

Not that I needed it.

Because sooner or later, she'll pay for what she's done.

I don't give a fuck if she's married or not.

That doesn't change the fact that she's fucking mine.

TWENTY-EIGHT

Naomi

CAN THE EARTH OPEN UP AND SWALLOW ME?

Better yet, can it spit me out in a parallel reality where I don't have to let my brain shackle my heart and soul?

Because at this rate, I'm heading to the point of no return.

My hand feels as cold as Kyoto's freezing winter as it snuggles in Akira's arm.

I want to pull away, to run, hide.

Run and hide and be chased.

But my brain keeps me planted in place with a makeshift smile taking over my lips.

I try to focus on the small talk Akira is making with Asher or on how Reina is asking me all sorts of questions, but it's impossible.

My attention flits back to Sebastian every time. To the way his mesmerizing eyes have turned glacial cold while the sharp edges of his handsome face have hardened. To how his jacket hugs his wide shoulders and narrow waist. To how a strand of his hair has fallen on his forehead or how a shadow falls over his cheekbones.

I can't stop looking at him.

Or observing him.

He awakened something inside me when he wrestled me and fucked me against the wood floor of his living room.

A beast that recognizes his prey.

A hungry being who simply can't get enough.

I spent a sleepless night tossing and turning in bed, replaying every detail in my battered head and torturing my starved body.

What we did was wrong, forbidden, and absolutely deviant on so many levels.

And yet, I've been aching for more.

And yet, it's all I've been able to think about.

Because that's the thing about forbidden fruit. One taste isn't enough. The desire keeps mounting and climbing, reaching heights that would only lead to demise once thrown off of it.

Maybe that's what I'm actually supposed to do.

Fall.

Dark red manicured fingers slip around Sebastian's bicep like a snake.

My head snaps up to see a beautiful redhead with full lips, a long, elegant neck, and striking hazel eyes. She's wearing a strapless golden dress that hugs her tall, slim figure. A figure that's currently snuggled up to Sebastian's side with easy familiarity.

A dazzling smile appears on her mouth and it's only directed at him.

And then something happens.

He smiles back.

It's like a knife slices through my dying heart and protrudes from my back. I never thought I'd feel this way after that black day, but the scene in front of me proves otherwise.

Logically, I know I don't have the right to be like this. I don't have the right to feel wounded or hurt or cut fucking open, but the need to curl into a ball and cry hits me out of nowhere.

I never thought I'd come to Sebastian's house under these circumstances. Or the house he grew up in, anyway. Money shines in every corner of the Weaver mansion, hinting at its owners' sophisticated taste. But it's cold—impersonal, even.

His grandparents gave the same vibe when Akira and I talked to them earlier. No wonder Sebastian turned out the way he is. Maybe it runs in the family.

"I see the circle has grown without me," the redhead tells Sebastian, and even her voice is as elegant as she is. "Introduce me, Bastian."

I suck in a breath at the intimate name she calls him and it takes everything in me to appear unaffected.

If the earth ever planned to suck me into a hole, this is the time to do so.

"Aspen," he says in his cold, unaffected tone. "This is Naomi and Akira."

My husband shakes her hand, then I do, too, contemplating if I could break it if I squeeze hard enough. I swiftly let go of her and the murderous thought. Or try to, anyway.

The chatter continues despite the simmering tension. Or maybe I'm the only one who's about to flare up and burst into flames.

The more Aspen glues herself to Sebastian's side, the closer I get to the point of combustion. It doesn't help that Sebastian completely ignores my existence and only indulges her.

But what did I expect anyway? That he'd swoop me up in his arms while everyone is watching?

That would be a disaster.

But then again, that's what we've always been, he and I. A sweet, cruel disaster that's impossible to end, no matter how much we try.

It might have started with that bet, but it was going on way before that. I thought the distance would lessen it, would eventually erase it, but it merely made it hotter, stronger, and absolutely unstoppable.

At least for me.

Reina grabs me by the arm and smiles at everyone. "Would you excuse us? Girl talk."

She doesn't wait for anyone's reply as she basically drags me around the corner.

Her gaze flits to either side of us and once she makes sure there's no one around, she releases me and places a hand on her hip.

Our queen bee has aged like fine wine, becoming elegant and a productive member of Blackwood. I heard she's into social work and organizes countless charitable events.

Heard as in stalked her social media. What? I had to keep myself in the loop, even from Japan. I'm a professional stalker who never leaves any likes or comments and just observes from a distance.

The former cheer squad captain silently judges me while looking me up and down.

"What's wrong, Reina?"

"I should be the one asking you that. Are you going to let that senior partner redhead witch steal Sebastian?"

I swallow the bile that has been rising in my throat ever since the redhead witch, Aspen, put her hand on Sebastian's arm and he smiled at her.

"There's nothing to steal. I'm married."

"I can't believe that either."

"Want to see the certificate? How about footage of our holy matrimony?"

"Good to know you're still a cynical asshole when you're cornered, Naomi, and no, I don't need to see the certificate to know that you're not doing the right thing."

"Funny coming from you when you were out to destroy our relationship back in college."

"It was the exact opposite, idiot."

"What?"

"I remembered why I even came up with that bet. I would've told you before if you hadn't ghosted all of our asses."

I grimace but say nothing, waiting for her explanation.

"I might have been somewhat of a bitch—"

"*Somewhat?*" I cut her off.

"Okay, a major bitch. But I always had reasons behind every-thing I did. Remember when Lucy had a crush on Prescott? I found out he shared those feelings, so I encouraged him to go for it. But then I saw him kissing that freshman and decided to out him. Until he told me he was drunk and mistook the girl for Lucy, and that's why I let him have a go again."

"Are you gloating about playing matchmaker for Lucy and Prescott? You should include that in your speech for their tenth anniversary."

"Stop being a sarcastic prick and listen. The point of the story is that I always had a reason, even when it came to you and Sebastian."

"What type of reason?"

"You had a huge crush on him."

"I… How the hell did you know that?"

"Because I watched everything, including how you secretly stole peeks at him or how you only looked at him among the en-tire football team."

"And here I thought I was being discreet."

"You were, but I made it my mission to be aware of every-one in my orbit. Once I noticed your interest, all the stars started to align, so I focused on Sebastian. He was a harder nut to crack since he was social as hell and camouflaged his emotions better than anyone I knew, but I saw it once. You were sitting at the fountain, headphones on, listening to that god-awful loud music and hum-ming while sketching in your notepad. Sebastian was standing by a tree, watching you and smiling. He wasn't passing by. He wasn't preoccupied with something else. He stayed there on purpose for several minutes."

My lips part. I didn't know about that. He never mentioned it, even when we talked during those black days in the cell.

"That's why I came up with the bet. And I don't care what you think because it was one of the best things I did."

"It doesn't matter anymore," I murmur.

"Of course it does! You were both the best versions of yourselves together. Sebastian was more relaxed while you were happy and laughed more than ever. Now, you're both just tragic."

Tragic.

That might be the best word to describe us.

But tragic is better than lethal.

Reina steps closer, her eyes drooping at the side like a mother who's worried about her child. "Are you happy, Naomi? Because Sebastian isn't."

"How…do you know that?"

"Unlike you, I've been here all this time and I've seen him slowly turn into a cold, aloof person whose sole purpose is to destroy others in court. He doesn't celebrate his wins either, just picks up another case and moves along like some sort of machine."

My eyes burn and I widen them to keep from letting the tears loose. Is it supposed to hurt this much, even though it's the most logical thing to do?

Is it supposed to feel as if my heart is being ripped out of my chest?

"Happiness is subjective, Reina. For me, that word means something entirely different than being with Sebastian."

"Is it worth being torn apart for? Because I've been there and it's the worst feeling I've ever had to go through. Asher and I were parallel lines, unable to collide for so long that I thought we would never be together."

"Parallel lines are safe."

"Parallel lines are torture."

"I can handle it."

"You're so different, Naomi."

"I know."

"I don't mean that as a compliment. I miss the Naomi who expressed everything on her mind without caring what others said about her. I wish you'd find her in you someday. I wish she'd claw her way out."

"I'll let you know how that works out." I smile, then it instantly disappears when I make out a very familiar face crossing the distance from the entrance.

Ren.

What the hell is he doing here? I know he's been working with Akira a lot lately, but my husband said he wouldn't be accompanying us tonight.

I made sure of it once I realized we'd be attending an event held by Sebastian's grandparents.

"I'll talk to you later, Reina…" I make some sort of an unintelligible excuse as I hasten my steps in Ren's direction.

He shouldn't be here. Not where Sebastian can see him. If he hears his voice, he'll recognize him from those days we spent in the cell.

And then Ren might be tempted to tell my father his spin on what he sees tonight, and my father can't be involved again.

My steps are long, despite my trembling legs. I'm not fast and it takes everything in me not to break into a jog and draw attention to myself.

Ren will go straight to Akira, who's standing with Sebastian. He'll recognize him and then he'll probably start being his usual mocking self. Whether he speaks in English or in Japanese, Sebastian will recognize him, too, and he might start a scene…

A hand grabs my arm and I squeal as I'm dragged into a room. One strong palm wraps around my throat, the other over my mouth.

"Not a fucking word."

TWENTY-NINE

Sebastian

MY KNEE PARTS NAOMI'S THIGHS AND MY CHEST FLATTENS her back as I shove her against the wall.

We're both breathing heavily; I'm not sure if the sound of harsh intakes of breath are hers or mine, or if the rise of my chest matches the fall of her back.

I breathe in the sweet scent of her lily and peaches perfume and the smell of her fear.

Fuck, how I love her fear. It's different from anyone else's. Hers is tangible and completely unique. Probably because it's mixed with a secret type of excitement.

Naomi doesn't fight me.

Her front slackens against the wall, even as she inhales and exhales in an uncontrollable rhythm.

For a moment, we remain like that, breathing in the thick air in silence. We're in Grandmother's tea party room, where she invites other influential wives and spends afternoons milking information out of them.

It's dark, though, so the only thing visible is the curve of

Naomi's throat and the soft line of her chin as she rests her cheek against the wall.

But I don't need to see her to feel her. Just like in the fucking cell, her warm body beneath mine is enough to cement her presence to my damn soul.

I release her mouth but wrap my fingers around her jaw, digging my nails into the softness of her flesh and feeling her pulse against my skin.

"Sebastian…" she breathes out in what resembles relief.

The sound sends a straight zap to my dick, and it strains against my pants and her ass cheeks. No matter how much I hate her, no matter how much I plan to destroy her, I can't stop wanting to fuck her.

Ruin her.

Own her.

In that goddamn order.

"Were you expecting your husband, my slut?"

"No, I just…"

"You just walked into my grandparents' house on his arm to fucking jab me?"

"I didn't want to come here."

"But you did. Surely you're well aware of the consequences," I speak harshly against the shell of her ear and she shudders, her breath catching.

I love the fucking sounds she makes when I rattle her to her bones.

When I'm the only thing she can think about.

I grab her tit and pinch the hard nipple through the material and she jolts on a broken gasp and a strangled moan.

"No…" she whispers. "Don't…Sebastian…"

"Don't what?"

"Don't…"

"Don't touch you? Fuck you? Don't make you come so hard

your tool of a husband will hear you scream my name? Because you'll scream, Naomi. *Loud.*"

"No…" The word is choked, almost inaudible.

I pinch, then twist her nipple with the same violence that's been bubbling in my veins since she walked into my grandparents' house.

Or maybe since she came back after being invisible for years.

"No…Sebastian…no…"

"You know how much that word turns me the fuck on, Naomi. Is that why you're saying it after giving me fuck-me eyes all evening?"

"I…didn't."

"Yes, you did, my slut. You were watching me while being on your husband's arm, probably fantasizing about how I'll tear through that tight cunt of yours and fuck it right. Should I take you on the floor like a dirty whore? Or maybe I'll do it outside against one of the trees and give everyone a show. Your fucking husband included."

A low whimper rips from her and I have no clue if it's because of my words or the relentless way I keep torturing her nipples.

I don't care either way.

Because I'm close to losing my fucking mind right now.

Turning into my beast might be the best option, but I'm lingering in that phase between the pathetic human and the unfeeling monster.

I bite down on the shell of her ear, causing her to cry out.

The sound douses me with the need for more.

More violence.

More carnal desire.

More of her taste.

The taste I haven't been able to forget, despite trying to. The taste that's become my aphrodisiac and my fucking kryptonite.

I lick the lobe of her ear, then bite down again before I whisper, "I'll start by taking you against the wall."

Her body goes slack, like every time she's surprised or lost for words.

I release her nipple, keeping my powerful hold around her neck.

Then I shove her dress up to her waist and yank down her panties so that they're looped around her ankles.

Her yelp echoes in the air, mixing with the low chatter and the music playing outside.

I thrust two fingers into her tight cunt and grunt when her arousal immediately swallows them in. I add a third and pound the three of them inside her, slapping the heel of my palm against her swollen clit.

Naomi whimpers, her head jolting back and her body tightening further around mine.

"Stay still."

"That…hurts…" she moans.

"Don't tempt me into adding another one."

"It really hurts…God…it hurts…"

"It's supposed to."

"Sebastian…"

"Don't say my fucking name in that tone."

"Sebastian…please…"

"Please what? More?"

"Please…"

"You love it when it hurts, don't you, my dirty little slut?"

She purses her lips even as her arousal echoes in the air with each of my savage thrusts.

Her tiny body shakes with the impact and her moans turn throatier and deeper. Whether they're in pleasure or in pain, I have no clue.

"Say it, Naomi. Say you love it when it hurts."

"No…"

I pull out of her in one go, ripping a noisy protest from her lips. She doesn't move even after I fully release her, remaining in position, her legs slightly parted, her lips open.

It takes me a moment I don't have to unbuckle my belt, unzip my pants, and free my engorged dick.

A drop of precum slides down my hand as I push her into the wall and slap her thighs apart.

She cries out but opens them the farthest possible with her panties looped around her ankles.

I slide my dick against her sensitive folds, grunting when her juices coat me, pulling me in and inviting me to go all the way inside.

"Say you love it when I hurt you, Naomi. Say you love the sting of pain and the twisted monstrosity of it all."

"Oh, God..."

"Those aren't the words I asked for. Try again."

She rolls her hips as I slide the crown to her opening. It's swallowing me in so I'll fuck it and Naomi until neither of us can move.

And as much as my dick wants to, I deny it and myself the pleasure.

This might be about sex, but it's also about proving a point to her.

And myself.

So I slide out and rub my dick against her folds instead. "Feel that, my slut? That's your greedy cunt luring me in to tear through it and fuck it all night long."

"Sebastian..." The sound of my name is caught between frustration and a plea.

"Say the words, Naomi, or I'll leave you unsatisfied and aching."

"Please..."

"I didn't ask you to beg."

"Please...please..."

"Stop begging me and admit it, Naomi. Admit that you love the pain."

"I do."

"I didn't hear that. Speak louder."

"I do." She sobs. "I love the pain. I love when you lash it out of me and make me breathless with your intensity, so please...please... Sebastian. Don't torture me anymore."

"Maybe I'm in the mood to. Maybe I plan to keep you on the

edge all night long, then leave you a wanton mess, unable to get off. You'll finger your tight pussy to the memory of me all night long, but you won't get the satisfaction your body needs."

"No…please."

I slide my dick through her inviting folds, down to her opening, and then up to her clit. But I don't give her enough friction to get off, and although it's faltering with how much I want to own her all night long, I hold on to my control.

But the need to torment her pulses through me in waves. I want to keep her hanging onto the idea of me, of us, even if it means I'll be torturing myself, too.

"Maybe I'm in the mood to never give you my dick again."

Up.

Down.

Up.

Down.

"Maybe I'll make you beg for it, then deny you the pleasure."

Up.

Down.

Rub.

"Maybe I'll use your mouth, then toss you aside because you mean fucking nothing."

She sobs, a low, raw sound that pierces through my chest, and for some reason, it doesn't feel like it's due to the lack of sexual satisfaction.

"Sebastian…please stop…"

"Stop what?"

"Stop this madness…please."

"That word doesn't stop me and you know it."

I wait for her to use the word that actually does stop me, but she doesn't.

Not even when her sniffles and sobs fill the air. Not even when she's flat out shaking.

This time, when her cunt swallows me, I thrust all the way in.

Naomi's startled gasp mixes with my deep grunt as I power into her tight heat. I tell myself that I'll savor it this time, that I'll take it slow and moderate. But the moment her cunt strangles me, I lose every last shred of my control.

The fact that I thought I would hold on to it feels cartoonish now—laughable, even.

I drive into her with a force that rattles us both. But she takes it all, her pulse quickening and her body quivering around mine.

"Fuck. Look at how your wet cunt is strangling my dick, you dirty little slut. Do you soak your husband's dick, too? Does he fuck you rough like you want or do you finger yourself afterward to get off?"

"Don't…bring him up…"

"Why? Hit a nerve?"

She doesn't say anything, but the image I've built in my own head magnifies and I take her savagely.

I release her neck and bunch her hair around my fist, then yank her head back so that her face is a breath away from mine. "Tell me."

She shakes her head, eyes shining with tears in the darkness.

I dart my tongue out and lick their saltiness. But that's not all I taste. There's also her perversion, her arousal, and her surrender.

I've always loved her pleasure fucking tears. It's like she can't contain everything that's going on inside her and has to purge it out somehow.

Her lips part and the harder I thrust, the deeper I dig my fingers into her hips, the more broken her moans become.

I keep going on and on, needing to engrave this moment where we're one into my memory.

Her body unravels around me like it was always meant to. I can tell she's close to her orgasm with the way her hips roll back and how she bucks against me, soaking in the roughness of my movements.

"Say it, Naomi," I growl against her ear. "Does he satisfy you?"

"No," she croaks as she clenches around me.

It's a single word.

One hushed word.

And yet it erupts like a fucking volcano inside me. My muscles grow stiff and my balls tighten for the impact.

I come the hardest I have in a long time, shooting load after load of my cum inside her.

The orgasm goes on for so long that I think it won't end. The more Naomi tightens around me, the closer I am to starting the fucked-up symphony all over again.

My weight falls on her back as she sags against the wall. I don't release her, my hand still lost in her hair and my dick pulsing inside her.

Our harsh pants and the smell of sex fill the air. It's potent and familiar.

Just like when we used to remain in each other's embrace in the past.

But we're not in the past.

Gradually, the outside world filters back in. The music. The chatter.

Reality.

I slide out of her and take my time watching the line of my cum dripping down her inner thigh to her ankle. It's one of my favorite sights—a sign of my ownership over her body. That cum means she belongs to me and not anyone else.

My vision darkens. Even though I just finishing fucking the living daylights out of her, it's not enough to ward off the anger.

The rage.

The fucking reality.

I let her go and tuck myself in.

Naomi slowly turns around and pulls her underwear up. Even though I'm focused on buckling my belt, I can make out her hesitancy. I don't have to see it to feel it.

I'm that fucking attuned to this damn woman.

And I hate it.

I want to fucking punish her for it.

She reaches a hand for me, her palm cradling my cheek as she goes up on her toes and seals her lips to mine. They're soft and tentative yet full and damning.

Just like seven years ago.

Only, she's not the same Naomi from seven fucking years ago.

I grab her by a fistful of her hair and yank her back, causing her to cry out.

"Why the fuck do you think you have the right to kiss me?"

She trembles in my hold and I shove her away before I change my mind and devour her lips and then conquer her mouth.

Before I kidnap her the fuck out of here so we're no longer in this reality.

But even that won't drive away the rage.

Even that won't be enough.

A piercing sob echoes in the air, and just like that, Naomi slides to the ground, pulling her knees to her chest.

Her palms hide her face as she flat out starts bawling. There's no other word to describe how her raw cries fill the air.

I've never seen her break down like this, not even in that fucking cell.

My gut twists and a feeling I never wanted to have again rushes to the surface.

Concern.

The fucking need to hold and console her. To wipe away her tears and tell her it'll all be okay.

But that would be a fucking lie.

We're not okay.

And never will be.

Still, I can't force myself to move as her hollow, haunted sobs fill my ears. They're different from when she's orgasming or enjoying the lash of pain.

These are for another type of pain.

They're emotional.

I reach a hand out toward her head, wanting to touch her, wanting to just…be there for her.

But she's never been there for you.

I pull it back, jaw flexing. "Come to my apartment tomorrow."

Her sniffles pause as she looks up at me through teary eyes. "Why?"

"Because if you don't, I'll tell your husband about this."

Then I turn around and leave, her fresh cries following behind me.

I close the door and remain there, making sure no one else hears or sees her this way.

Broken.

Vulnerable.

Desperate.

I should feel triumph, but all that lurks in my bones is resounding fucking defeat.

THIRTY

Akira

Dear Yuki-Onna,

    You need to stop visiting me in my dreams. It used to be new and fun; now it's just annoying.

    And creepy.

    You keep touching me, giving me blowjobs, and taking my dick to the highest levels of heaven just to drop him back in hell.

    That's not cool. At all.

    It's just torturous at this point.

    You already dropped me out of your life, so how about you disappear, huh? Or, here's a better idea, you can come back, explain yourself, and then fuck off.

    Do I sound desperate? That's because I probably am.

    I don't like you molesting me in my sleep and making me wake up with a hard-on that I have to fuck the mattress to get rid of.

    I certainly dislike the way your fucking eyes look at me while you swallow my cum, as if you're inviting me to a different place that I can't find because you fucking disappeared.

    What I hate the most, however, is that I can't touch you. No matter how much I try to, you just vanish and haul me out of an uncomfortable sleep into an even worse reality.

Why show up when you never actually intended to stay?

Is this your invisible middle finger because you know I won't be able to flip it back?

In that case, fuck you very much, Naomi. And, no, I'm not bitter or enraged or fucking dramatic.

I just want to sleep at night without obsessing about how I will come down your throat when you visit at night or how I will attempt to stay in that fucking imaginary world.

I just want you to go.

So do us both a favor and leave me alone.

Or at least stay after you exorcise my soul through my fucking dick.

You'll never read this, but I'll still sign it with as little love as possible and with the right amount of hate,
Akira

THIRTY-ONE
Naomi

I NEVER THOUGHT THAT THE ONE THING ABLE TO LIFT ME up would be the same thing that could break me down.

I never stopped to consider that my own Achilles heel would enable me to touch heaven even while living through hell.

It's been a few weeks since the charity event at Senator Weaver's house.

A few weeks since I hit rock bottom, burned, and rose from the ashes.

I don't know why I broke down that night. Could be because of the physical torment or the psychological pain. Could be because Sebastian made me so happy, then rejected me so cruelly afterward.

Could be all of those combined.

I didn't even feel it when I fell to the floor and let the thing that festered inside me out in the open.

It was a moment of weakness, but I moved past it.

Or I pretended to, anyway.

My affair with Sebastian is a different story altogether.

Every other day, I've gone to his apartment, where he ambushes and fucks me. He comes up with different ways to catch me off guard and it never gets old. Not the waiting time or the thrill that comes with it. Not the adrenaline rush or the sinking into the unknown.

The moment he grabs me, I fight, I really do, but it's always useless. Not only because he overpowers me, but also because I love it when he does.

I love it when he pushes me down and uses me so thoroughly, as if he can't get enough of me. Or when he takes me roughly and unapologetically, whispering dirty words to me.

"You're such a filthy girl, aren't you, my slut?"

"Look how your greedy cunt wants more of my dick."

"Open your legs wider, let me see my pussy."

"No touching yourself or I'll come all over your face."

"Feel that? Feel how you stretch around me, inviting me in?"

"Does your husband smell me on you when he touches you? Does he see my dried cum between your legs and in your every pore? Does he notice the marks I leave on your tits and ass or do you hide them?"

It should turn me off, should give me the courage to finally say the safe word, but I don't.

I can't.

Because those words, no matter how wrong they are, turn me ablaze with a wildfire.

And Sebastian is the reason behind the flames. He's the damn volcano.

Every evening, I say this time will be the last. That I'll bid him farewell and voice that damn word.

Every night, I come prepared for the end and armed with the will that kept me going for seven years.

But every time he touches me, every time he calls my name and fucks me like he hates me yet still wants me, I forget all about it.

I tell myself that we're safe and no one will find out about us. Akira thinks I'm busy with the fashion house and Father couldn't care less as long as he has his deal with my husband.

Ren has been watching me close lately, but Akira keeps him busy, annoyed, and agitated, so he can't possibly be following me.

Besides, if that asshole had found out about me and Sebastian, he would've told my father and I would have already seen the consequences of my actions. Kai, however, is a mystery. I'm not naive to think he's in the dark about this entire situation since he's in the know about everything. However, he seems to be turning a blind eye. He didn't even ask me to stay away from Sebastian as he did when I first got back here.

So, for now, I choose to be in this temporary phase for as long as I can.

Even if I'm well aware that it won't last.

Even if I know it will hurt like a mother when it all ends.

Stopping in front of Sebastian's door, I remove my wedding band and slide it into my bag.

I've been doing it since we started our screwed-up relationship. Not that Sebastian commented on it. He's never once told me to leave Akira, even when he taunts me about him sexually.

But then again, we'd have to have actual conversations for that to happen. All we do is fuck, then I gather my clothes and leave without a word.

I stopped trying to seek affection from him after he brutally rejected me that night. Now, we're just two hollow souls using each other.

And despite the emptiness of it sometimes, it's still better than nothing.

I tap in his apartment's code. He gave it to me so he could ambush me upon my entrance. Some days, he waits until I'm a few steps inside before he takes me. Others, he drags me to the shower and fucks me under the stream of water.

My spine tingles with anticipation of what he'll do today.

He changes his methods often enough that I have no clue what he has in store for me. It's part of the thrill and the reason why no one could ever replace him.

Sebastian is the only one who knows my needs and can satisfy them without my having to voice them.

I come to a halt inside the door of the apartment when I notice the lights are on.

In all of the times I've been coming here, it's usually pitch-black, like in some horror movie.

His apartment is really empty. Aside from a TV, there's absolutely nothing.

A female voice comes from the direction of his bedroom and I freeze, an acid-like sensation rising to my throat.

Please don't tell me Aspen is here.

I've seen him with her at the countless social events Akira and I have been attending. She's often happily on Sebastian's arm, and even though I'm not sure whether they're in a relationship or not, I know there's something going on.

I've felt bad for the times that Sebastian has grabbed me and dragged me into a secluded place so he could fuck me. Sometimes, I feel like such a bitch for being the other woman.

But other times, when I recall that all of this is temporary, I just embrace that bitch and take what I need from him.

Just like he takes everything from me.

Finding Aspen in his apartment is a different story, though.

The wisest option would be to leave, but my legs subconsciously carry me in the direction of his bedroom.

Sebastian's voice filters through the hall, its baritone a direct stimulation to my ears. The fact that he could use it to talk dirty to someone else turns my blood green with envy.

I stop in the doorway of the bedroom, ready to spoil their fun and be an actual jerk.

But it's not Aspen I find perched on Sebastian's bed.

It's a familiar face I saw at Weaver & Shaw that day. His assistant.

She confiscates a bottle of whisky from Sebastian and forces him back to lie on the bed. He's dressed in a plain white T-shirt that hugs his chest muscles and gray sweatpants. His chaotic hair appears to be half-damp as it falls across his forehead.

He's pale, his lips dry and his face worn out. He wasn't that way two days ago.

"You need to rest," his assistant says in a reproachable tone.

Sebastian's gaze strays toward me as if he's known I was there all along. I swallow thickly, fighting the need to fidget. I'm twenty-eight, but I still feel like that starstruck teenager I was ten years ago when I first saw him.

Will this feeling ever go away?

His assistant, Candice, follows his field of vision and smiles. She flips her braided hair back. "You didn't tell me you'd be having someone take care of you."

"I don't," he croaks.

"Well, now you do." She places the bottle on the nightstand. "Take care of this big baby."

"Me?" I look to either side of me, making sure she's not actually talking to someone else.

"Who else is here, girl?" She grabs her purse and addresses Sebastian. "Don't even think about showing your sickly face at the office tomorrow."

"Don't go…" he whispers, and he sounds sick—feverish, even.

"Some of us have kids to take care of." She steps to me and whispers, "Don't let him drink when he's sick."

"What happened?" I ask in a low voice.

"He showed up to work like he's a survivor of the zombie apocalypse shows my youngest loves to watch. The doctor said he's come down with a nasty cold and that his temperature should be monitored. He doesn't get colds often, but when he does, they turn him into a corpse. His meds are on the nightstand and I'm 1 on his speed dial if you need anything. But please don't. I want some action with my man tonight and that won't be happening if my demanding boss calls."

I smile. "I'll make sure he doesn't."

"Thank you. I owe you one."

She leaves before I can ask her about food or what else I should be doing.

Sebastian is reaching for the bottle of whiskey, even though his arm seems to lack energy. I jog to it and grab it.

He groans, remaining in what looks like an uncomfortable leaning position. "Give it."

"Candice said no drinking when you're sick."

"Candice doesn't tell me what to do."

"Forget about Candice. You shouldn't be drinking when you're sick."

"Are you a fucking doctor?"

"One doesn't need to be a doctor to be logical."

"Thanks for your unnecessary opinion. Now give me that."

"No."

"The bottle, Naomi."

"I said no." I keep it behind me as he groans again, losing his balance and falling on his back.

Sebastian stares at me through thick lashes that shadow his light, enthralling eyes, but even those lack life today. "Since when are you the alcohol police?"

"Since you're sick."

"Why the fuck would you care?" He closes his eyes. "Leave…"

His lips twist and his chest rises and falls at an alarming pace. I wait a few seconds to make sure he's asleep before I touch his forehead. It's hot and slightly damp. He definitely has a fever.

I put the bottle of whisky away and place my bag on the foot of the bed. Then I go to the bathroom, wet a washrag, and return.

After putting it on his forehead, I pause. This brings back awful memories from when I struggled to keep him alive back in that damn cell. There were moments where I thought about what could've happened back then and all the wrong ways it could've ended.

My hand trembles as I slowly release him, not wanting to let the negativity slip back in. I read the directions on the medicine, which state it needs to be taken after eating.

Before I go to the kitchen to see what's there, I adjust the rag on his forehead.

A strong hand wraps around my wrist and hauls me back on the mattress. Jeez. Sebastian's strong for someone so sick. His thumb strokes the sensitive flesh of my wrist and I gulp as his eyes slowly open. They're clear, albeit dark. "Nao…"

My breath hitches at hearing my nickname from his lips. God. No one has called me that since Mom's death. Even Mio calls me big sister and Kai prefers *Ojou-sama* to my actual name.

"Yeah?" I try to control my breathing and fail.

"Why are you still here?" His voice is low, husky, and tired.

"Because you're sick."

"Why now? Why not seven years ago when I was shot and in the hospital?"

"Sebastian…"

"I need to know the reason. Tell me why I meant so little to you that you left me over the fucking phone."

"You're feverish, just rest." I try to pull my hand away, but he grips it hard and slams my palm against his chest.

His wild heartbeat makes my lips part. "Hear that? That's the sound of my fucking heart ever since you returned. Because no matter how much I tell the fucker you betrayed it, he doesn't understand. Make him fucking understand."

Tears sting my eyes as the weight of his words settle in. "I… didn't betray you."

"The seven years I spent without you while you were on another man's arm would testify otherwise."

"I didn't…"

"Then what was it? Did you have sex with that fucker, Ren, and didn't want to face me? Did you really think so little of me? That I would toss you aside because you fucked another man to fucking save me? If anything, I would've been indebted to you."

"I don't want you indebted to me." I pause for shallow, torturous seconds. "And I never had sex with Ren."

I can at least tell him that much.

His thick brows draw together over his darkened eyes. "What the fuck is that supposed to mean?"

"It never happened. I managed to leave without doing that."

The line deepens in his forehead. "Then why the fuck did you make me believe that for all this time? The last image of you I have in my head is you being raped for *my* sake. Being traumatized for *me*! Did you enjoy tormenting me and coming over in my nightmares abused and bloodied?"

"Of course not!"

"Then why? Tell me why you did it? Why you left me?"

"I just...wanted to," I mutter in a helpless attempt to have him drop the subject.

"*Wanted* to? I suppose you happened to marry Akira after you promised yourself to me because you also wanted to? Did you love him after you confessed your fake feelings to me, or was it before?"

"They were never fake."

"Shut the fuck up and get the fuck out. I don't even want to look at your face anymore."

He throws my hand away and turns to his side, giving me his back.

I swallow the burn of his words and stand up. I don't leave, though, because no matter how much he hates me, I don't hate him.

Never did. Not even when he hurt me.

I'm at the door when his tired voice filters after me.

"I wish I'd never met you. I wish you'd never returned."

I'm starting to wish that, too.

I always thought we were two unique pieces that fit together perfectly, but maybe we've been forcibly jamming ourselves into molds that don't fit us.

Two wrongs don't make a right.

And we're too deviant and forbidden to ever be right.

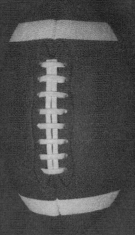

THIRTY-TWO

Sebastian

BEING ILL SUCKS LIKE A BITCH. AN INEXPERIENCED ONE who seems to be blowing your patience instead of your dick.

I groan as I open my eyes, then pause when I inhale the scent of lilies. A scent that shouldn't be in my bed.

It doesn't take me long to find the source. A small figure is huddled against my side in a fetal position. Her hands are wrapped around a towel and her long lashes flutter on her flushed cheeks.

The blue neon numbers on the clock on the nightstand read 3:24 a.m.

She stayed.

My mind is a blur of events and emotions, but I know I said some fucked-up shit that would make anyone bolt. Especially with her habit of leaving whenever she sees fit.

I meant each of those words, and yet, I slowly turn so I'm lying on my side, facing her.

She's on the edge of the mattress, far enough away that she's not touching me, but her warmth still douses me.

It's different from the fever. Hers is potent, mixed with twisted emotions and carnal need.

It doesn't matter how much I roughen her up or how long I take her. It doesn't matter that I've fucked her in more positions than I can count or that I've filled her every hole with my cum.

The moment I'm done, I'm always in the mood to start again. To fuck her again. Own her again. Relieve my fucked-up emotions again.

But that's the thing. The part about relieving emotions never happens. If anything, my rage has been blackening each time she walks out of the fucking door.

Back to her life.

To her damn husband.

I reach a hand out and stroke a strand of her ink-colored hair out of her face. She looks so peaceful when she's asleep, like a porcelain doll.

And just like a doll, she's breakable.

Still, discovering the fact that she was never forced to have sex with Ren seven years ago brought relief I didn't think I would ever feel.

All this time, I haven't been able to stop thinking about the sacrifices she made at the time or the way she shook when she left.

She held her head high, even though she was trembling with fear. And my last sight of her was her back as she walked out the door.

Naomi mumbles something in her sleep before her eyes flutter open. They're unfocused at first, dark with confusion. She blinks twice and her lips part.

Probably lost for words again.

We remain like that for a moment, with my hand in her hair and her eyes locked on mine.

It feels intimate in a fucking normal kind of way.

Like we've been waking up to each other's faces for the past seven years.

"You didn't leave," I say slowly, carefully.

"You're sick." She reaches a hand out, then pauses. "I'm just going to check your temperature."

She puts her palm against my forehead and my breathing deepens at the contact. She quickly retrieves it. "I think your fever's gone."

Her voice is light—joyous, even. And I don't know why I want to catch it and trap it somewhere.

Naomi slowly sits up on her haunches by my side, making me release her. "You need to eat something and take another dose of your medicine." She grabs a container of food off the nightstand. "The oatmeal I made earlier is still warm."

After opening the container, she picks up a spoon and a bottle of pills. "Here."

I don't take them but sit up against the headboard, watching her swift, precise movements. She's one of those people who does everything fast, as if she's in a race against time. I haven't noticed that about her before.

"You said a second dose. I don't remember taking the first one."

Her ears heat. "I helped you."

"Helped me how?"

"I poured the contents of the capsule on a spoon of oatmeal and…"

"And what?"

"And just helped you swallow it."

"By sticking your tongue at the back of my throat?"

"I didn't need to go that far…and I wasn't trying to kiss you. I just had to make you eat and swallow your medicine."

"I don't believe you." I'm taunting her, but I can't help it. She's flustered, her unsteady fingers opening and closing the container over and over. I don't think she even realizes she's doing it.

"I don't know how to make you believe it."

"Do it again."

Her wide eyes meet mine. "W-what?"

"Repeat what you did and I'll be the judge."

"That's just ridiculous."

"We won't know unless you go with it."

She remains still for a long moment, then releases a defeated sigh. Naomi opens the capsule into the container, mixes the medicine with the food, then takes a spoonful.

Her eyes meet mine as she places the oatmeal on her tongue, slightly sticking it out, then leans in and grabs my chin with her thumb and forefinger.

My lips part as my dick jumps to life.

She slowly thrusts her tongue inside my mouth, surprisingly not spilling much of the oatmeal, and carefully rubs it against my tongue.

In the midst of food, I taste her and her tentative strokes. She sweeps it to the back of my tongue and her lips brush against mine. I swallow the oatmeal and she stills before she attempts to pull back.

I grab her by the back of her neck and feast on her tongue, sucking on it open-mouthed before I lick her lips and hit the roof of her mouth. I kiss her savagely and out of control so that the only sounds she releases are strangled, surprised moans.

I kiss her like I've never kissed before. Like this kiss will be the last I have. My nails sink into the back of her neck and I slam the front of her body against mine.

Naomi squeals, her hand gripping my bicep for balance, but she opens up to me. Her tongue meets mine stroke for each damn stroke as we both tumble into madness.

I pull back, reluctantly releasing her.

Naomi's panting harshly, her cheeks painted red. "Why did you do that?"

"Do what?"

"Kiss me."

"I was only getting the oatmeal." I lick my lips and her eyes follow the movement before she shakes her head and shoves the container in my lap and the spoon in my fingers.

"You can do the rest yourself." She stands and her dress rides up her pale thighs.

I tighten my hold on the container to keep from grabbing her and repeating what we just did.

Or maybe taking it a step further.

"Leaving?" I sound unaffected when I'm barely holding on to my calm.

She grabs the duvet and covers my legs with it. "Stop kicking me out. I'll leave in the morning."

"Won't your husband ask about you?"

"I already called him."

"What's your excuse this time? All-nighter at the office again?"

She lifts her chin. "I'm staying with a friend."

"We're friends now?"

"We…were."

"*Really?*"

"We used to tell each other things we didn't tell the rest of the world. That's what friends do."

"Then why don't you tell me things now?"

I expect her to brush me off, but she sits on the bed, on the far edge so she's out of my reach. "What do you want to know? Aside from everything that happened seven years ago, because I won't talk about that."

"So I'm free to ask anything aside from what I want to know the most? When did you become so cruel?"

"Since you," she whispers.

I let out a mocking sound. "That's rich coming from you."

"Are you going to be throwing jabs all night or is there anything you want to know?"

"Why did you marry him?"

"It was an arranged marriage between our families."

I don't know why that makes me breathe a little easier. She didn't choose him. It was an arranged marriage.

"Akira is an influential man and my father wanted him as an ally."

"Your father?"

"I found him." She smiles, but her shoulders hunch and her eyes shine with haunting sadness. "Or more like, he found me."

"Is he everything you imagined?"

"Worse." She takes the spoon from my hand and I think she just needs something to touch, but she fills it with oatmeal and places it in front of my mouth.

I can eat on my own, but I open up and let her feed me. This is the most domesticated I've seen her and it touches a part of me I didn't know existed.

"I wish I'd believed Mom when she said I should stay away. I wish I'd appreciated her more when she was alive. She died feeling uneasy that I was with Dad."

"May she rest in peace." A gloomy aura falls over us. The thought of the stern but kind Riko being dead leaves a heavy weight at the base of my chest.

She was always happy whenever I spent time with Naomi or went to pick her up. Once, she told me she was thrilled her daughter was finally having a great relationship.

Naomi shoves another spoonful at my mouth and twists her lips as moisture shines along her lids.

"Do you like working in her fashion house?"

"Not really. I'm just keeping it as a legacy."

"Do you still sketch?"

Her eyes shine and she smiles. "Whenever I have time. I'll show you…if you want."

"Sure."

Naomi takes the container and the spoon and places them on the nightstand. Then she rolls to her side, reaches for her bag, and retrieves a small pad.

After she hugs it to her chest for a second, she passes it to me.

I study her sketches—people, faces, some shadows. Cocking

my head, I study the patterns and how they all seem like a varia-
tion of one person. It's a lot more mature than back in high school,
not that she was ever immature. Just a bit innocent, and now all of
that innocence is completely gone.

"Laugh at them and I will kill you," she says defensively.

I chuckle, "Tsundere."

Her eyes widen and I pause. Fuck. I meant to never use that
nickname again.

"Your technique has gotten so much better. And you're still
doing what you love, even if not professionally."

"I changed my mind. I don't want to pursue this as a profes-
sion, because it would probably kill my creativity. I'd rather keep
it as a hobby."

"I see."

She removes the pad from my hands, slowly stroking its edges.
"What about you? Are you doing what you love?"

"Yeah. The adrenaline rush I get from smashing someone in
court chases away the urges. Even if only temporarily."

"I never imagined you as a lawyer, though I should've suspected
it, considering your perceptive nature and warped sense of justice.
And, hey, you don't make minimum wage like a detective. Wow,
you're living the dream."

She remembers. We once talked about how I had people-reading
skills and she suggested I become a detective to put that gift to use,
but I vehemently refused to put so much effort for little pay. What
she doesn't know is that I did look into cultivating and growing my
skills, which is why I chose to practice law.

The fact that she remembers our conversations from back then
fills me with a sense of warmth I haven't felt in a very long time.

"I see you haven't really lost your cynical nature."

"It comes out when someone like you provokes it."

"Someone like me?"

"A soldier of dark justice."

"You call it dark justice, I call it my own version of it. Nothing is black and white and everything can be turned gray."

"Why am I not surprised that's your motto?"

"People don't really change."

"You have." She stares at her sketchpad.

"I have?"

"Yeah."

"How so?"

"Your apartment. for one. It's so empty."

"I don't need things." Because I don't want to be attached to anything, but I don't tell her that.

"You're colder and untouchable, too. You're as far as the night sky and just as…scary sometimes."

"Who made me that way?" It could be because I'm sick and can't filter my words or that I'm just too fucking tired of the back and forth, but I don't regret the words when they come out.

If it's madness, I might as well indulge.

Naomi's grip tightens on the pad and she visibly winces. Good. At least she recognizes what her actions have done. I hope she burns inside hotter and darker than I fucking do.

"Sebastian…"

"What, Naomi? What do you have to say?"

"Nothing."

"Fuck that. I've known darkness since I was six years old and I learned early on not to fight it and, eventually, I learned to blend with it. Being black was fine, even if it felt empty. Then you came along, and I wanted fucking gray. Now, I'm just colorless, so don't sit there and tell me you have nothing to fucking say."

Her lips tremble. "I'm sorry."

"Your apologies don't give me back the years I've lost, so fucking save them."

"I lost those years, too."

"Doesn't look like it." I motion at her bare ring finger. "Did you think hiding it would make me think of your marriage any less?"

She goes rigid, her hand tightening on her sketchpad and discomfort turning her skin sickly pale. I should stop, should shoo her away and reunite with the bitter asshole I became seven years ago and start a self-pity party, but I don't.

I can't.

I've already ripped the stitches open, so I might as well bleed out properly this time.

"Do you love him?"

She swallows again, runs her fingers on the pad again, avoids eye contact fucking again. "It's…complicated."

"There's nothing complicated about a fucking yes or no question."

"I need him," she murmurs.

"So that's a yes."

"No! Sebastian, please don't go there. Take that as if I'm begging you. *Please*."

I want to go there. I want her to say the words that will put me out of my fucking misery. Whether they kill me or free me, I'll at least have some sort of closure. That's all I needed all this time. That's what I searched for during all the fights in the bars—a fucking finale.

But maybe I don't want closure.

Maybe being colorless isn't so bad, after all.

Or, most probably, this cold is messing up my thinking process.

I lie on my back and she releases a long breath, sniffling.

I close my eyes and soon after, she lies in the nook of my body, her arm wrapping around my shoulder.

It's tentative, her touch, as if she's scared of my reaction. And she should be. Why the hell does she keep trying to touch me this intimately even after she broke us to fucking pieces?

I stiffen, but I don't attempt to peel her off me.

Naomi must've taken it differently because she burrows her face in my chest, her breathing shattering against my skyrocketing heartbeat.

"Don't touch me," I say without opening my eyes.

"Please let me. Just this once."

"I said don't touch me, Naomi. When you do, I picture these fucking hands on him and your face buried in his chest. When you do, I imagine your scent clinging to him and his on you, so don't fucking touch me with the same hands you touch him with."

She shakes her head in my chest and I feel the wetness of her tears on my T-shirt as her tiny gasps fill the air. "Just a moment…"

"One condition."

"Anything."

"Don't go back to him."

"W-what?"

"In the morning, stay here. Don't fucking go back to him."

Her leg hooks over mine and she snuggles closer so her whole body is looped around mine.

I turn around and hug her.

For the first time in seven years, I sleep without nightmares of Naomi turning her back on me.

THIRTY-THREE

Naomi

I GO HOME.

I step on my fucking bleeding heart and leave.

The tears came as soon as I was out of Sebastian's apartment and they were there during the whole drive home.

But no matter how much my heart begged me to turn around and return, I just jammed the knife in deeper and didn't listen.

Last night was magical, peaceful, and a little bit painful, too. It was the first time we didn't have sex, but he's never been as deep inside me as when he talked to me and hugged me.

He's never felt as close as he did in that moment.

Everything that happened might not be perfect, but it was ours and I enjoyed every second of it.

But like any magic, there's a timeframe for the spell to run its course.

I reached that moment.

When Sebastian told me not to go home, I wanted to say yes, I wanted to make a small place in any corner of his life and stay there.

But that's just the emotional side of me speaking. The logical side that has allowed us to survive all this time is what should be taking the reins.

I stay in my car for a few minutes once I stop in front of Akira's house. I fix my makeup in an attempt to chase away the puffiness of my eyes.

That damn husband of mine can't see me at my lowest, not when he makes it his mission to exploit everyone's weaknesses to drag them down.

I thought I could be in Sebastian's vicinity, fuck him, be with him while staying married to someone else.

But I was wrong. Utterly and devastatingly so.

I need to somehow turn the tables on Akira so he'll be forced to let me go.

But that would be as hard as breaking his cool façade. Besides, there's also the threat of my father and what he'll do to Mio if I defy him.

And then there's Kai, but I'm never sure if that sly snake is on my side or if he's only using me to get in my father's good graces.

My head hurts.

I step out of the car and remove my shoes at the entrance, then put on my slippers. Instead of going to my room, I make a turn and head to Akira's.

It could be due to the crying, the sadness, or the need for any semblance of hope. But I have to take a chance and talk to Akira.

Surprisingly, he's kept to himself about Sebastian. I expected him to threaten and demand he works for him, but it's been weeks and he hasn't made an offer yet.

It should make me happy, but for some reason, I'm just apprehensive about his next move. Akira's silence is never good. It means he's plotting someone's ruin and building another person's hell.

A familiar sound causes me to halt in front of his bedroom. The door is ajar, which is why I'm able to hear what's happening inside.

I carefully push it open, my fingers sweaty. The scene that unfolds in front of me nearly drops my jaw to the ground.

Akira stands in the middle of his black-themed bedroom in direct view of the rays of the sun that are slipping through the window.

He's wearing his yukata, but it's open, revealing his lean muscled chest and his cock as he rams it into the mouth of the last person I expected.

Ren.

My father's guard is on his knees in front of my husband, his shirt open, his face flushed, and his wrists are wrapped in thick rope behind his back.

One of Akira's hands is grabbing Ren by the hair while the other has a knife in it. The blade shines in the air with droplets of blood before he runs it down Ren's neck, over the tattoos on his nape, and then back to his pulse point.

The sound of his cock driving in and out of the guard's mouth is savage and relentless, like he's on a mission to break his jaw.

"Open wider," Akira grunts, lust audible in his voice, but he somehow still sounds like he holds his usual calm. "Make it good."

Ren's eyes are defiant, but his face is red and he's fucking bleeding due to Akira's knife. Red soaks his shirt, his skin, and even drips onto the floor.

"Do it right or I'll use your ass, Ren. Actually, I'm using it anyway, but whether I take it easy or tear through you while you scream depends on how you please me," Akira warns, his pace increasing by the second.

The scene is like the weirdest nightmare. My husband Akira, the damn liar, and my nemesis Ren, who I've been metaphorically stabbing in my brain.

How? When?

Though I should've suspected something was going on when Akira insisted on working with him instead of Kai, and Ren's reaction to it.

Or the endless hours they spend together.

Or everything in between, really.

My hand shakes as I retrieve my phone and snap a picture of what's happening in front of me. The flash goes off.

Shit.

Both Akira's and Ren's attention are directed at me. Akira's bored and a bit annoyed. Ren's wide and frantic, as if he's been caught masturbating in public.

I feign calm as I slip my phone back in my bag and lean against the doorframe, acting cool. "Don't let me stop you."

Ren jerks backward, releasing Akira's very big and very unsatisfied shaft. Spit, precum, and blood trickle down his chin as he scrambles across the floor, then stands up.

A few cuts mar his chest, abdomen, and neck and soak the collar of his white shirt.

Ouch. That looks painful.

"Untie me," he hisses at Akira.

My husband, who's been watching his frantic movements while toying with the knife, releases a breath. "Know your fucking place. I'm the one who gives the orders, not the other way around."

"Akira," he mutters.

"Say it right."

"*Onegai…*" Ren pleads under his breath, then blurts the honorific term, "*Desu.*"

"Good. Now say that again and mean it."

Ren's dark eyes snap to mine before he bows his head and murmurs, "Your wife is here."

"Don't mind me. Take all the time you need." I pretend to be studying my black nails.

Ren frowns, then holds his head high, even while he begs Akira to let him go. A dark gleam covers my husband's features as he tilts his head to the side and closely watches Ren scrambling for words.

Color me surprised. Akira is actually having fun.

He also seems to be egging Ren on just to hear him deal with being out of his element.

And the ever-collected Ren is playing right into his hands like a marionette.

I never thought I needed this scene until I witnessed it.

Akira finally cuts Ren's ropes and the younger man closes his shirt with a hand as he storms to the door.

He stops in front of me, his chest heaving and his face still covered with blood and spit and drops of semen.

There's shame there, embarrassment, and I revel in every negative emotion he feels, because no matter how dark they are, they can't be as painful as what I felt when he shot Sebastian seven years ago.

Or when he continued to threaten his life, per his boss's order.

"I…" He swallows. "I'm…"

"Save it." I square my shoulders. "I have evidence of your preferences, Ren. Something that will get you kicked out of the Yakuza and have you killed by Kai's sword."

"No! He made me!" He points a finger at Akira, who's merely watching us with a tilted head.

"He's lying," Akira says with a gentle shrug of his shoulder. "His mouth wanted my dick as much as his body begged for my knife."

Red creeps up Ren's neck. "If you show Boss evidence, Akira will be implicated, too."

"Not if I simply crop out his face from the picture."

Ren stares between Akira's calm expression and my taunting one. "You're both in on this? Did you make him do that to me just to trap me?"

"You trapped yourself the day you shot Sebastian and nearly killed him." I point a finger at his shoulder. "Mess with him or with me again, even under my father's orders, and you can kiss your fucking career—and life—goodbye. I heard Kai likes to torture first before cutting people to pieces."

"Fuck. You."

"What did I say about that language?" Akira asks in a disapproving tone.

"And you!" Ren snarls at him. "Fuck you both, you weird fuckers."

I tap my chin. "You might want to wipe all the blood and cum off before saying that."

Ren snarls again, and as he storms past me, Akira calls after him, "You better be prepared for your punishment, brat."

The guard pauses, his lips pursing before he leaves, his angry steps echoing down the hall.

I stare at Akira and then at his hard cock. "That must be painful and unsatisfying."

"It wouldn't be if you hadn't shown up."

"So it's *my* fault?"

"You think it's mine?"

"I'd offer a hand, but I'd rather have it cut off."

He points at his cock that's losing its erection, then wraps his yukata closed. "The thought of your hand is enough to turn a sinner into a priest."

"Screw you."

"Again, I would've screwed someone if you hadn't come in here."

"I thought you were asexual."

"I thought so, too. Turns out, I'm just selective."

"And Ren of all people is the one you selected?"

He smiles, it's rare and filled with pure sadism. "He could use some discipline. A lot, actually."

"He's loyal to my father."

"If I want it, his loyalty and everything he has to offer will only belong to me."

"That's not how it works. He's a high-ranking member of the Yakuza and he breathes that reckless lifestyle. If you try to force him to join you in peaceful Kyoto, he'll probably blow your car up."

"He would." His lips pull in a smirk that holds so much pride. "But let me worry about him."

"Since when are you into knife play?"

"I've always loved knives and flesh. Oh, and blood."

I frown. "When we talked through the letters, you never mentioned knife play, only breath play."

He pauses, fingering his yukata's belt. "I've developed a fetish."

"You realize I'll use that picture against you, too, right? I'm glad you found your drive and your choices, knife included. No hard feelings. I'm just looking out for myself."

"And Sebastian, obviously."

I ignore the sharp twist in my stomach and hold on to my cool. "Don't bring him into this."

Akira approaches me, then sniffs me like a dog. "I can smell him on you, wife. You've been carrying his scent and his marks for fucking weeks. You really thought I wouldn't notice?"

"You...knew."

"Of course."

"Then why didn't you do anything?"

"In the early Edo period, there was a famous rônin samurai named Miyamoto Musashi who was known both for his skill and his quirkiness. Many other renowned samurais challenged him to a duel, but they were all killed even though they were better skilled than him. Do you know why he won every time? It's because he changed his tactics to fit each opponent's weakness. If they were stern, he was playful. If they were playful, he was rigid. Being fluid and ever-changing is what gets things done, whereas brute force will sooner or later lead to someone's ruin."

"What's your tactic for us then?"

"I'm still watching, just like Musashi did before his duals."

"Don't you dare hurt him."

"Don't you dare threaten me again and we'll talk."

"I mean it, Akira. If you do him any harm, your family will receive the picture. Your father is still alive, so you can't own the Mori fortune just yet. He can still strip you of the leading position and hand it to your brother on a gold platter. Don't force my hand to ruin the empire you've been building all these years."

"My, Naomi. I didn't know you had this much fire inside you."

"I have a fucking volcano, if you want to see."

He smiles, but it quickly vanishes. "There'll be no divorce. Play your role or I will throw you to Abe's wolves."

"Then I will just bury you and Ren in return. You're not the only one who knows my weakness."

"You better check on your weakness then."

The adrenaline wave slowly dissipates. I dislike Akira's apathetic tone and face. I've known him long enough to realize that means he's pissed and will soon become vindictive.

When I found the chance to threaten him, I couldn't possibly let it pass. But maybe coming on this strong wasn't such a bright idea.

Still, I hold on to my strength, even when my stomach tightens. "Why?"

"My gift should've reached him by now."

"What type of gift?"

"No bombs, don't worry. Just expensive Japanese essential oils that I'm sure he'll appreciate since he was born in Japan. He'll love the note more than the oils, though."

"Wait. What? Sebastian was born in Japan?" How come I didn't know that? I was aware that his grandparents shunned his parents and they had to go away, but I didn't know it was to Japan.

"Maybe you're not as tight as you think you are if he never told you he was Japanese-born. He lived in Tokyo for six years until his parents died."

"Why do you know all of that?"

"I like the power it gives me. But that's not the end of it."

"What is that supposed to mean?"

"You might want to pay more attention the next time you're in your father's office."

I spend the entire day obsessing over Akira's words. Sebastian's origins. The note with the essential oils.

My husband was a damn asshole and refused to divulge more—no surprise there.

As I sit behind my desk at Mom's company, I contemplate calling Sebastian and asking, but the way I left this morning stops me.

I practically snuck out like a thief. Besides, he's probably still groggy with the cold. The fever had gone down when I checked it before I left, but he could still be sick.

Shaking my head, I attempt to focus on the documents in front of me, but I end up sketching instead.

The whole day is spent in an unproductive funk and even Amanda shakes her head at me due to how unfocused I am. I call it a day around seven p.m. I'm really not in the mood to face Akira again, but I can pester him, make his life hell, and even cockblock him until he gives me the answers I need.

I'm driving on a secluded road when I notice a car following behind me. Its headlights are blinding, so I can't make out the model or the color.

Rolling my eyes, I step on the brakes, drawing my car to a halt. I'm really in no mood for Father's and Akira's guards tonight.

I told them not to follow me as if I'm a sheltered little princess.

After closing my car door harder than needed, I march to the other car, which unsurprisingly stopped right behind mine.

I knock on the Audi's tinted window. "Open up."

No answer.

"Ren, is that you? I swear to God, I'm going to start getting really nasty really fast if you don't stop playing around."

The door opens and I startle, my heel catching on the asphalt as I meet those tropical eyes. He's dressed in a black hoodie and sweatpants, and the early evening's lack of light casts a shadow on his face.

"Sebastian? What are you doing here?"

"Following you, obviously." I don't like the coldness in his voice, even though I know where it's coming from.

"Shouldn't you be resting?"

"Maybe. But you were also supposed to stay this morning." He reaches out and grabs me by the wrist, then yanks me over. I yelp as I land on his lap.

"Sebastian! What are you doing?"

His eyes rage as he whispers in threatening dark words, "I asked you nicely to stay, but you don't want nice, Naomi. You want me to fucking kidnap you."

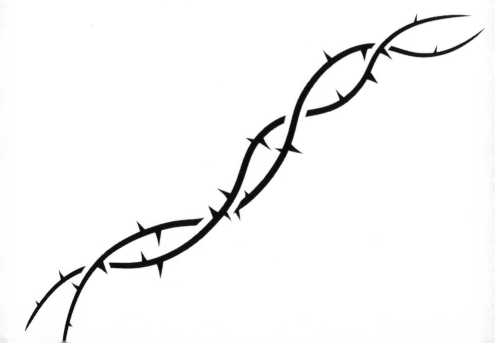

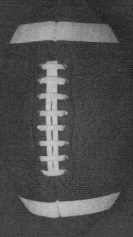

THIRTY-FOUR

Sebastian

YOU MIGHT BE FUCKING HER, BUT I'M THE ONE SHE COMES *back to every night.*
   Mori A.

That's the card I got with the package of essential oils that showed up at my apartment this morning.

Right after Naomi fucking left.

I didn't think she'd stay just like that, but I'd hoped she would at least talk to me about it, not disappear like she did seven fucking years ago.

She won't be disappearing now.

I slide my attention to her as she grabs the seatbelt with both hands while watching the road.

When I followed her from her company, I meant to go all the way to her house and kiss her in front of the fucker before I kidnapped her.

There's been a slight change in plans, but my intention still stands.

Aside from her initial fight, she's been quiet all the way here, just watching the road with her dark, haunting eyes.

"We…did we just pass the sign to Blackwood?"

I remain silent, tapping my forefinger on the steering wheel.

"Sebastian! Why are we back in Blackwood?"

"This is where it all started. Seems like a perfect crime site, don't you think?"

She pushes back in her seat, her delicate throat bobbing with a gulp and her cheeks paling.

Fear radiates off her in waves.

Good. She needs to be fucking scared.

"What are you going to do, Sebastian?"

"Have you ever seen a kidnapper share his plan with his victim?"

"Is this about how I left this morning? I…couldn't just stay."

"Yes, you could have, and I don't just mean today. I also mean seven fucking years ago."

"You're only judging me from your perspective without even knowing mine."

"Because you refuse to fucking share it. But I'm done coaxing you into this."

I swerve the car to a dirt road and she squeals, digging her black-painted nails into the seatbelt.

Then she freezes as she makes out our surroundings.

"Sebastian…no…not here…"

"Yes. Fucking here."

I stop the car, kill the headlights, and step out of it, then round to her side. She tries to scramble away, but I grab her by the elbow, undo her seatbelt, and drag her out.

The scene is like déjà vu.

"Remember Blackwood's forest, Naomi? Turns out, the mafia does use it to bury corpses, after all. Reina was found assaulted and on the brink of death right here. Doesn't that bring back memories?"

"No…no!" She hits my chest with a closed fist as she wiggles and tries to push me off her.

"Save the fight for when I'm pinning you against the fucking ground."

"Why did you bring us back to the forest? It's where you were shot and they took us."

"It's also where I chased you the first time, and I'm in the mood to repeat it."

"You're out of your mind if you think I'll run now."

"You're talking as if you have a choice. Run or I'll leave you here."

"You...wouldn't."

"Try me."

"We're not twenty-one anymore, Sebastian!"

"What? You've lost your stamina?"

"I'm wearing heels."

"All the better. I can catch you faster." I release her and she steps backward, but her wild gaze remains on me, her hair in disarray, framing her soft, pale face.

"And then what? What if you don't catch me?"

"Oh, I'll catch you. Whether I do it sooner or later is up to you."

"I hate you sometimes."

At least it's not all the time. "That makes two of us. Now, run."

She startles, but like in the fucking past, she turns around and runs.

Her movements aren't as fast as back then, probably because of the shoes.

I jog behind her, my muscles tightening with the need to hunt. To fucking chase and conquer.

And eventually hurt.

I don't fantasize about inflicting violence on everyone. Just her. My Naomi.

One of her shoes falls off her foot and she stops for a fraction of a second before she kicks the other one away. Her pace picks up when barefoot, and she starts darting between the trees, going in a zigzag line in an attempt to lose me.

It works for a mere moment before I'm on her tail again, feeding off the prey pheromones she's emanating.

My beast claws its way to the surface, magnifying and expanding with every step that brings me closer to her.

I inhale the scent of her, lilies and thrilled fear, and I know I'm a breath away from grabbing her petite body and throwing it down, then fucking her thoroughly.

It doesn't matter that I was sick just last night. Tonight, I feel stronger than the fucking devil.

Naomi chances a glance over her shoulder and squeals, the sound echoing in the dark silence before her frantic movements spiral out of control.

She's acting on pure survival mode now, pushing her muscles to their limits and probably consuming a week's worth of oxygen.

My own wave of energy kicks in and my leg muscles move fluidly and with purpose. The more she darts between trees, the more determined my beast becomes.

The clearer her scent becomes, the faster I chase her.

She pauses when we come to a clearing. The rock we used to talk and fuck on is still there, a natural witness of our fucked-up darkness.

An unmovable object that stayed there even when we didn't.

And now, we're just back to square one.

I use her hesitation and grab her with my arm around her waist, singlehandedly lifting her up.

She yelps, her throaty voice reverberating in the air as her tiny body claws, squirms, and kicks in my hold.

Her groans are pure and primal, just like my harsh breathing.

I wrap my other arm around her and carry her to the rock as she fights to get out of my grip, even as her whole body seems to catch a burning fire.

Fuck the fight in this woman.

No one but her would kick and claw me even when their eyes are shining with lust for me.

This is part of the reason why I could never move on from her, not even if I wanted to.

I shove her body against the rock so that she's bending over with her tits on the flat edge. Naomi yelps and scrambles forward, attempting to escape. I slap her on the ass three consecutive times.

Her shriek is fucking music to my ears as it fills the forest, its spirits the only witness to our depravity. Our fucking reality.

The spanking doesn't kill her fight, although it lessens it, she still tries to swat my hand away.

I grab both her wrists and imprison them behind her back, then yank her head back by a fistful of her hair. "Stay fucking still."

"No…nooo, let me go!"

"Scream all you like. No one will hear you here. It's only you and me, my dirty little slut. Did you really think I wouldn't catch you? You can run for a fucking decade and I'll still grab you by the throat."

"I didn't run…"

Her words start a fire at the base of my spine. "Stop saying shit like that when you fucking did."

"No…you idiot. I didn't!" Tears shine along her lids, and I have no clue whether they're crocodile tears or pained ones.

I release her wrists and her hair, and Naomi falls back against the rock with a gasp. But I don't let her get comfortable. I want to be all over and around her and fucking inside her every goddamn second and never let her the fuck go.

Reaching to her front, I unzip her pants, then lower them and her panties.

My hand comes down on her ass at the same time as I thrust three fingers inside her. She's soaking from the chase, but her shriek pierces the air.

Her nails scratch against the rock's surface, probably to find a reprieve from me, but there's none.

There's no saving the lamb from the wolf.

I fuck her with my fingers and stimulate her clit hard enough to make her jolt and moan.

Still thrusting my fingers in and out of her wet cunt, I retrieve the vial of essential oil from my pocket. It's been burning since I put it there after I planned for its perfect use.

I remove my hand from her pussy and she groans, a disappointed sound that's like a musical masterpiece to my ears.

"Stay in fucking place," I order, then pour the oil on both of my hands. Its strong notes of cedarwood, rosemary, and pine fill the air as I throw the glass bottle onto the dirt.

My palm lathers her cunt and she moans, even if there's still a fight in her tense muscles. "Your husband thought it was a genius idea to send me oils and remind me that he's the one you go back to every night. So I'm going to fill your holes with his precious oils, so when he smells them and sees my cum on your cunt, he'll know who you actually belong to."

She writhes on the rock, not out of fight, but out of a need for friction.

"Such a greedy little whore, my Naomi. Do you need this pussy filled?"

"Mmm…"

"How about your other hole?"

I part her ass cheeks and thrust an oiled finger inside. She goes rigid, her spine jerking up before she relaxes around me.

"He'll smell me and his fucking oils on your ass, too. He'll see me everywhere in you."

Her breath breaks and I know she's close to orgasming, but I don't give her that pleasure and pull out my fingers.

"Sebastian…" she pleads, her aroused voice a fucking aphrodisiac to my starved dick.

I lower my sweatpants and lather my length with the fucking oils.

"Beg for my dick to fill your cunt, Naomi."

"Please…" she murmurs, the word barely audible.

"More."

"Please fill me."

"I didn't hear that."

"Please fill me with your cock. Please, I want it. I need it. Please…"

Her whispered moans, the brokenness of them, does me in. I drive inside her with a deep groan, then watch where we're joined as I add another finger in her ass. "Your cunt is fucking made for me, baby. Isn't it?"

"Yes! Yes!"

"Now tell me to fuck you the way we both want it."

"Harder…faster…rougher…make me take your whole dick… punish me…own me…give me everything you have to offer even if I can't take it…"

"Fuuuuck!" I nearly come then and there, but I hold it in and drive into her with the pace that's made us Sebastian and Naomi.

We're twisted. We're fucked up. But we're us.

"More…please…take me, Sebastian. Please. Don't hold back. Make me as filthy and as dirty as you want me…"

I pull out almost immediately, then slam back in, making her scream.

Holding her nape with one hand, I move the other one in her ass, covering it with oil and thrusting deep. I match my dick's frantic pace until a depraved sense of pleasure is all I can feel.

She clenches around me, shaking with an orgasm, and I slide out of her cunt. Her thighs are quivering and her legs are barely carrying her.

I part her ass cheeks and thrust my rock-hard dick inside, groaning at how tight she is.

Naomi cries out, even as she wiggles her ass, taking more of my thick length inside her.

I twist her clit, then pound three fingers into her cunt as I fuck her in the ass. I do it savagely, roughly, out of fucking control.

She's sobbing now, begging me to stop, but then she murmurs, "More, please more…"

And I give it to her.

I give her everything in me, and it's not only about sex.

I give her the fractured parts of me that I haven't been able to mend together ever since she turned her back on me in that fucking cell. I give her the side of me I don't even like.

"Sebastian…oh, please, please…no."

"Please no? Do you want me to leave you high and dry, baby?"

"No…"

"Then say the right words.

"Yes…Please…yes…yes!"

My pace increases until she's begging and sobbing and clenching all around me. I grab her by the hair, then by the throat as I roll my hips and drive into her. My tongue finds her cheek and I lick her tears before sliding down to feast on her quivering lips.

She kisses me, her tongue meeting mine and her whole body melting against me.

I come then. My cum shooting deep into her back hole as she shudders and releases the most erotic sounds I've ever heard.

"On second thought, you're never going back to him," I growl against her ear, panting harshly. "No one but me will ever fuck you again."

"No one has." She pants, her dark, teary eyes meeting mine. "No one has fucked me since you."

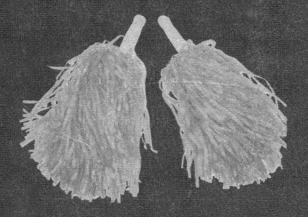

THIRTY-FIVE
Naomi

IT'S STRANGE HOW EASILY THE WORDS LEAVE ME. I never thought we'd be back here, at Blackwood's forest, at the rock we called ours. But here we are. And that's part of the reason why I spoke up.

Maybe all the depraved sex went to my head. Maybe the chase loosened my tongue.

But as soon as I say it, it's like I've broken a spell.

The cold air forms goosebumps over my skin and draws a chill down my spine.

Sebastian's chest leaves my back, his lips no longer tormenting my ears or whispering filthy words.

He pulls out of me and I moan softly at the loss of him. I survived without him for seven years, but now that he's back to touching me and being one with me, it's torture to be away from him even for a minute.

The moment he releases me, I force myself upright, wincing due to the bumps the rock has left on my chest and shoulders. It's probably already bruising.

My hands shake as I pull my underwear and pants up. I've always been a mess whenever Sebastian has unleashed his beast on me. He knows all the right places to touch and the best ways to make me insane.

I can feel his attention on my back, looming over me like some sort of threat.

"What did you just say?" The tenor of his voice is low, but it's rough and deep.

I carefully turn around to face him. He's all tucked into his sweatpants, his shoulders tense. The lack of light turns his face into an impenetrable shadow. "I never had sex with Akira or anyone else."

If I expected relief, joy, or any sort of reaction, there's none of those. Only his narrowed eyes greet me. "You never had sex with your husband of seven years?"

"No."

"Why?"

"Akira would kill me if he knew I'd told you this, but I'm done hiding. I…just want it all out."

"Want what out?"

"He's asexual—or was asexual. I think he's on the spectrum for that. Anyway, he's gay. He'd never look in a woman's direction."

Sebastian is silent for a moment as the revelation sinks in. His brows are still knit together and the sharp lines of his face tighten under the moonlight. I want to reach out and touch him, to kiss him and seek his warmth, but it's definitely not the time for that.

So I lean against the rock, just to have something touch, and wince when my ass touches the surface. Well, damn. We're back to the stage where I need daily care after his ruthless fucking.

I touch my forehead, stroking my hair away from my face. "Aren't you going to say anything?"

"What do you want me to say, Naomi? Do you want me to be happy that he never looked in your direction when you looked in his?"

"Stop being defensive, damn you! And I never thought of him

that way. Akira and I had an agreement since the beginning. I'm his image for his traditional family and he's my image for my own family. We weren't to get involved in each other's sexual lives either. We're in an open marriage."

"Open marriage is still a fucking marriage. You still go back to his house and have meals with him. You still appear in public on his fucking arm, have his last name, and wear his goddamn ring. So don't expect me to rejoice at the news, Naomi. Don't expect me to be a gentleman and say 'you did the right thing,' because you fucking didn't. It should've been *my* name attached to yours. My ring on your finger. My fucking arm around yours. You were my Naomi first. *My* fucking woman. But you went ahead and ruined it."

I taste salt, and it's then I realize a tear has escaped my lids. The strength in his emotions leaves me breathless, feeling suffocated and with no way out. I've never seen Sebastian so down, so hurt.

I've never seen him so angry.

But his anger wraps a noose around mine and drags it out.

Because he has no right to be. Not after everything I've been through.

"Who do you think I did it for?" I jam a finger at his chest. "Do you think I enjoy being on Akira's arm or that I'm delighted to wear his ring and have his goddamn name? I don't! But I had to *for you.*"

"Me? Oh, that explains it all. Thanks."

"Shut up, you fucking idiot. For once, just shut up and listen. You know the father I found? He's Abe Hitori, as in, the head of the Yakuza in New York. It was by his order that you were shot that day in the forest and held in the cell. He did that to break me in and make me into his obedient daughter. And it worked. It fucking *worked.* If you hadn't gotten medical care, you would've died, Sebastian. You would've disappeared as if you'd never existed. They would've buried you in some damn hole and no one would've found your body. So yes, you asshole, I did it to save you. I left and married Akira so you'd survive."

Sebastian's eyes widen and he steps closer, reaching a hand

toward me, but I push him away. "No! Let me finish. You wanted to know everything that happened. So here it is, Sebastian. Here's the fucking truth I've been swallowing like a bitter pill every damn day. When Ren and Kai, my father's men, gave me the choice of following his orders or witnessing you die, I didn't think twice about it. I was ready to sell my body and my fucking soul if it meant seeing you safe and sound. That's how much you meant to me. That's how much I cared about you. But that's not all. My father would've sold my younger sister, Mio, who was only fourteen at the time, without batting an eye. But Akira wanted to marry me and my father needed the Mori family's power, so that's where I came in. The only reason my father even looked in my direction was because I'd be able to secure an alliance for him."

"Why didn't you tell me?" He sounds a bit broken, a bit emotional. "Why did you think it was a better fucking idea to leave me, break us, fucking destroy what we had."

"I told you it was to protect you! To protect us, even if we didn't exist anymore. I was so lost back then and scared and nothing I did seemed enough or right. Nothing I did could've brought me back to you."

"Nao…"

"Don't Nao me." I push away from him, letting the tears loose. "I cried like a baby when I thought they would leave you for dead in that damn cell. I cried just as hard after I broke up with you on the phone and ended what we had with the fucking safe word. The night I married someone else, I lost a part of my soul. Ever since then, I've been only living but have never felt alive. I survived on reading articles about you and the thought that you were well and breathing. And you know what? I don't regret what I did. I don't regret saving you from my father's wrath and continuing to do so until now, because if he finds out I'm endangering his precious alliance with Akira, he won't hesitate to kill you this time."

His hand touches my shoulder and I push it away. I'm a crying mess and my breathing is all over the place. Tears blur my vision until all I see are shadows. Sebastian doesn't stop trying to reach for me, even though I wiggle free every time.

"Come here." He wraps an arm around my back and I bang both fists against his chest.

However, my fight is short-lived as he engulfs me in a strong embrace. My nails dig into the material of his hoodie and I break.

In the middle of the forest.

In the darkness.

I let all the pain loose. Sharp pieces splinter into my heart and everything overflows to the surface.

Snot and tears stain my face and Sebastian's clothes, but he holds me close, his hand drawing soothing circles on my back as he squeezes me.

"And my mom died around then…" I choke on the words. "It broke me harder because I was slapped with the reality that I was on my own… You weren't there… Mom wasn't there… Akira is cold and never attempts to be a friend… My father keeps threatening me with Mio's life… She's so young and sheltered, and I feel like I'm responsible for her, you know. I don't want her to end up like me. I don't want her to be Father's pawn and marry a man she doesn't love and then suffer because of it every day…with every damn breath she takes…because that's how it felt without you, Sebastian. Breathing was a chore. Waking up every day, putting a smile on my face, and pretending I was fine was a damn struggle. I'm tired… I'm so tired."

"I was tired, too, Naomi. I was hurt and bitter and a general asshole to everyone because the girl I thought was mine left me over a fucking text. You cut me open that day and I never managed to sew myself together again. You at least knew why you left, I didn't. All this time, I thought you blamed me, I thought I was a motherfucking loser for not being able to protect you back then."

"No, Sebastian, no…don't think that way."

"But I did, Naomi. For seven fucking years, that's all I could think about. And then, you waltz back in on another man's arm."

"I just told you…"

"I know. But that doesn't mean it didn't shatter the pieces I've been trying to pick off the floor for years. The rusty knife you left inside me cut me deeper and harsher to the point where I thought I wouldn't survive it this time."

"I'm sorry...hurting is the last thing I wanted..."

"I'm sorry, too, baby." His voice is low, pained. "I'm so sorry you had to go through that on your own. I wish I'd been there."

His words make me sob harder and I snuggle into his embrace, sniffling and ugly crying.

Because maybe those are the words that I wanted to hear from Sebastian. That he wished he'd been there.

That he really wanted to be there for me and help me carry the burden.

I don't know how long I stay like that, but Sebastian holds me the entire time, stroking my hair, my back, and being the rock I've needed all along.

"The only time I've been able to breathe was when I got back, when I saw you at that party the first time, even though you hated me."

"Oh, baby, I never hated you. I hated what you did. I hated that you broke up with me over a text message and a phone call. I hated the person I became without you—grouchy, cold, and hollow. I hated a lot of things, including your fucking husband, whom I fantasized about killing a thousand times, but I never managed to hate you. Not for one second. Not for a single fucking breath."

Oh, God.

It's like I'm levitating out of my own body and finally living in that alternate reality I've been wishing for.

"Sebastian..." I stare up at him, his name caught between awe and pain.

"What is it?"

"I can't do this anymore. I can't pretend my heart and soul aren't with you."

"You won't have to, baby. I promise."

I don't know how long I cry.

But it's long enough that my eyes feel swollen and my breaths start hitching.

It goes on for what seems like hours, yet Sebastian doesn't release me for even one second.

When I'm spent, he drives us out of the forest, but something tells me it's not going to be our last time here.

This place was our beginning and has some of my best memories, and there's nothing that will erase that.

I tell him to go to my house.

Or rather, Mom's.

We step inside and I deactivate the alarm. The place is still the same as it was seven years ago. Nothing's changed, not even the alarm code. I've been having a maid clean it up monthly, but this is the first time I've stepped foot in here since I left Blackwood.

I stand in the middle of the living room and hug myself as memories of Mom hit me out of nowhere.

I can imagine her standing in front of a mannequin and being a perfectionist.

The smell of her cigarette is at the tip of my nose, even though the place is spotlessly clean.

Images of the two of us eating and watching TV together assault me, and fresh tears spring to my eyes.

I'm such an emotional mess today.

Strong arms wrap around me from behind and I release a cracked breath.

"I didn't know you kept it," he whispers.

"I thought about selling it, but I just couldn't. This is the last thing I have of Mom. The fashion house doesn't count, that's just work. This place is…full of memories of her and…us."

"And your true crime shows," he teases.

I laugh despite the tears. "And those, too. Though I haven't watched one for seven years."

He turns me around to face him. "Why not?"

"They brought the memories back and turned me into an emotional mess."

"Let's go get you a shower and then we'll watch one."

"We will?"

"The fucking things grew on me."

"I told you they would."

"I only like them because they remind me of you."

My cheeks burn and I look away. "Do all the women fall for that?"

"Most of them do, Tsundere."

I bite my lip to reign in the burning pit of jealousy hollowing the bottom of my stomach. I know I shouldn't be feeling this way when I'm married, and I didn't think he'd be celibate for seven years when I'm the one who broke his heart.

But I can't help it.

"Is…Aspen one of them?"

"Could be."

"She's pretty."

"She is."

"Reina called her a redhead witch."

"Reina is still a bitch sometimes. Aspen is a beautiful woman."

"Then go back to your *beautiful* Aspen."

"I'll see her at the firm once my sick leave is over."

"Well, good luck."

"Thanks."

"You're not supposed to agree with that."

"But you're the one who was saying she's pretty and wishing me good luck."

"It's just figure of speech, asshole."

"You're the definition of Tsundere."

"Shut up." I pull away from him and place a hand on my hip. "You have to do something about her. I don't want to share you."

"Are you going to do something about your husband?"

I bite my lower lip.

"You can't ask me to be exclusive with you while you're on another man's arm, Naomi. That's not how it works."

"I…know."

"What do you know? Do you know about how fucking enraged I become when I see you with him? You were smiling at the motherfucker in all the pictures online."

"It was an act."

"One you pulled so well."

"Do you want me to cry then?"

"I want you to leave him once and for all. This is not up for fucking negotiation."

"I want to leave him, too and I'm plotting something. Akira needs to be the one who divorces me while still being Father's ally. If I initiate it, my father will come after you."

"I don't give a fuck about that."

"No, Sebastian. No! I didn't sacrifice seven damn years just to crash and burn now."

He grabs me by the arm and pulls me close, his eyes darkening like a lethal storm. "I won't see you on his fucking arm again, Naomi. Do you hear me? I don't care if he's gay. He still puts his fucking hands on you. He still touches you. I'll kidnap you and get us both killed instead of seeing that scene again. You're fucking mine and that means you belong with me, not with some other asshole."

"Then get rid of Aspen, too. The next time I see her on your arm, I'll kick you in the balls."

"You will, huh?"

"Yes! And you know what else I'll do? I won't let you chase me."

"Now, that is pure torture."

"Torture is seeing you with another woman and not being able to do anything about it."

"There's no other woman, baby."

"Huh?"

"Aspen and I are in a strictly professional relationship."

"Then…why is she always on your arm?"

"Because I wanted to hurt you as much as you hurt me."

"That's just…cruel."

"You were cruel, too."

I release an involuntary breath that comes after too much crying. "Aren't we so toxic?"

"We are?"

"Yeah, we keep hurting one another."

"Not anymore."

"But it hurts, Sebastian. Thinking about you with Aspen and other women hurts."

"There haven't been any other women."

"W-what?"

"I've never been in a relationship since you."

"Oh."

"Not even for sex. I wanted to that first year, just so I could erase you, but I couldn't get it up for anyone. Except for the memory of you while I was in the shower. Thanks for the world's longest cockblock."

"Wait…you never had sex with anyone else?"

"Not since Owen's party. My dick blames you for his strained relationship with my hand, by the way."

I smile, my heart feeling lighter than it has in years.

"What are you smiling at, Tsundere? My dick's issue is a real one. That's why I nearly broke you that first time after you came back."

I wrap my arms around his neck. "I'm just happy."

"Wow. You're happy for my dick's misery? Now he'll really hate-fuck you."

I laugh. "No, I'm happy because you never forgot about me. It makes everything worth it."

"Who'll make up for my slaughtered sex drive?"

I lick my lips. "I'll apologize with my lips. They're friends with your cock."

"That would be a good start. But hate-fucking is still on the menu."

"Isn't it always on the menu?"

"We'll take it up a notch this time."

I hop up his body and Sebastian staggers backward as my legs and arms wrap around him.

He holds me steadily with an arm and smiles. "Is this an invitation, baby?"

"For you? I'm always asking for it."

I squeal as I jump off of him and he eats up the distance between us in a fraction of a second. I turn and take the stairs, then I break out in laughter as we strip each other and tumble into the shower.

Happiness.

This is what happiness feels like and I wish I could stay in it forever.

Even if I know it won't last.

THIRTY-SIX

Akira

Dear Yuki-Onna,

I touched you.

In my dream, I mean. Let's take a moment to thank the Lord and all of his angels that I didn't think I would ever be grateful to.

For the first time since forever, you didn't vanish into thin air right after you blew me and you let me sink my fingers into your inky hair. I want to be a dick and say that it resembles Sadako from The Ring, but I will rein in the assholish tendencies today.

Because your hair? Yeah, it definitely felt like smooth silk and all the beautiful shit I didn't think I believed in.

Apparently, I'm that fucking sappy and I totally believe in pretty things. Or maybe I only believe in them when it comes to you. Give me my grumpy self back, Naomi.

Anyway, you slowly slid up my hot and bothered body like a kitten and I swear to fuck, I can almost hear you purring. Oh, and did I mention you were naked? Nice to meet you, Naomi's body, we're definitely going to be buddies going forward.

You should've told me you had tits that could turn a saint into a sinner and a nun into a whore because, holy fuck, I totally wanted to stuff my face in them and never come out for air. But I settled with only touching them and teasing you until you moaned. And, yes, I was careful, not because I didn't want to give us what we both wanted, but because I was dreading the moment you'd vanish and I would have to wake up all alone without your tits—I mean you.

But you didn't go.

You even dry humped me, making me hard in an instant all over again, and fuck, I never liked something I should be so embarrassed about. And I had to drag you to my camp and yank away the seductive look in your eyes and rise up to the challenge you were taunting me with.

So I grabbed you by the arm and flipped you onto your stomach and then ate you out. I feasted on your pussy as if I were a dying man and you were my last fucking meal. And your taste? Yeah, it's something I will be telling stories about to my Grim Reaper.

But what I loved the most is the erotic sounds you made. The way you moaned, "Please, more...please, fuck me, make me cum....I'm all yours. This pussy is yours..."

And fuck me, those sounds almost made me ejaculate without friction. But I didn't, because I had a mission; one that included ripping all the sounds from you. So when I felt you clenching around my tongue, I released your pussy, parted your ass cheeks, and moved on to your back hole, then thrust my fingers into your dripping cunt.

Yes, I'm filthy, but not as much as you are because you came around my tongue moments after I ate your ass.

Best oral I've ever given. And I'm not a giver.

I was so ready to let my dick have his turn with your soaked cunt, but then you disappeared. Fucking again. And I had to wake up, dripping in sweat and with my hands strangling my cock. Oh, and I had cum all over my stomach.

Not cool, Naomi.

Next time, the least you can do is stay until the end.

Preferably never let me wake up.

Your dirty, **dirty** pen pal,
Akira

THIRTY-SEVEN

Naomi

WE SPEND THE NIGHT IN MOM'S HOUSE.

It's so different from the past but still feels the same.

We're still those college kids who snuggled up together in front of the TV while Sebastian tried to touch me inappropriately at any given moment. We're still as comfortable in the silence as when we're having a conversation.

But it's different now, more jaded, broken.

We're both hurt, haunted, and both spent a long time hollow.

Being filled all at once is both thrilling and painful.

But it's never felt so…rewarding.

After taking a shower together, where Sebastian took me against the wall, we lay down to watch a true crime show.

But we didn't really pay attention to it, we just faced each other and talked.

About the pain.

About the longing.

About everything.

I kept it all inside and when it came out, it was uncensored and unrestrained.

It was like purging.

Sebastian told me about how he passed the bar and severed his relationship with his grandparents. He told me about the role Nate played in his new life and the friends he has in the firm. He told me about how he used work to escape his emotions.

In a way, it was the same for me, so I spoke about that and how my life in Japan was. I tell him about the new family I found and that Mio—and sometimes Kai—is the only thing I like about it.

The night went on and we barely slept. Between the talking and the cuddling and the slow hum of the TV in the background, we were just in our own world.

And then the light of day slipped through the window.

I groan, hiding my face in Sebastian's naked pectoral muscle. "I want it to be nighttime again."

He chuckles, the hum of his chest creating a vibration against my hardening nipples. "It'll be night in a few hours."

"I want it now."

"Used to the darkness, baby?"

"I'm more comfortable in it, I guess."

"That's why we're compatible."

Inhaling his bergamot scent, I run my fingers over the two tattooed lines over his chest and then trace them to the scar from the bullet wound on his shoulder. The thought that I could've lost him still fills me with an incomparable amount of fear.

Probably because it could happen again.

"I hate that we have to go back to real life."

"We don't have to, baby."

"You're a hotshot lawyer and I don't want Nate to hate me because I'm taking you away from the firm."

"I see you're still starstruck by Nate."

"What? He's cool."

"Don't say that fucking word about another man."

"He's your uncle, jerk."

"Still a man."

"You're impossible." I laugh.

"Not more than you."

"Me?"

"You said you don't share, remember?"

"Well, I don't."

He tightens his arms around me. "Then I'm not sharing either. I'll just kidnap you until you file for divorce."

"Kidnap me in my own home?"

"Even kinkier."

I playfully hit his shoulder. "Stop it."

"Not until you're officially mine."

"It'll take time."

"That's why I'm keeping you. There's no going back to Japan or that fucker again."

"Hey. Japan is beautiful."

"I'm well aware of that."

"Because…you were born there?"

"How do you know that?"

"I just do. Why didn't you tell me?"

"Reasons."

"What type of reasons?"

"If you haven't figured it out, I won't spell it out for you—at least not yet."

"That's unfair."

He grins and I stop and stare as my chest flutters. It doesn't matter how many years have passed, he's still the only man able to twist my stomach and make me fall head over heels. I met ten years ago, and I still have a major crush on him.

I don't think I'll ever stop.

Running my fingers over the hard ridges of his chest, I say, "We have so much in common. I'm Japanese but American-born and you're American but Japanese-born."

"Fucking fate throwing a Tsundere my way, huh?"

I laugh. "Shut up, asshole."

"I love it when you show me tough love."

I elbow him and he winces. "Have you ever thought about going back to Japan?"

"No. It reminds me of my parents' deaths."

"I'm sorry."

"I'll go with you, though."

"Really?"

"I'd go anywhere in the fucking world with you, baby."

I can tell I'm blushing without looking at myself in the mirror. I'm twenty-eight, yet he still makes me blush like the teenager I was the first time I saw him.

"You would?" I whisper.

"I'll fucking chase you this time."

I pull away from him. "What about now?"

His eyes darken with that haze that I love so much about him. "You want me to chase you now?"

"I don't know." I inch to the edge of the sofa.

"Maybe I'll fuck you harder this time."

"Oh, yeah?"

"I'll fuck you good, fuck you right until you scream."

"You will?"

"It'll hurt."

"Mmm."

"I'll be rough."

"Yes, please."

"It'll be out of fucking control."

"Yeah?"

"It'll be everything you need and more."

"What are you waiting for? Catch me," I whisper in a sultry voice and bolt.

Sebastian's grunt follows after me as I head toward the stairs, then stop and change direction toward the kitchen's back balcony.

If he catches me on the stairs, I don't have a damn chance.

He's right behind me and I can feel him closing in on me.

I don't stop as I open the balcony door with shaking fingers and sprint around the built-in table on the porch.

Thankfully, only the trees and a few faraway houses are in sight, but any of the neighbors could come out and see me naked.

A large hand grips me by the elbow and I shriek, then try to butt his chin. Sebastian evades me and pushes me on my back on the table. "Got you, baby."

"No, no…let me go!"

I hit at his naked chest, leaving scratch marks, but he easily subdues my wrists and slams them at the top of my head.

"I'm going to fuck you so thoroughly, you won't be able to move, let alone leave."

"Let me go!"

"Scream louder for the neighbors to hear how much of a greedy slut you are. *My* slut."

His chest covers mine as he kicks my legs apart and thrusts inside me. He does it with no preparation whatsoever, and it's so fucking delicious.

The burn turns me speechless as my body takes all of him in.

I'm wet from the small chase and I moan loudly as he drives into me with a force that pushes me across the table.

I flex my fingers above my head, but they barely move with his savage hold on my wrists.

He's like the beast, crushing me, taking me, owning me.

Making my every desire come true.

"Sebastian!"

"Yes, baby. Call my name."

"Sebastian!"

"Call me the way you did seven years ago."

"What?"

He rolls his hips, hitting deeper as pressure builds inside me at a maddening rhythm and then it's relief and then it's pressure again.

"You know. Say it."

"Baby?"

He thickens inside me and his rhythm spirals out of control. "Say it again."

"Fuck me, baby. Take me."

"How should I take you?"

"Rough, hard…give it to me, please…"

"Who's the only one who gets to fuck your tight little cunt?"

"You…"

"Who's the only one you unravel around?"

"You!"

"Who the fuck do you belong to?"

"You, Sebastian! You!" The words match his maddening rhythm and they're so liberating, so freeing that I wish I'd said them before.

"Now tell me what you said back then, Naomi. Right before you left the cell."

"I…"

"Say them, Naomi."

"I love you!" I scream as my orgasm hits me and wetness like I've never felt before pours out of me and soaks my thighs. But I don't focus on the embarrassment as I scream, "I love you, Sebastian!"

"Only me?"

"Only you."

Sebastian fucks me harder as he looks over my shoulder. "Heard that, motherfucker?"

I roll my head back, catching sight of none other than Akira. He stands behind us, watching the show with his usual penetrating gaze. His posture is so still, he can be mistaken for a statue.

Mortification grips me at being watched this way, whether by him or anyone else.

True, my nakedness is fully covered by Sebastian's body, but still.

He doesn't stop, though. He fucks me rougher, faster, ripping a moan from deep inside me.

At that moment, no one else matters. Not Akira, not anyone. It's just me and Sebastian.

I moan his name, riding the pleasure until he empties deep inside me. And then I'm coming again with his name at the tip of my tongue.

Jesus. I'm so depraved.

I just had sex with Sebastian in front of my husband, yet all I feel is the need for more.

THIRTY-EIGHT

Sebastian

I STARE UP IN THE ONYX EYES OF AKIRA FUCKING MORI.

The man who didn't only marry my Naomi, but also stayed with her for years.

The man who saw her every day, talked to her every day, touched her every day when I didn't even know where she was.

Naomi stays limp underneath me as my front covers hers and my cum and her juices drip down her thighs.

Akira snuck up to the porch as I was driving into her and stood there, silent, watching with a slight rise in his brow.

The most logical thing to do would've been to stop and hide her from him.

But I didn't.

He had to see that she only belongs to me.

That she fucking loves me.

That he'll only ever be a phase in her life. A fucked-up one at that.

She's mine, neither he nor anyone else will take her away from me again.

After the way she broke down last night, I swore that I'd never leave her to battle the pain alone. I'll be with her every step of the way.

Until last night, I'd been suffocating with each passing second. I'd been dying and she was the only air I could breathe.

She was taken away for years. Seven. And she spent them by this fucker's side.

"I'm sorry, should I be clapping right now?" said fucker asks. "Maybe shout a bravo or two."

"Get the fuck out of here." I hold on to my calm while wrapping a hand around Naomi's waist.

"I'm afraid I didn't come just to leave. As much as I appreciate the voyeuristic shows my wife and I keep giving each other, it's not the reason I had her followed and came here. We need to go, Naomi."

"Like fuck she will."

"We promised to have breakfast with your father, remember?"

Naomi stiffens at the mention of her dad and I stroke my thumb on the wrists that I'm still holding.

"I'm not going," she whispers.

"Really now? Hitori-san will be upset, and I suppose Mio-chan will have to pay." He steps closer, then brushes past me to the house. "Come inside whenever you're ready, Nao."

Her lips twist when he disappears through the door. "Let me talk to him."

"I'm going with you."

She sighs but says nothing as I slide out of her and carry her. Her frail arms wrap around my neck and she buries her head in the nook of my shoulder, releasing a satisfied sound.

I want her to make those sounds for the rest of our lives.

Instead of following the path Akira took, I walk around the house and slip inside through another back entrance.

We go upstairs and I clean her and then myself, making sure the fucker waits until we're both fully dressed.

I even sit her down in front of a vanity and brush her hair, letting the thick black strands slip through my hands.

Naomi smiles at me through the mirror. "We have to go down, Sebastian."

"Or we can stay here until he gives up and leaves."

"Akira? Give up? Those words don't exist in his perfectionist vocabulary. He'll just pester us and even come up here."

"Or I can pummel the fucker's face against the wall."

"No. Don't. He'll take it personally and make sure you pay ten times worse." She turns around, forcing me to release her hair as she stands up and strokes my cheek. "Let me do the talking. I'm used to his stupid antics."

I grunt, but I lead her out of the bedroom.

Akira has made himself at home and has sat down on the sofa as he checks his phone. Naomi stands on tiptoes to see what he's focused on as a small smirk lifts his mouth.

Upon noticing us, he tucks his phone away and smiles in that fake, political way. "There you are. I thought you went for another round."

Naomi sits on the chair across from him, but instead of taking the other available chair, I sit on the armrest and wrap an arm around her slender shoulder. Her breathing slows for a bit and she flashes me a small smile.

"We would've if you'd left," I tell Akira.

"So it appears I cockblocked you just like my wife did not so long ago. Now, where was I? Right. Naomi. Have you forgotten our deal?"

"No, but I also don't want to do this anymore. I won't be accompanying you at public events either."

I stroke her shoulder but remain silent. I understand her need to personally do this, so I just support her through it.

Akira leans forward in his seat, intertwining his fingers. "The point of keeping an image is to appear in public together."

"We won't need to, because you'll divorce me."

"And if I say no?"

"I already made my threat. I won't repeat it."

"You don't want to stand in the way of my plans, Naomi. I can and will crush you both. It wouldn't feel so great if Weaver here dies of an accident similar to his parents, would it?"

I stiffen. "How the fuck do you know about that?"

"Because I have connections. Don't make me use them."

Naomi lifts her chin. "Don't make me use what I know either."

"Is this your final decision?"

"Yes." She doesn't hesitate.

"I hope you're ready for the consequences."

I jerk up, march over to him, and grab him by the collar. "Threaten her again and I will fucking kill you."

He merely smirks as he shoves me away, then looks at her. "Making an enemy out of me is a grave mistake and you know it, my dear wife."

"Get the fuck out." I motion at the door.

He nods at her and leaves, walking as slowly as physically possible.

After the door closes behind him, Naomi slumps in her chair, holding her head in her hands.

I go to her and gather her in my arms. She doesn't fight as her trembling body snuggles against my chest. "It's going to be okay, baby."

"No, it won't. There's also Mio. I can't let her pay the price for my actions."

"She won't."

"You don't know my father, she most definitely will. I...I have to talk to Akira. He's the only one who can help."

"I will not send you back his way."

"It's not like that. I just need to use his weakness against him."

"And what's that?"

"His interest in Ren. He was looking at his pictures just now."

My brows furrow. "The same Ren who abducted us?"

"Yeah. He's one of my father's men."

"And Akira is interested in him?"

"More than interested. He's no longer asexual because of him."

"Why didn't you use it before?"

"Because I only just found out about it. They've met a few times before this year, but this is the first time Akira has acted on his sexual desires. As far as I know."

"I still don't like this."

"It'll be fine. I promise. Just give me a few days."

"One day."

"Sebastian!"

"*One*. I can't stay away from you more than that. Not after I finally have you again."

She rolls her eyes but drops her head on my chest and absentmindedly strokes my arm. I breathe her in, reveling in the peaceful moment.

It took us so long to get to this point and I'll do everything in my power to protect our new beginning.

It's still fragile, but it's ours. Mine and Naomi's.

My phone vibrates and I retrieve it, thinking it's work.

But it's a text from an unknown number.

This is Akira. I forgot to share something earlier. Fine, I didn't forget. I just enjoy playing with you. Here's the thing. Naomi thinks I'm the one who sent her those letters. The ones you used to send through your old Japanese address. See, my family owns that building and I was curious when I learned someone from the United States had rented a PO box with my first name on it and made a request that his letters be sent from that Japanese address back to the States. I thought to myself, there must be a story there. And what a story it was. I read your letters, then put them back into the envelopes and personally handled the shipping. Aren't I a good cupid? But then I thought it would be a beautiful twist of fate if I was the one to have her. As it happened, her father was seeking my alliance and I found the golden opportunity to use her for my own benefit. Don't you think it's a wonderful coincidence that your middle name and my first name are the same, Sebastian Akira Weaver?

THIRTY-NINE

Sebastian

T HOUGH LETTING NAOMI GO IS THE LAST THING I WANT, I do it anyway.

We parted ways as soon as we got to Brooklyn and I might have made out with her for long minutes in public and gave people a show they don't need.

It took a lot of coercing for me to let her go. She's insistent on dealing with the situation herself. I don't fucking want her to. I meant it when I said I'd rather kidnap her and keep her for myself.

If it were up to me, she'd be chained to my bed, where I'd only let her go to chase her.

But the last time one of us decided to handle the whole situation on our own, we were separated for seven fucking years.

Seven years of loneliness.

Of rage.

Of fucking wasted time.

And that won't be the case going forward.

Besides, Naomi needs this for closure. I might have lived on negative emotions all this time, but she suffered, too. Silently. Alone.

And she needs to rip the stitches from her wound on her own. And when she falls, when it hurts, I'll be the one to carry her through it all.

The other reason is Akira's fucking text. He knew about the letters. The asshole was well aware of everything that started ten years ago.

He also knows about my past and my Japanese middle name my grandparents prefer not to mention unless they absolutely have to.

Why do I get the impression that the reason Akira played that card isn't only to taunt me but also because he has a hidden agenda?

But what?

After going back to my apartment and changing clothes, I head to the firm. My head still hurts from the cold, but it's nothing pain-killers can't take care of.

The moment I walk in, I find it in a state of chaos.

Daniel sits on Candice's desk, talking to the new interns and grinning for the sole purpose of showing his godamn dimples.

"I know you guys meant to go into my office and made the small mistake of walking into the wrong one." He snaps his fingers. "Come on, Kate, Omar. Grab your things and come to my world of fun."

They look between Daniel and Candice, who's standing by her office, crossing her arms and tapping her leg on the floor.

"Like hell they are," she snaps. "You should leave, Mr. Sterling."

"Stay out of it, Candice." He doesn't pay her any attention as he continues his grinning session. "I promise more fun than the cold-hearted idiot."

"Mr. Sterling, please get off my desk so we can work."

"One sec, Candice. Don't you have a sick boss to take care of?" He winks at Kate and Omar. "I never get sick, because my physique is strong. See these muscles? I played football in high school. Soccer for you guys."

Candice raises a brow. "And Sebastian played football, *real* football, in both high school and college."

"It's not real football, love. The real one has the right name. Foot and ball. Not hand and whatever ball." He directs his smile at the interns. "Lunch later? I'm more generous than your current boss."

My assistant taps her foot manically at this point. "Are you going to get out or should I call Mr. Weaver? The *senior* Mr. Weaver who owns this whole place."

"Jesus, Candice. Does Sebastian pay you extra to hold down the fort in his absence?"

"I don't, but I'll start to." I walk inside Candice's office and both interns stand up in greeting, still flustered by my colleague's advances.

I give a hand gesture, so they sit back down.

"Aren't you supposed to be sick?" Daniel jumps off from the desk, not bothering to hide his displeasure.

"You are." Candice directs her no-nonsense gaze at me. "You should be resting."

"I have important things to do. But first, Candice, take Kate and Omar to a late breakfast."

My assistant gives Daniel the side-eye as if telling him, 'See?'

"Hey, not fair—"

Daniel hasn't finished his sentence when I grab him by the collar of his jacket and drag him with me into my office.

As I kick the door shut, he pulls away and fixes his jacket, grumbling, "I'm suing you for assault."

"Really? Physical assault because I dragged you?"

"No. Assault against fashion. The envy is real, mate."

"Is that why you were trying to take my interns?"

"I was getting back what should've been originally mine. You stole them."

"Don't admit defeat then. Now, tell me how far you've gotten with information on Akira Mori?"

Daniel sits on the chair's armrest and fingers the pencils on my desk. "The man is a sodding fort. There's nothing to get."

"How about Knox?"

"He doesn't have much either. Just some shady transactions here and others there, which he only managed to get info about by pulling strings back home. His foster father doesn't like digging into his partners' personal lives."

"So he's spotless?"

"Legally? Squeaky clean."

"Morally?"

"He has dubious relations with the Yakuza, but they use phantom LLCs all the time. So even if there's a legal way to prove involvement, it'll take decades—that is if you stay alive during the process."

Fuck.

All this time, I had some sort of hope that Akira could be taken care of legally.

Or at least, he could be hurt.

"What's your deal with Akira, anyway?" Daniel tilts his head. "This whole thing can't be because you want to secure a client. You don't even search for new people like Knox and me, who, by the way, are always on hunting missions for fresh blood."

I've gone on a hunt, countless times, but it was never for a client.

"It's the wife, isn't it?" He grins, a sly one that makes the sharp lines of his face harsher.

"She's not his wife." Or at least, she won't be soon.

"I always wondered who would be your type. Never thought it would be a married woman."

"And what's your type? A skirt?"

"Brunettes in a skirt. Abso-fucking-lutely."

"A blonde broke your heart?"

His lips twist in what resembles disgust before he smirks. "Not as much as Akira's wife broke yours."

"Stop calling her that."

"Hit a nerve? This shit's got my interest piqued and I need the inside scoop. Which of the rumors is true?"

"What rumors?"

"They say you broke her heart in college and she married some-one more powerful than you and threw it in your face."

"That's not true."

"Pity. I would've done that." His usually joyous features scrunch into a frown. "If someone betrayed me, I'd make sure to slowly de-stroy their lives until they fell to their knees at my feet."

"Someone betrayed you? Is it the blonde?"

"*Maaaybe.*" He shakes his head, seeming to pull himself out of a trance. "But this isn't about me. This is about you and your Japanese princess. Sorry, I mean, Akira Mori's princess."

"Call her that again and I'll punch your face so hard, no doc-tor will be able to put it back together."

"Bloody hell, mate. Not the face! This shit is real estate."

"Then don't make me destroy it."

"I'm just warning you so you don't get yourself and us in trou-ble. If you're gone, Nate won't have his beloved prince and we won't have anyone to throw under the bus when we screw up."

I raise a brow but say nothing.

"Anyway, do what you like, but don't forget who Akira Mori is. He might be new to the States, but he's something entirely dif-ferent internationally. The Mori family is very influential domes-tically. Not only because of their bloodline, but also because they have direct relations with the emperor of Japan and other business tycoons across Asia. And let's not forget his recent black diamond fortune that I told you about."

I couldn't give two fucks about his power. Either he lets Naomi go or we'll both die while trying to free her from him.

The door of my office opens and my uncle comes in, his hard gaze taking in the scene in front of him.

Daniel grins. "Nate! I was just telling Sebastian that you're my favorite boss."

"Save the ass-kissing for Van Doren, Sterling."

"Thanks for putting that weird image in my head." Daniel makes a face and points at me. "I'll throw you the best funeral when you get yourself killed, Weaver Prince. And then I'm taking away your interns."

He leaves with an evil laugh that I shake my head to as I fall into the seat behind my desk.

My uncle doesn't sit down. Instead, he merely places a hand in his pocket as he observes me closely.

"What is it, Nate?"

"I was told you came to work when you're still on a sick leave."

"I'm fine."

"Die someplace else that isn't my firm, Rascal."

"You'll get good press out of it."

"Not if the cause of death is exhaustion." He narrows his eyes at me. "What are you up to?"

"A lot of things and nothing at the same time."

"Let me guess, it has something to do with Naomi?"

Everything has had to do with Naomi since the day I said yes to that fucking bet. I've fought it over the course of time, but that doesn't change the place she currently occupies in my life.

Or that she should've been in seven fucking years ago.

Nate takes my silence as affirmation and sighs. "I knew you'd get yourself in trouble because of her the day you kissed her on TV without caring if Mr. and Mrs. Weaver saw you."

I grin. "Remember how Mrs. Weaver clutched her pearls? Priceless."

"Her reaction doesn't make you less impulsive. Or stupid."

"Stupidity is accepting that she was gone. Besides, getting back what was originally mine isn't impulsive, Uncle."

"It certainly is if you lose control of your head for it."

"You're only saying that because you've never loved someone so much that being apart from them feels like drowning and burning alive at the same time. You've never stayed up all night, staring at the fucking sky with the minuscule hope that she's also staring at it from a different nook in the world. You've never loved, period,

Uncle. You're nearing your forties and still are a cold-blooded bach-elor with no settling down in sight."

"Why settle down when you can be free? And you're right, I've never loved and I don't plan to. It's all a stupid idea of nothingness that fools like you believe in. It's not real. Not tangible. And cer-tainly not lucrative."

"If Mrs. Weaver hears you say that, she'll have a stroke."

He smiles, but it soon vanishes. "What do you plan to do now?"

"The only thing I can do. Bring down Akira."

"That's not wise."

"And neither is being hollow for seven years."

"Akira has dangerous allies, Sebastian."

"I'm not a kid anymore."

"You don't understand." He places a palm on the desk and leans forward. "He has allies you should never cross paths with."

"I won't know until I take my chances."

"You will stop this nonsense of going against Akira and that's fucking final."

"No."

"Sebastian…"

"No, Uncle. I'm not going to stand back this time and then lose my mind when she fucking disappears again."

"This is about *your* life."

"I'm well aware of the risks."

"No, you're not. I didn't want to tell you this, but you need to know what you're getting yourself into."

"What are you talking about?"

Nate unbuttons his jacket and sits across from my desk. "Your parents didn't really die due to an accident."

"I kind of figured that out on my own. Mom embezzled some-thing and she paid for it with her and Dad's lives."

"How do you know that?"

"The day they passed, I overhead them when we were in the car. As I grew up, I connected the dots."

"That's not the end of it. Do you know who Julia stole from?"

"Who?"

"The Yakuza. I don't know if it's the same branch Akira's connected to, but it could be."

My pulse quickens as the pieces of the puzzle start falling together. The fact that Ren knew about my tattoos and the accident back then all point in one direction, but I don't want to think about its relation to Naomi.

So I say, "My parents already paid for it."

"They did, but you were supposed to die with them. Instead, you were held prisoner in the hospital for ransom."

"I was what?"

"You were kidnapped in Japan. They called Mr. and Mrs. Weaver and told them that if they didn't pay, they wouldn't be seeing their grandchild again."

"They...paid?"

"Of course they did. They might have cut Nick off when he chose to be with Julia, but they always had this misconception that sooner or later, he'd come crawling back into their laps. So when they learned their precious eldest son had died, it devastated them. You were all they had left of Nick, therefore, they didn't hesitate to pay the kidnappers."

"But it's done. They released me."

"With a final note that said, 'His life is ours now. Make sure he keeps his mouth and eyes shut if you don't want him to end up like his parents.' Mrs. Weaver burned that note and put the whole incident behind her as if it never happened. But I knew there'd come a time when you'd cross those people's paths again. And here we are. Nick and Julia lost their lives because they messed with the wrong crowd. Don't repeat your parents' mistake, Sebastian. Don't walk toward death with your own two feet."

I lean back in my chair and let the information sink it, then I release a sigh. "But that's the thing, Uncle. I'd rather die than live without being alive."

FORTY

Naomi

I MAKE IT TO MY FATHER'S HOUSE.

Though I'm late, so the whole breakfast thing is over and everyone has moved on to doing their chores.

Mio tells me that Akira is with Father in his office and invites me to join her while she trains.

"Not this time." My attention is focused on the second story where my father's office is.

My sister's shoulders hunch and she fingers her bamboo sword. "Is something wrong, *Onee-chan?*"

"Nah," I say absentmindedly.

"Are you mad at me because I agreed to marry the Russian?"

I break eye contact with the building and stare back at her. Sometimes, I forget just how delicate my little sister is, and I don't only mean physically. Yes, she has soft cheekbones, a small nose and lips, and huge almond eyes, but she's also fragile on the inside.

Despite her love for kendo, Mio is the type who bawls her eyes out while watching an emotional scene in a movie. She's also a bit naive, always finding the best in people before the worst. No clue where she got that trait from, because everyone surrounding her is monstrous. My father is at the top of that list.

"No, of course not, Mio. I'm mad at Father, not you."

"But I agreed to it. I'm fine with it."

"You think you're fine with it, but you don't know those people or how dangerous they are."

"I can take care of myself. I'm not a baby."

It's useless to tell her that she doesn't know what she's getting herself into. She might be sheltered, but she's as determined and rigid as one of her damn swords. She takes after our bastard father.

So I'll just work on resolving this from the background without getting her involved.

"Okay, fine."

She narrows her eyes. "You're brushing me off."

"How could I do that to my cute little Mio?" I take her chin and shake her by it, causing her to smile before she pulls away.

"You're doing it again, *Nee-chan*."

"Doing what again?"

"Treating me like I'm a little girl."

"Sorry. I guess you'll always be my baby sister."

"I'm grown up."

"Yes, you are." And that's not a good thing. Knowing my father, he'll eventually find a way to thrust her into a situation that will break her.

But not if I'm there for her.

"*Nee-chan?*"

"Yeah?"

"I…saw him."

"Who?"

"The man Papa wants me to marry. His name is Damien Orlov and he's a leader in the Bratva."

"How the hell did you see him?"

"I just…did."

"You don't even go out, Mio."

She bites her lower lip. "I do sometimes."

"And? How did you see this Damien?"

"I happened to run into him." I don't miss the hesitation at the end or how her throat bobs with a swallow.

"Mio…did he do something to you?"

"He was big, *Onee-chan*. Like *huge*. He was bigger than anyone I've seen. He's even bigger than Kai. I didn't think anyone could be bigger than Kai."

"That's because you don't know the world."

"But I want to." A spark shines in her eyes and she fingers her sword. "I need to, *Nee-chan*, and if I stay with Papa, I won't be able to."

"And you think marrying this Damien would be the magical solution?"

"No, but at least it would be my choice."

It's not. It's Father's choice, but I don't get to tell her that as she excuses herself and leaves, her shoulders snapped in a line.

As soon as she disappears from view, I let my smile drop and take the steps two at a time until I reach my father's office.

Ren stands in front of it wearing a suit without a tie. He touches his black dot earring when I come into view and glares at me.

I let my lips stretch into a taunting smile. "Are you here for Father or your lover?"

"Shut the fuck up," he hisses, searching his surroundings. "And that psycho isn't my lover."

"Looked like it when he was cutting you up while doing… other things."

"You obviously liked watching. Are you a psycho as well?"

"I could be, especially after what you did seven years ago. How does it feel to be helpless and at the mercy of someone stronger than you, Ren? Does it burn? Does it *hurt*? Do you feel like your insides will explode from frustration?"

"I'm not helpless. I can kill the bastard anytime I want."

"And be killed by my father in return?"

"Maybe it'd be worth it to get rid of the vermin."

"Maybe you're lying to yourself, because if you wanted to kill Akira, you would've done so already."

"Or maybe I'm biding my time."

I place a hand on his shoulder and lean close enough to make his eyes widen and his mind probably question what I'm doing.

"I pity you for gaining Akira's interest, Ren. I really do. But if you get in my way or threaten me and Sebastian again, whether solo or under your bosses' orders, I'll destroy you like you did me seven years ago. I fucking promise you that."

"Am I included in that threat?" Kai's suave voice cuts through the tension between me and Ren. I step back, but only after I know he's gotten the message loud and clear.

Ren stiffens, probably wondering how much Kai has heard. I can tell he's ashamed of his unorthodox liaisons with Akira. And on top of that, he's aware that if my father's second-in-command learns about it, he'll definitely cut him to pieces.

"I don't know." I face Kai and cross my arms over my chest. "You saved my life, but you stole it away from me later, so it's always a gray area with you. But if you get Sebastian involved again, I won't hesitate to bury you, just as I will Ren."

"You're wise, *Ojou-sama*, but you might want to save that talk for the one who matters." He motions at the door of the office.

With a deep breath, I knock, then go inside without waiting for approval.

The office is done in shades of green and brown. There are bookshelves stuffed with more antiques than actual books, and countless paintings and calligraphies decorate the walls. Kai once told me that my father got those priceless paintings from the black market and sometimes uses them as transaction money instead of actual cash.

Some of them have values that go into the hundreds of thousands. As a wedding gift, my father gave us calligraphy that cost millions of dollars.

I don't know where Akira put it or if he even kept it. I've sure as hell never asked about it.

My father and my husband sit around the coffee table, drinking tea and talking animatedly in Japanese.

When they notice me, their conversation comes to halt. A bright spark shines in my future ex-husband's eyes. He probably thinks I came here for him and to honor the deal we made seven years ago.

Well, he has another thing coming.

"Breakfast was half an hour ago, Naomi," my father reprimands.

"She had an emergency, Hitori-san," Akira lies on my behalf.

"Not really. I just don't see why I should have breakfast with you when I hate you, Father."

His cheeks redden and he grips the teacup tighter. If there's anything Abe Hitori despises more than being defied, it's being disrespected, especially in public where it's considered a humiliation. Due to his control-freak tendencies and role in the Yakuza, he's used to having his demands met.

"Do you have a death wish?" he grinds out.

Maybe that's exactly what I have, because right now, pressure is building inside me. Or maybe it's been festering there for years. Either way, it needs a release.

I need a release.

I need to finally drop the mask and be me again.

I need to be the Naomi who didn't let anyone walk all over her, because that's what her mom taught her.

"Akira and I need to talk," I say.

"We already talked, dear wife, and you chose to disobey me, so I had Abe here send for your lover. We don't want her to ruin our partnership, do we, Hitori-san?"

"Indeed, Mori-san." My father glares at me. "You should've known better than to test us."

My legs shake and it takes everything in me to not fall to the ground. "S-send for him? What do you mean by *send for him?*"

"It means he's in our custody." My father reaches for a remote and turns on the TV. I cease breathing when a cell comes into view.

And not just any cell.

The same cell that Sebastian and I were locked in seven years ago. Only, this time, I'm not there. Sebastian is. Alone.

On the ground.

Unmoving.

Oh, God.

No, no, no…

For years, I had nightmares about this same scene every single night. In my dreams, I would miss him so much and have a moment of weakness and go to him. I would kiss him, touch him, sleep in his arms, but then my father and Akira would *always* kill him.

Right in front of me so I would learn a lesson.

The reason I had to resist Sebastian was for this exact reason. I preferred breaking and stomping all over my own heart so he wouldn't end up in this position again.

I foolishly believed I could change things. That I could finally be with him despite everything.

But I'm late.

Too late.

My hands tremble and my eyes sting with unshed tears as I stare at the screen. A burning sensation rushes to the surface, threatening to spill over.

No. Please.

Please, Sebastian. You can't leave me now after I finally found you again.

"He's not dead," Akira announces. "But he will be if you don't keep your part of the deal."

A tinge of relief expands in my chest, but it's short-lived at the lurking threat behind Akira's words.

I knew he disliked being threatened, that he hates not having the upper hand and the control that comes with it, but I pushed his buttons anyway and now he's making me pay.

"Neither you nor anyone else will threaten my business, Naomi. Do you hear me?" My father points at the screen, at Sebastian's inert body. "That little bastard should've died twenty-two years ago for his parents' sin, but I spared his life for his grandparents' money. Turns out, it was never worth it and he should've joined his thieving mother."

I stare between Akira and my father, dumbfounded.

"I told you. It goes way back." My husband motions at a calligraphy hidden by the plant in the corner of the office.

My eyes widen when I read the words in Japanese.

The weak are meat. The strong eat.

Those are the exact words on Sebastian's Japanese tattoo. The same words that he lived by all this time—probably since he was a kid.

"You knew Sebastian's parents?" I ask in a choked voice.

"Only his thieving mother." My father takes a sip of his tea. "She was an assistant at one of our branches that we use as a front to ship illegal paintings. When she found out about that painting which was worth three million at the time, she got greedy and stole it right after the art expert announced its authenticity. She was smart enough to replace it with a forgery and we didn't know until the buyer hired his expert and he told him it was a fake. We figured out she was the thief and hired the truck that hit them. The cause of death was a car accident. As easy as that."

I stumble and catch myself at the last second. The reality of my father's words hit me hard and fast. He killed Sebastian's parents. My father is the reason he was orphaned at a young age and turned out the way he is now.

"You're a monster! How could you do that to a child?"

"His mother stole from me. No one fucking steals from me."

"But Sebastian was there! He was only six years old."

"And he was supposed to die, too, but we used him to milk ransom money from his rich grandparents. Now, I'm thinking that wasn't a very good idea. Don't you agree, Mori-san?"

"No, probably not. We wouldn't have been in this predicament if he'd died at that time. But then again, it wouldn't be this much fun either."

Fun.

Does he really think all of this is *fun?*

I'll show him what fun is like.

"Are you going to get in line, Naomi?" my father asks in a calm tone. "Or should I finish off the life I spared?"

"I'll do as you want. Let him go." My voice is apathetic, but it's not defeated. Sheer determination like I've never felt before pulses in my veins and flows through my raging bloodstream.

This time, it won't go as they dictate.

"No. Not until Akira signs the contract he's here for and you go back to Japan. And we make sure you're not keeping in touch with him."

"But that could take weeks!"

"So be it." He raises his teacup to Akira, who returns the gesture.

I glare at them both, then turn around and leave.

As soon as I close the door behind me, I'm tempted to slide to the ground and weep.

That's what I did seven years ago.

The day of my wedding, I locked myself in a closet and cried for hours.

But that didn't bring me a solution. That didn't let me live in peace or bring me back what I'd lost.

Action does. And it's time I take it.

I stare at Ren and he stares right back, though warily. He touches his pierced ear, then the tattoos on his neck.

"What do you want, *Ojou-sama?*" he asks in a mocking tone, even though he's clearly wary of me.

"A truce."

"Ha. A *truce?* You just threatened me."

"Which is why I'm asking for a truce."

"And what makes you think I want it?"

"You have as much to lose in this as I do. Akira has the upper hand in your relationship, doesn't he?"

His jaw clenches. "Are you sure this is you asking for a truce?"

"Yes. Because I understand what he can be like. He must've

gathered all your weaknesses in a neat file that he uses to threaten you with whenever he thinks you've crossed a line. He's controlling you and playing with you, and you hate it. After all, you're a free spirit not meant to be shackled, caged, or controlled."

Ren's lips purse.

I step closer, softening my voice. "He doesn't *feel*, Ren. Take it from me. I've lived with him for seven years. So when the fun he's having with you is over, he'll just toss you aside as if you never existed. By that time, he'll make sure to break both your dignity and spirit so you have nothing left. And just like that, he'll move on to his next pastime."

Though Akira is capable of all of those things and more, he wouldn't do that to Ren. I know it's different with him—I can sense it—but I need to rile Ren up so he's on my side. Besides, I was right about how much Ren hates Akira's controlling nature. He was always a rebellious soul and my soon-to-be ex-husband is killing that part of him.

My father's guard clenches and unclenches his fists before he releases a long sigh. "What do you want?"

"I'm glad you asked."

I lean over to whisper the plan in his ear. After this, I have to pay a visit to the only people who will help Sebastian.

Even if it means throwing my dignity out the window for it.

FORTY-ONE

Akira

Dear Yuki-Onna,

　　For the first time, you'll receive this as a series of text messages instead of a letter in a black envelope.

　　You must be wondering how I got your number, but it's already saved under my name in capital letters.

　　I've rummaged through it and saw what you call me between you and yourself, my little minx.

　　At this point, you must've stopped whatever you were doing and are questioning why I started my text with the opening you received in letters for damn years.

　　The answer is simple, but not really.

　　See, Naomi. You've been living a lie fed to you by that fucker husband of yours whose murder I'm plotting as we speak.

　　He told you he was me, Akira, your pen pal that you wrote to ever since we were eighteen. But he's only a pervert who read the letters we wrote to each other and then used them to keep us apart and worm himself into your life.

The day I saw you crying then smiling, I fucking had to get close to you, but I didn't want to get too close because I get bored easily.

I didn't want to get bored of you.

The idea of Akira came when I overheard you telling Lucy that you'll one day marry a Japanese.

Here's the thing, I felt a twist in my gut when you said that, but at the same time, I had this idea of becoming what you were looking for.

Don't judge, it really sounded fucking genius at the time.

So I sat down in my room and wrote you that first letter by hand. Then I typed it out because I didn't want you to somehow recognize my handwriting and call me out for being a stupid geek.

Then, I went through all the trouble of renting a PO box in Japan using my middle name, Akira—which also happens to be the first name of your bastard husband, the one he used to get to you. Fucker.

Anyway, I didn't think you'd write back. I was throwing tasteless bait in open water, not really believing I would catch any fish.

But you latched onto that fucking bait and replied.

I wasn't lying that time. I really did grin like a kid who saw boobs for the first time and had a mini hard-on.

Talking to you through those letters was different than I imagined. You were open, more open than anyone I knew in my life.

At some point, I wanted to get close, to grab you by the arm on campus and tell you I'm the same Akira you ask for porn site recommendations. The same Akira you friendzoned so hard that you don't think of him as a man.

That's what stopped me. The fact that you considered me a friend. I thought it was enough at the time. I didn't want to lose the only meaningful friendship I had and the only person I can be my dickish self with and be told off about it.

I even loved how we talked about mundane things without thinking of consequences or what the other thought. We were judgment-free and that was liberating in my closed off, calculated life with my grandparents.

Sappy, I know.

But then, that bet happened and I got to know you in a different way. Not as the nerdy jerk you friendzoned into the following planet, but as the man whose crazy matched yours.

I've got to admit, I was a little mad that you never told Akira that you had those dark fantasies. I felt betrayed as your friend, which is why I turned into a judgy little bitch—and I might be a tiny bit sorry about that.

But at the same time, I felt special as Sebastian because I was the only one who got to see you that way. I got to touch you and fuck you like no other man ever would or could.

Akira still felt bitter and bitchy, though.

Yeah, I know. Jealous of myself much?

I was having an identity crisis. I was so sure you'd figure out I was the same person, so I spiced up the asshole parameter a notch so you'd never put two and two together.

But at some point, the line blurred even for me. I wanted to be the Akira you flipped the finger off to while you spoke to him about everything and I wanted to be the Sebastian that you look at with fuck-me eyes and let him fulfill your every fucked-up fantasy.

When I tried to tell you I'm Akira, though, the timing wasn't right. You found out about the fucking bet and turned your back on me.

I couldn't lose you as Akira, too, so I decided to never associate the two versions of myself to always be in touch with you.

But you ended up leaving us both, anyway.

And to make things worse, your husband used my alter ego to get close to you. I'm wounded that you thought the fucking asshole was me, baby. And you have to make it up to me for the rest of our lives.

Because, here's the thing, I might be as Tsundere as you. Whether as Sebastian or Akira, the only woman who has ever managed to flip my world upside down is you.

And you bet your sweet ass that I will hold you accountable to it for as long as we live.

The one you named BABE on your contact list is the same pen pal who will send you black envelopes on our anniversaries.

He's the pervert who's fucking proud of your eclectic taste in porn.

He's the person you understood and he understood you back.
He's the friend who smiles when reading your words late at night.

He's the man who fucking loves you with everything he has and doesn't have.
Sebastian Akira Weaver

FORTY-TWO

Naomi

I STARE AT THE TEXTS WITH MY LIPS PARTED AND MY JAW practically hitting the floor.

When I went to my father's house this morning, I didn't check my messages or my phone, because my entire focus has been on outsmarting my father and Akira.

But now, when I'm about to call Nate, I noticed the series of texts Sebastian sent me.

Or more like, Akira.

The nerdy pen pal that I always pictured to be quiet and introverted with some sort of a behavioral problem isn't my husband. He's not the man I married, distrusting every word he said in his letters because of his elusive nature.

Akira is none other than Sebastian.

I read and re-read his words, thinking I've missed something or that it's a figment of my imagination. Maybe I'm so worried about Sebastian's state that I'm starting to see things.

But the words in front of me don't lie. Every confession aligns with what I've known about Akira all along. And it's not only his way of talking, but also the little things that have stood out over the years for me when it came to Akira—my husband—and I brushed them off as unimportant.

Such as his lack of a sense of humor. My husband is cold and calculated, and no one can accuse him of being playful. There's also the age part and how he's not from Tokyo, and lately, I discovered he's into knife play, not breath play like Akira from the letters—Sebastian.

All of those things should've been signs, but I wouldn't have suspected him, not when he was being judgmental over my fantasies that he himself triggered. *Asshole.*

And yet, a smile breaks on my lips and my nose tingles as moisture gathers in my lids.

Akira from the letters is Sebastian.

He's not my unfeeling husband. When I thought he was, I mourned the friendship we could've had but didn't.

Turns out, it's been an entirely different person all along.

I'm mad about the whole double identity thing, but at the same time, I can't help the giddiness at knowing he was there for me from the beginning. Even before we were officially together.

"Something good?"

I lift my head from my phone to stare at Kai. He's driving the car after he insisted on escorting me to wherever I wished to go.

There's a chance he's doing this to spy on me for my father, but there's a reason I'm risking having him with me.

I drop the phone in my bag and stare at him. "Nothing you need to worry about."

His lips twitch slightly as if he's well aware of everything going on and is just watching it unfold. "If you say so."

"Why are you here, Kai? Shouldn't you be torturing Sebastian, per your boss's orders?"

"Do you want me to torture him?"

"That's not what I meant." The mere thought of him being hurt causes my stomach to cramp.

"Then what do you mean?"

"You shouldn't be helping me."

"Too late for that. Besides, I'm along for the ride and to see what you'll do."

"You heard me talking to Ren, didn't you?"

"Maybe."

"Are you going to tattle?"

"Tattling is Ren's characteristic, not mine."

"Are you mad at him for selling out Akira and, therefore, endangering your alliance?"

"I don't get mad, *Ojou-sama*. You should know that about me by now."

"You must feel something for what Ren did."

"Hmm." He taps his finger against the steering wheel as he takes a sharp turn to the left that surprisingly doesn't jolt me from my seat. He drives like he lives, always on the edge but without actually making a fatal mistake.

"What does 'hmm' mean?"

"The only feeling I have about Ren's actions is curiosity. He's dug himself into deep holes on all fronts and it'll be nearly impossible for him to escape them all with his head in place, no matter how otherworldly he thinks he is. It'll be fun to watch."

"That's all?"

"That's all."

"Are you telling me you wouldn't punish him?"

"If Abe orders it, of course I'll cut him limb from limb and feed him to my dogs."

"So much for loyalty."

"I'm loyal to principles, not to people, as Ren should've been." He brings the car to an abrupt halt. "We're here."

My insides knot as I stare through the window at the grandiose mansion sitting on a large piece of land. I've been here before, but it was under different circumstances.

I suck in a sharp breath, then step out of the car. Kai

accompanies me as I stand in front of the large metal gate and retrieve my phone.

My hand trembles when I dial Nate's number. I called him as soon as I found out about Sebastian's captivity and convinced him to be the meditator between me and his parents.

I could tell Sebastian's uncle doesn't like to be in debt to his parents, but since it's about his nephew, he agreed.

Nate picks up after one ring. "Are you here?"

"Yeah."

"Come inside."

The line goes dead as the gate opens with a creaking sound. I hesitate and Kai watches me closely as if ready to catch me if I fall, even though both his hands are inert by his sides. He's armed, though. He always is.

"I can go on my own," I say.

"Nonsense."

I lift my chin. "You don't think I can do this alone?"

"Of course I do, but you'll do it faster if they think you could pose a threat."

"This isn't the Yakuza, Kai. Brian Weaver is a politician."

"Which is another word for a mobster." He motions inside. "Come on."

We walk from the gate to the entrance, and although it's not really far, it feels like it takes forever.

A petite woman with a guarded expression opens the door and welcomes us inside.

As soon as we step in, Nate appears in the entrance. He's aged like fine wine and is heading in the silver fox category with flying colors. I'll always respect and adore him for the role he played and continues to do so in Sebastian's life.

He stares at Kai for a beat with his critical gaze, then directs it at me. "Remember what I told you on the phone. Don't try to play on their sympathy. Just their pride."

I nod, even though I have no clue how I would do that. One

would think that when they realize their grandson is in danger, the most logical thing would be to try to save him, regardless of the price.

Apparently, that doesn't apply to the Weavers.

Nate leads me and Kai to what appears to be a reception area. Brian Weaver, who's wearing khaki pants with a white shirt, sits on a chair and is reading from a newspaper. His wife, Debra, is glowing in a designer skirt suit. Pearls surround her neck and dangle from her ears and her golden hair is gathered in a sophisticated bun.

She's sipping from a cup of tea that she places on the table next to her upon our arrival. Brian stares at us from over the top of his newspaper, but he doesn't put it down.

"Hello there," Debra says in a honeyed voice, with a smile that is so fake yet she doesn't attempt to hide. "After your audacious appearance in the charity event, I didn't believe we'd meet again under these circumstances, or any circumstances, really. Don't you think you have some nerve to show up here?"

Nate stands in the middle of the room between us and his parents, his jaw flexing. "Naomi is here because Sebastian has been abducted again, and she knows of a way to save him."

"Save him, then." Brian pierces me with his gaze. "You're obviously the reason he's in this predicament, and the least you can do is get him out of it."

I grind my teeth to hold on to my patience. "If it were that easy, I wouldn't have shown up at your door."

"Why have you, then?" Debra clicks her tongue as she takes a sip of her tea and mutters under her breath, "I told Sebastian a seamstress's daughter isn't fit for him, but he never listens."

"Tsk." Kai shakes his head at them. "Don't talk to her that way or disrespect her again, or you won't live to see the headlines written about you."

Brian folds the newspaper as a red mist crawls up his skin. "Are you threatening me and my wife in my own house?"

"I'm merely relaying ground rules. Naomi has a family behind her, one that is a lot more powerful than your little senate. If you and your wife wish to escape our wrath, do not speak to her in a holier-than-thou tone."

I elbow Kai. I know where he's coming from, but threatening the people whose help I need isn't how I planned to go about this.

Surprisingly, though, Brian straightens and Debra clears her throat. Nate smiles a little, seeming to be enjoying their discomfort a bit too much.

"What do you want?" Brian asks me.

"I know of a way to help Sebastian, and that can be done by blocking my husband's business ventures. You're the only one with enough power to do it fast and efficiently."

"Why should we do that?" It's Debra who asks, her voice hardening with every word. "From what Nathaniel told us, it's your father's doing. The same man who not only murdered my eldest son but has also been threatening my only grandson's life."

"You're not doing this for me, you're doing it for your grandson. Your own flesh and blood whom you gloat about all the time. You owe him that."

"Do not lecture us, young lady." Brian stands up, his shoulders crowding with tension.

"I'm not lecturing you. I'm asking you to do the right thing and help Sebastian."

"And then what?" Debra takes a sip of her tea. "Say we do as you suggest, will you leave this time?"

"Mom…" Nate warns.

"What? Her father killed Nicholas!"

"After *you* sent him away. After *you* disowned him because of your foolish pride. You're as guilty as the killer."

Her lips tremble. "Blame me all you like, but the murderer's daughter doesn't get to be with my grandson. Surely even you can see how messed up this whole thing is."

"That's for her and Sebastian to decide, not you. Stop meddling, stop trying to make your word law, and stop being an unpleasant presence. Just *stop*."

Debra's hand shakes and some tea spills over the rim of the cup she is holding as she places the saucer on the table. She stares at Nate as if he's grown three heads. "Nathaniel! Did you call my presence unpleasant?"

"Do the right thing." Nate's gaze flits between his parents. "For once in your self-indulgent lives, do something for someone other than yourselves."

The tension in the air could be cut with a knife. Both Brian and Debra seem like they want to hit Nate for his insolence and he appears to be waiting for any move just so he can hit back.

"I know you care about Sebastian," I say quietly as they keep glaring at each other. "And while I can't promise to stay away from him, I promise to get your grandson back. So please help me help him."

It's late when Kai and I leave the Weaver mansion. Brian and Debra are still making calls and pulling strings, and while I'd rather stay there and make sure everything's going according to plan, it's obvious that our presence isn't appreciated.

As a compromise, Nate remained behind to keep an eye on his parents and will send us updates when everything's done.

At this rate, Sebastian will spend the night in the cell, all alone and cold, just like seven years ago.

The thought of what my father—and Akira—would do to him just to prove a point drops my blood pressure and makes me feel faint.

"Do you think they're torturing him?" I ask Kai as he drives down a deserted road.

"Could be."

The world closes in on me from all sides. My stomach churns and nausea assaults me in blinding waves. "Stop the car."

Kai hits the brakes and I struggle with the handle before I nearly throw myself out. I use the door for balance to keep myself standing and suck in long intakes of fresh air.

It manages to chase away the nausea, but it doesn't erase the constant ache in my stomach.

Kai appears in front of me, one hand in his pocket and the other offering me a handkerchief. That's when I realize tears are sliding down my cheeks.

I wipe them away fast, not wanting him to see me this weak and out of sorts.

"You care about him that much?"

I bunch the handkerchief in a fist. "Why else would I sacrifice seven years of my life?"

"I figured it was because of Mio."

"She's not the only reason."

"Why him? His family thinks so little of you, and not only that, your father was the reason he was orphaned."

"We don't really get to choose who. It just happens. Like it just happened that you saved me nineteen years ago."

"That was neither coincidence nor fate. I decided to take action."

"Then take it again." I release a long breath, trying not to sound helpless or like I planned this all along when I allowed him to come. "Help me, Kai."

His features remain unchanged, though he tilts his head to the side slightly as if that will allow him a better view of me. "With what?"

"I have something on Akira, an image I can threaten him with for the rest of his life, but I don't have anything on my father. In fact, he has Mio to hold over my head. Even if I get Sebastian out this time, there's no guarantee that he won't kill him just to put me in my place. And I can't…" I gulp past the lump that's gathered in my throat. "I can't live in that type of fear anymore."

"I don't see where I come into this."

"You can give me something to use against him."

"Let's say I do have that something. Why would I hand my boss's weakness over to you?"

"Because you care about me."

"You flatter yourself, *Ojou-sama*. I care about no one. I'm merely curious."

"You do care. It might not be conventional or normal, but you always have since that day you killed Sam to save me. It was your first kill and you told me yourself that act holds a special place in everyone's lives. Yours included."

"Let's presume I do. That doesn't give me a reason to divulge Abe's secret."

"Is my life reason enough?"

He narrows his eyes and a gust of air causes his long hair that's tied at his nape to fly in the wind. "Your life?"

"The same life you've taken pride in saving all these years like you do with your hard-earned swords. I know you see me as some sort of an accomplishment, Kai. Probably the first thing you ever considered to have value. And I hate to end that just to force your hand."

"Is that a threat, *Ojou-sama*?"

"No, I'm merely telling you how it will go if I don't live with Sebastian. I love him, Kai, and you might not understand what that means, but for me, that love is what makes my life wholesome. I can no longer live away from him or be content with watching him from afar. So if you're scheming with my father to shove me back with Akira, then I'll kill myself and finish the life you take so much pride in."

I'm breathing harshly, my limbs shaking due to the force of my words. Kai remains inert, unmoving, as if I hadn't said anything.

"Well played, *Ojou-sama*. I knew I saw something in you even when you were nine."

"Does that mean you'll help me?"

He reaches into his jacket and I think he'll retrieve a gun and shoot me for thinking I could threaten him, but he produces a small black leather notebook and slips it into my bag.

"What's…that?"

"Abe's little black book."

"What?"

"Your father has a system of scamming his most important clients. Once every few years, he'll sell them a forgery among many genuine paintings. They're used to the best quality from him, so they never suspect it. Even when the paintings are found out to be fake, they blame their own people, not Abe. It's a fine line so he can't scam the same person twice or the same group of people within a close timeframe. When he was younger, he used to do this proficiently and even kept us, his closest circle, out of it so he could reap all the profits. I only found out about this practice when he started to keep a record due to his faulty memory a few years ago. That little black book contains the names of the paintings, the people he's scammed, and the years it happened. He's been agitated since he lost it and stopped the whole scamming business altogether. That's why he's desperate about the alliance with Akira. It's for protection more than anything because even though he stopped, he's still in grave danger if that ledger comes to light. We're talking about other powerful crime organization leaders and influential figures who wouldn't hesitate to torture and kill him."

My mouth falls open, then closes. "And you're giving it to me?"

"You asked for something to use against your father. That's his biggest weakness."

"But you could've used it to push him out of power and then become the leader."

"I'm not interested in being on the front line, *Ojou-sama*. Real leadership is done from the background."

Why am I not surprised that he'd rather be the one to pull the strings without showing his face? Kai is a strategist, after all, and even though my father is the head of the Yakuza, Kai might've been the power behind it all along.

"Don't speak a word about having the ledger," he continues. "Let me do the talking with Abe. I'll tell him Akira somehow got hold of it and gave it to you. That way, Abe will always be wary of both of you and wouldn't dare to threaten you again."

"Thank you, Kai."

"You'll only be holding it for me. When I want it back, you'll give it."

"And when will that be?"

He lifts a shoulder. "When I'm sick of using Abe as a front."

"You'll kill him?"

"Why? You don't want that?"

"I don't care as long as Sebastian, Mio, and I are out of this."

"You and Sebastian are debatable. Mio isn't. She wants the marriage and no one will stop her."

"Not even you?"

"Not even me." He stares at his watch. "But shouldn't you be worrying about Sebastian?"

My upset stomach tightens at the mention of him and the thought of what he must be going through.

The unknown awaits us, but this time, I won't let it rip us apart.

FORTY-THREE
Sebastian

MY EYES SLOWLY CREAK OPEN.
Pain assaults the back of my skull and black dots form in my vision even as I slowly get used to my surroundings.

Where the fuck is this place?

The last thing I remember is writing that text to Naomi, the last one as Akira, then I headed to the parking garage because my headache was getting strong and I needed to sleep it off before meeting her later. But when I got there some sort of a bag was thrown over my head.

After that…nothing.

There was absolutely nothing.

I blink a few times and inhale deeply, only to be assaulted by the stench of piss. Grunting, I place my palms on the ground and sit up.

My head pulses with pain and my tongue feels too big for my mouth. A bitter taste floods my throat with each swallow.

The gray walls circle around me and the world spins. Or maybe I'm the one who's spinning.

I shake my head, closing and opening my eyes a few times so I can focus better.

The blur covering my vision slowly disappears and the place I'm being kept in comes into focus. My memory kicks in with a vengeance.

I couldn't forget this hellhole even if I lived a thousand years.

This is where Naomi and I were kept and emotionally tortured. This is where they broke her so she'd play into their hands without any second thoughts.

The metal door that she walked through stares back at me with the same sturdiness as before, as if it's mocking me.

As if telling me it's happening again.

Or maybe it's already happened.

I search my surroundings, but there's no trace of my Naomi.

Did they take her, too? Is she being kept in a separate place?

Using the wall for balance, I stagger to my feet and walk to the door.

I bang on it the hardest I can. "Open up! Open the fuck up!"

There's no sound or movement from outside, but I kick and punch it with both hands until I bust my knuckles.

I don't stop to think about the pain.

Or the grogginess.

I don't stop to consider anything but my Naomi. There's no way in fuck I'll stand by as they torture or threaten her.

Before, I believed the facts instead of believing in us.

I let my insecurities take control and wholeheartedly thought she'd left me.

Not now.

Now, I'll fight for her.

I'll be there if it means my fucking death.

The door creaks and I jump back, ready to punch whoever is coming in. Either I save her or I die trying.

A man with Asian looks steps in. He's tall and has long hair, and sharp eye contact that only people in a high position of power, such as my grandfather, possess.

He stares at me for a second and I stare back, my hands balled into fists.

He doesn't have a weapon or any guards with him, so I could possibly overpower him and step past him—

"I wouldn't recommend it," he cuts off my train of thought. "If you touch me, I'll cut you, and even if by a miracle you manage to move past me, this place is full of guards. Armed guards."

"What the fuck do you want? Where's Naomi?"

"My name is Kai and I will be your host for the day." He slides his attention to his watch. "Or for the next few minutes, anyway."

I walk closer, squaring my shoulders. "I don't care who the fuck you are."

"You should. My name will be engraved in your memories, because that's what will come to mind if you think about hurting Naomi. If you look at another woman, I'll be there. If you make her cry, I'll also be there. The glint of my sword will be the last thing you see before life leaves your miserable limbs."

"You don't scare me." I stare at him square in the eyes. "How Naomi and I treat each other is only up to us."

"It'll be up to me, too."

"Who the fuck do you think you are?"

"The one who saved her from assault when you weren't even in the picture. I killed for her once and doing it again will be my pleasure."

"You...killed Riko's boyfriend, Sam?"

"Ex-boyfriend, since he's rotting as we speak."

So the reason I haven't been able to find the miserable bastard isn't because he moved to another country, but because he's already dead.

He was killed by this man. Kai. Somehow, that makes me see him in a different light. He's the reason why she wasn't scarred to the point of no return and I can't help but respect him for that—regardless of his reasons for doing it.

"While I'm grateful for what you did for her in the past, she's mine and I won't allow you to get near her."

"I'm not interested in her that way. She's our princess and I'm merely her guardian angel—a fallen one, at that."

"Where's is she? Take me to her."

"No need." He sighs. "She went through all this trouble to get you out. First, she figured out Akira's bids for his next business venture by playing that fool, Ren. Then she took it to your grandparents with the help of your uncle."

"Naomi went to see my grandparents?"

"Yes, and she begged them to help you by blocking Akira's investment from behind the scenes. Of course, your grandparents weren't thrilled to have to pull out the big guns and wanted her to end your relationship, but she didn't agree. Instead, she told your grandmother that they won't lose you like they lost your father, and that was the deciding point for them. Once Akira's plots were halted, he lost it and might have taken it out on Ren." He pauses and smiles as if reliving an image. "Anyway, in exchange for her to stop blocking Akira's projects, she made him agree to divorce her while remaining an ally to her father. She's currently threatening Abe that if he uses her or you—or her sister—she'll make Akira withdraw the alliance and all his funds. Among other things that she now has over him."

My lips part as I listen to Kai's retelling of the events. I can't believe she did all of that on her own.

Naomi isn't the same, after all. She was always strong, but she's now a force to be reckoned with.

"Speechless? Good." Kai grabs me by the shoulder hard. So hard that it feels like he'll break my bones, then whispers in a low, calm but threatening tone, "You'd better remember her sacrifices until the day you die. Or I'll be there to make sure you take your last breaths."

"Sebastian!"

My gaze snaps to the flash of movement behind Kai. Naomi runs toward me, her fair cheeks flushed and her red lipstick making her appear paler, softer, and so fucking beautiful.

Her black hair flies behind her as she rushes forward and physically pushes Kai out of the way.

"Go away, Kai," she tells him impatiently.

He steps back, then gives me one final warning look before he turns around and leaves.

Naomi grabs me by the arms, her gaze searching everywhere, for a wound, I suppose. The last time we were here, I nearly died. But I didn't, because of her.

Seven years later, this one hell of a woman saved me for the second time. And I will make sure she doesn't have to do it again for as long as we live.

"I'm okay," I say softly, my voice full of emotion.

"Oh, thank God. When I saw you through the footage, I thought the bastards hit you or did something."

"I'm really fine."

She doesn't stop touching me—running her fingers over my bicep, then up my side, chest, and shoulder as if she needs to make sure for herself.

"Nao."

She's focused on my torso, my hand, my arm. Anywhere but my face.

"Baby, look at me."

She finally lifts her eyes and they're filled with tears. They blur the dark color of her irises and then cascade down her pink cheeks.

I reach a hand out and wipe them away with a thumb, my palm lingering on the swell of her cheek. "Why are you crying?"

"Because you're okay. Because it's finally over."

"Kai told me. I can't believe you went to my grandparents and did everything in between. You're so strong, so goddamn beautiful."

"It was all scary, but I would do it all over again for you, Sebastian. I would go to hell if it means I get to be with you."

"Good because I have a special spot in there."

She smiles through her tears and it's the most beautiful fucking smile I've ever seen on her.

"I'm free," she whispers as if not believing the words. "I'm free of Akira. I'm free to be with you…I mean, if you…want to."

"Of course I fucking want to. I needed to be with you a lifetime ago."

Her own palm grabs my cheek, a whirlwind of emotions darkening her gaze. "Seven years, Sebastian."

"Seven fucking years."

"Promise me we'll never be apart again."

"Oh, I promise to chase you to the end of the world, baby."

"Yeah?"

"Fuck yeah. Also, you'll keep the promise you made seven years ago in this same place."

Her breath hitches. "What…promise?"

"You'll marry me. For real this time."

She bites her lower lip, staring at me from beneath her lashes. "You still want to marry me?"

"I never fucking stopped. You're the only woman I ever wanted to be my wife and that will never change, not even when you had a bastard for a husband before me."

"Akira never counted for me."

"As he shouldn't. Fuck that guy."

"Fuck that whole marriage. If it were up to me, you would be my only husband."

"Well, it's up to you now."

"Oh, Sebastian. Of course I will marry you."

"Good. Because that wasn't a question." And then I'm kissing her—savagely, wildly, like the animal I actually am.

And Naomi kisses me back like the prey she is.

EPILOGUE 1
Naomi

Six months later

TODAY'S THE DAY I'VE BEEN DREAMING ABOUT FOR YEARS.
The day I thought would never be a reality.
My wedding day to Sebastian.

I feel as if I'm walking on air, reaching and touching the stars. It's like levitating out of my own body although my feet are on the ground and I'm heading toward the aisle.

This is the second time I've done this, but I don't even remember the first. All the memories I have of that day are tears and blurry images of metaphorically burying myself.

That marriage was nothing.

This one is everything.

My fingers tighten around the roses I'm holding in my hand and I inhale their scent and let the whole setting sink in.

We decided to get married in the back garden of my old house. This is where we've been living for the past couple of months and will continue to. Just the two of us.

We'll erase the bad memories that linger here and replace them with new, happy ones.

Sebastian and I will start a new page in both of our lives.

Only our closest family and friends are attending. And that means my father isn't here.

We're estranged now and if it weren't for Mio, I'd never see him again. He's still allied with Akira and that's all that matters to him.

My ex-husband stayed Japan after we finalized the divorce and he gave me my freedom.

Ren went with him, or more accurately, Akira threatened him to either accompany him or he'll lose his head at Father's hands. On the other hand, my father, who now believes that Akira is plotting against him because of that ledger, wanted Ren with Akira to keep tabs on my ex-husband. So both of them are using the guard. I feel bad for him sometimes, but it's not like he can't take care of himself.

The only members present from my family are Mio and Kai. My father's second-in-command insisted on being a part of my life, even if it's from the shadows.

I'd rather have no relation whatsoever with my father and the Yakuza and their dirty business. But ever since that red night about twenty years ago, Kai has been different. Like a big brother of sorts. A fucked-up one at that, but it still counts.

The other attendees include Reina, Asher, Owen, Lucy, and Prescott, and when they smile as I walk down the aisle, I smile back.

We've all been getting together over the last couple of months, and it feels…normal. I have friends; I have a life here.

I'm not lonely and miserable.

I'm not sad.

If anything, it's the absolute opposite.

I nod at Debra, Brian, and Nate, who are seated in the front row. The senator and his wife insisted on attending their only grand-child's wedding even though Sebastian wasn't really keen on inviting them. They're not the best of friends with Nate and Sebastian, but I know they care about them in their own snobbish way. They're also a bit scared of me after Kai's threat so they don't dare to voice their displeasure about me anymore.

Sebastian's co-workers are also here—Aspen included. I still don't like her, but it's probably my irrational jealousy. Candice smiles at me and wipes a tear with her handkerchief.

I love that woman so much. She's been a huge help with all the wedding preparations and 'keeping her boss's head in the game,' as she called it.

All of these people are here to witness our wedding.

Mine and Sebastian's.

I finally see him. He's standing at the altar, wearing a dashing black tuxedo that makes him look like a model.

A strand escapes his styled hair and the small imperfection makes him even more perfect.

More…irresistible.

That man stole my heart when I was eighteen and has never given it back.

He confiscated my body when I was twenty-one and turned each of my fantasies into a reality.

And along the way, he also stole my soul.

He took my innocence and twisted it into something absolutely addictive and never gave it back to me.

My feet come to a halt in front of him and he takes my hands in his, pulling me toward him.

"You're so fucking beautiful," he whispers in my ear. "I want to claim you here and now, baby."

"Stop it." I laugh, biting my lower lip.

"I mean it. You're killing me, Tsundere."

"Be patient."

"And what do I get in return?"

"Chasing me?" I whisper.

"In your wedding dress. In the forest."

I nod eagerly.

Sebastian never stopped chasing me or pushing my buttons. He gives us both what we need and more.

The night I got him out of the cell once and for all, we moved into this house. Sebastian had absolutely no attachment to his apartment anyway.

And that same night, he chased me.

It was one of the best chases of my life and I came more times than I could count. Probably because I knew there was no longer anything standing between us.

That I was his as much as he was mine.

Or maybe it was because he kept calling me his fiancée as he fucked me hard and fast.

After we say 'I do' and we put on each other's rings, Sebastian's lips meet mine, and he kisses me with a hunger that matches my own. I hug his neck to return it, to sink deeper into him.

I've lost so much time already and there's no way I'll let that happen again. I'll take advantage of every moment, every kiss, and every damn touch.

I squeal into Sebastian's mouth when he picks me up in his arms and walks in the direction of the house.

The crowd breaks out in laughter, and some teasing remarks echo in the air, but neither of us could care less.

Once we're inside, he kicks the door shut behind us and slams me against it. My legs wrap around his waist with my dress bunched over them. And then we make out as if we were still those hot-blooded college kids.

Maybe we are.

A part of us will always be trapped in that period of time when we became each other's addictions.

When we became best friends.

When we fell so deeply in love and never managed to crawl out.

Sebastian's mouth leaves mine with a groan. "I'm going to fuck you, Mrs. Weaver."

I smile, my heart thundering. "I like that."

"The fucking part or your new last name?"

"Both." I palm his cheek, staring deeply into his tropical eyes that I've used as a source of light in my darkest moments. "I can't believe we're actually married, Sebastian."

"I'll spend the rest of our lives reminding you of it."

"Promise?"

"I fucking promise."

"I love you so much. I loved you seven years ago and I love you even more now."

"I've been in love with the idea of you since we were fucking eighteen, Nao. Then three years later, I found the one woman who not only didn't judge me, but also embraced my crazy. I never stopped loving you, baby, not even when a part of me hated you. Not even when you left. And for the rest of our lives, I'll love you hard, love you fucking right."

"Oh, Sebastian…"

"Say you're mine, baby."

"I'm yours. Always have been."

"Even when you weren't with me?"

"Especially then."

His lips slam against mine and I close my eyes as laughter bubbles to the surface.

I'm happy.

I'm free.

I'm with the man I've always loved and forever will.

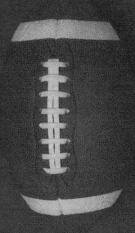

EPILOGUE 2
Sebastian

Three years later

"I CAN SMELL YOU, NAOMI."

Her small squeal of fear goes straight to my dick, hardening it until it's fucking painful.

A rustle comes from my right and I sprint in that direction. I can hear her harsh breathing, her sneakers crunching the leaves, and her involuntary gasps.

She's gotten good at hiding her movements. Like a good prey, she adapted to the environment and tries to make herself unnoticeable.

But never from me.

I can see her everywhere, smell her anywhere.

Find her anywhere.

Naomi zigzags across the ground in a useless attempt to lose me. But I've learned the forest by fucking heart. Just as she has.

And there's no way she'll be able to mislead a beast in his natural habitat.

She trips and I catch her by the elbow before she falls, but she pulls on my arm, crying out, and we both tumble to the dirt. She wrestles me, her nails digging into my arm and her delicate face reddening with the effort. The scratch marks on my neck burn, but they trigger my need for more.

The harder she scratches, the rougher I'll take her. The more she fights, the crazier we both become.

And fuck, how my beautiful wife fights.

It's our favorite game. Our fantasy. And we're the only ones who are allowed in it.

I grab her wrists and slam them against the ground above her head, but she doesn't stop trying to wiggle and kick.

She knows she'll never overpower me, but she still tries to anyway.

It makes my dick rock fucking hard.

"Stay still or I'll fuck you dry in the asshole, my slut."

"No! Let me go!" she shrieks, and I use my other hand to yank her skirt up her legs.

My hand meets her bare cunt and I grunt. "Looks like you came prepared to be taken like a filthy whore, didn't you?" I slap her on the pussy and she gasps, tears welling in her dark eyes.

"No, please...no. Please don't hurt me."

"But I will. I'll fuck you so hard, so deep, you won't be able to move."

"No...please...stop..."

She tries to wiggle free, but I slap her wet cunt again and she cries out, her hands flexing and relaxing in my hold.

I pull down my sweatpants and angle her leg up, then drive into her in one ruthless go that knocks the breath out of her and makes her moan. Loud. So loud that the whole forest echoes with it.

My thrusts are hard and merciless, just like we both love.

After a few minutes of brutal fucking and her body taking me in, I slow down.

"Please..." she cries, tears welling her eyes. "Please..."

"Please what, baby?"

"More, Sebastian. Please, more!"

I give her just that, fucking her hard, then slow, then hard again, until she's dazed while soaking my dick with her juices.

We come together, both groaning and calling each other's names.

We might be the beast and the prey, but we'll always be us. No matter how much time has passed.

I lie on the dirt and pull her on top of me so I'm not crushing her. Her erratic breathing matches the rhythm of the rise and fall of my chest.

We remain like that for a while, letting the fresh air engulf us as we each catch our breaths.

We've been married for three years and there hasn't been a day where I didn't worship at this woman's fucking altar.

There hasn't been a day where I didn't show her how fucking grateful I am for having her in my life again.

Falling back into each other's lives has been easier than either of us could've thought. It was like picking up where we left off.

Only, I'm no longer a star quarterback and she's no longer the outcast cheerleader.

I'm a lawyer and she's a successful businesswoman who's a perfectionist when it comes to her work but turns into the goofiest person when it's only the two of us.

We still watch true crime shows together and she's still scared of horror movies.

Akira, the asshole, is out of our lives for the most part, but whenever we bump into him, he still reminds me that she was his wife first.

The last time we saw him was when we went to Japan so I could visit my parents' graves for the first time.

Naomi felt so bad when she learned that her father had killed my parents and nearly killed me in the process, but I never blamed her for that.

It's not her fault that her father is a fucking murderer. I refuse to get caught up in the past after everything that's happened.

Akira then reminded me of the fucking letters. The ones he read as a hobby each week, the pervert.

When Naomi learned I was Akira—the original one, not the damn imposter—she had a lot of things to say about it.

First she cursed me for being a judgmental asshole.

Then she hugged me because she'd always shared a connection with Akira—*me*.

And then she kissed me because I found her first. I wrote to her first.

Akira was sort of my alter ego that I invented right after I saw her smiling while crying. I had to get close to her somehow and I heard her once mentioning to Lucy that she preferred Asian men.

I wished I was Asian back then, and that's how I got the idea of Akira. It was fitting that I was born in Japan and my parents gave me that middle name. A name that represents both the sun and the moon.

That's how I wormed myself into her life before we ever got together.

"Hey, Sebastian?"

"Yeah, baby?"

"Thank you for finding me. I don't want to imagine how my life would've been if you hadn't."

"Thank you for coming back to me." I kiss her forehead.

She looks up at me and smiles. Her whole face lights up when she does it. "Are you happy?"

"What type of fucking question is that? Of course I'm happy."

"But our family is so small."

"You're enough for me."

"What if I told you there's another member who wants to join?"

"What?"

She takes my hand and places it on her stomach. "I'm pregnant."

"You…are?"

"Yeah. Six weeks."

I sit up, taking her with me, and she wraps her arms around my neck. We agreed that we wouldn't have kids as soon as we got married so that we could make up for all the time we wasted.

But a few months back, Naomi went off birth control and has been upset whenever she gets her period.

Looks like she didn't this time.

And I knew it, but I didn't want to spoil her fun.

"We're going to be parents, Sebastian. Isn't that scary and exciting, but still scary?"

"Like us, you mean."

"Just like us." She kisses my cheek. "Thank you for being with me. Don't ever leave me, okay?"

"You'll never get rid of me, baby."

We're in this together and we will always be.

I'm her monster and she's my willing prey.

THE END

Next up is the standalone book that features Sebastian's uncle, Nathaniel. You can read this angsty age-gap, marriage of convenience romance in *Empire of Desire*.

Curious about Reina and Asher mentioned in this book? You can read their completed story in *All The Lies*.

WHAT'S NEXT?

Thank you so much for reading *Black Thorns*! If you liked it,
please leave a review.
Your support means the world to me.

If you're thirsty for more discussions with other readers
of the series, you can join the Facebook group, Rina
Kent's Spoilers Room.

Next up is the heart-pounding marriage of convenience, age gap,
father's best friend standalone, *Empire of Desire*.

ALSO BY RINA KENT

For more books by the author and a reading order, please visit:

www.rinakent.com/books

ABOUT THE AUTHOR

Rina Kent is a *USA Today*, international, and #1 Amazon bestselling author of everything enemies to lovers romance.

She's known to write unapologetic anti-heroes and villains because she often fell in love with men no one roots for. Her books are sprinkled with a touch of darkness, a pinch of angst, and an unhealthy dose of intensity.

She spends her private days in London laughing like an evil mastermind about adding mayhem to her expanding universe. When she's not writing, Rina travels, hikes, and spoils cats in a pure Cat Lady fashion.

Find Rina Below:

Website: www.rinakent.com

Neswsletter: www.subscribepage.com/rinakent

BookBub: www.bookbub.com/profile/rina-kent

Amazon: www.amazon.com/Rina-Kent/e/B07MM54G22

Goodreads: www.goodreads.com/author/show/18697906.
Rina_Kent

Instagram: www.instagram.com/author_rina

Facebook: www.facebook.com/rinaakent

Reader Group: www.facebook.com/groups/rinakent.club

Pinterest: www.pinterest.co.uk/AuthorRina/boards

Tiktok: www.tiktok.com/@rina.kent

Twitter: twitter.com/AuthorRina